"I want you to fir____
started."

The moment Erica saw ___ ___ ___
expression, she wanted t___ ___ ___ words back.
Then the corner of his mouth lifted in an odd little
smile and Erica forgot to breathe.

His scent drifted around her in a tangible embrace
and she was dizzied by his nearness. Then, when
his mouth was so near she could feel the sweet
warmth of his breath, she trembled once, parted
her lips and was swept away by the power of
his kiss.

Too soon, Roberto stepped away, seeming as awed
and shaken as she was. He gazed at her for a long
moment, then took a deep breath, whispered
"Good night" and went out the front door.

But Erica knew that he'd be back; and her life
would never be the same.

Dear Reader:

Romance readers have been enthusiastic about the Silhouette Special Editions for years. And that's not by accident: Special Editions were the first of their kind and continue to feature realistic stories with heightened romantic tension.

The longer stories, sophisticated style, greater sensual detail and variety that made Special Editions popular are the same elements that will make you want to read book after book.

We hope that you enjoy this Special Edition today, and will enjoy many more.

Please write to us:

Jane Nicholls
Silhouette Books
PO Box 236
Thornton Road
Croydon
Surrey
CR9 3RU

The Avenger
DIANA WHITNEY

SILHOUETTE

SPECIAL EDITION

*First published in Great Britain 1996
by Silhouette Books, Eton House, 18-24 Paradise Road,
Richmond, Surrey TW9 1SR*

© Diana Hinz 1995

*Silhouette, Silhouette Special Edition and Colophon are
Trade Marks of Harlequin Enterprises II B.V.*

ISBN 0 373 09984 3

23-9602

Made and printed in Great Britain

To the world's fatherless children, with the prayer that each and every one will find a Daddy to cherish.

DIANA WHITNEY

says she loves "fat babies and warm puppies, mountain streams and California sunshine, camping, hiking and gold prospecting. Not to mention strong romantic heroes!" She married her own real-life hero twenty years ago. With his encouragement, she left her long-time career as a finance director and pursued the dream that had haunted her since childhood—writing. To Diana, writing is a joy, the ultimate satisfaction. Reading, too, is her passion, from spine-chilling thrillers to sweeping sagas, but nothing can compare to the magic and wonder of romance.

Other Silhouette Books by Diana Whitney

Silhouette Sensation

Still Married
Midnight Stranger

Silhouette Special Edition
Cast a Tall Shadow
Yesterday's Child
One Lost Winter
Child of the Storm
The Secret
*The Adventurer

*The Blackthorn Brotherhood

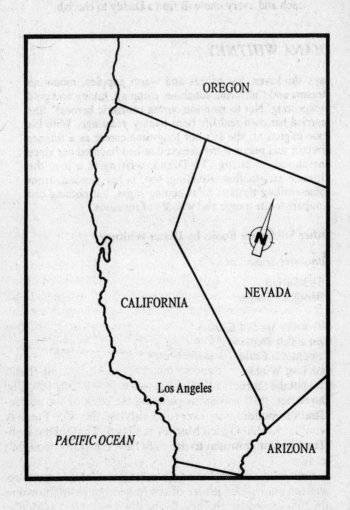

Prologue

His heart was racing. His palms were wet. His ten-year-old belly rumbled with fear. Crouched at his appointed observation spot, he peered around the corner of Blackthorn Hall's administration building. The quad was deserted, but he continued to scan the clipped grounds with narrowed eyes and fierce determination.

Roberto Arroya was the sentry.

Being a sentry sounded real important, but all things considered, Roberto thought it was a pretty sissy job. The important stuff was spray painting the back of the administration building so everyone driving the 405 Freeway would read that Ogden Marlow is a Nazi. That's what Roberto had really wanted to do, only Devon Monroe wouldn't let him.

Dev, who was twelve and almost completely grown-up, was the undisputed leader of the four roommates known as the Blackthorn Brotherhood. The other two, Larkin McKay and Tommy Murdock, were both eleven, and so tight with each other that sometimes Roberto wondered if they were joined at the hip or something. Lark and Tommy were always together but Roberto didn't much care because Devon Monroe was his very own best friend.

As far as Roberto was concerned, Dev was the smartest and bravest kid in the whole world, even tougher than the bangers who hung out in the *barrio* where Roberto used to live. Geez, Dev had even survived two days in the Box, a four-by-four concrete vault that Chancellor Ogden Marlow—dubbed Hogman by the facility's inmates—put kids in who had the guts to stand up for their rights.

As far as old Hogman was concerned, nobody at Blackthorn Hall had any rights. But when he saw the Brotherhood's sign, he'd probably have a stroke or something. It'd serve him right, too.

Roberto thought the whole sign idea was super cool, the neatest thing any Hall resident had ever done, and it ticked him off that all he got to do was squat here like a stupid monkey, staring at nothing.

Bored now, he poked a fuzzy dandelion ball with a twig. Air caught the feathery remnants, carrying them over the chain link fence at the edge of the compound. They were free. Roberto felt better.

Glancing back over his shoulder, he saw his three friends engaged in whispered argument and took a quick look at the sloppy blue words that were dripping across the red brick. "Aw, man," he muttered to himself. Cripes, any dork knew that *Nazi* only had one *z*. Any dork except Tommy Murdock.

Roberto figured that asthma medicine Tommy was always sucking must have pickled the poor kid's brain. Tommy was a neat guy, but he sure as hell wasn't gonna be no rocket scientist. Not that it mattered much. Roberto's IQ was supposed to be somewhere in the genius range, for all the good it had done him. Tommy was always razzing him about that, too, saying stuff like if he was really so smart, how come he'd ended up at Blackthorn Hall in the first place?

Roberto never bothered to answer because Tommy already knew. Everyone did. It was on account of Roberto's mother wanting booze and drugs more than she did her own kid—

The thought dissipated when a sudden movement caught his eye. He stiffened as the office door opened. Ogden Marlow and another man stepped out.

Roberto leapt back, flattened against the wall and hissed a warning to his friends.

Larkin dropped his spray can.

Tommy shoved the asthma inhaler back in his shirt pocket.

Devon frantically pointed toward a bank of concealing bushes below the freeway fence.

All four boys sprinted across the grass.

Roberto dived into the nearest shrub, then crawled on his belly into the heart of the thicket. When he turned around, he saw Dev and Lark crouched right in front of him, but Tommy was sprawled facedown on the lawn.

Larkin swore and would've run to help, except Dev grabbed his shoulder and shoved him back into the bushes. It was too late. Hogman and the other guy were already dragging Tommy away.

An hour later, Larkin stared glumly out the dorm room window. "They shoulda been back by now."

Roberto sat on the thin cot, absently tossing a tennis ball from one hand to the other. "Dev isn't gonna be back. At least, not today."

Lark frowned. "Why not?"

Frustrated, Roberto flung the ball at the nearest wall, ducking as it ricocheted back past his head. "'Cause Dev's gonna turn himself in, that's why not. Hogman'll put him in the Box for sure."

"Aw, hell, Bobby, Dev ain't gonna do such a stupid thing. He's just gonna take back the inhaler Tommy dropped and say that Tommy was chasing the guys who really did it."

"Yeah?" Roberto flopped on his back, tucking his hands behind his head. "So what makes you think they're gonna go for that?"

Lark shrugged. "Dev said they would."

Staring at the ceiling, Roberto felt a familiar fury build in his skinny chest. "Dev just said that so you wouldn't get all torqued out and stuff. Hogman's gonna make someone burn for what happened. If it isn't Tommy, it's gonna have to be Dev."

Unable to dispute that logic, Larkin ruffled the stick-straight thatch of surfer blond hair that Roberto had always admired, folded his arms and stared at the scratched linoleum floor. "So that means they'll let Tommy go, right?"

Roberto threw his roommate a killing look. "You don't give a damn about Dev, do you?"

Stung, Larkin flinched but didn't look up. "You know better'n that. It's just that Tommy's always so sick and everything...." With a pained sigh, he let the words evaporate and refocused his gaze out the window. There was no need to finish the sentence. Both boys understood what he meant.

Despite a ready smile and slick sense of humor, the ponytailed Tommy Murdock had always been kind of puny, although anyone who said so to his face would risk a punch in the nose. The most important thing in Tommy's life was trying to be like other kids; only he wasn't like other kids, and that was what got him busted in the first place. He and his homeboys had been running from the cops when Tommy had had an asthma attack. His homies got away; Tommy didn't. Just like today.

Roberto slid a glance at Larkin and saw the poor guy was really bummed. Roberto felt kind of bad to have accused him of not caring about Devon, so he went over and tossed an arm around his roommate's husky shoulders. "It'll be okay," he told the despondent boy. "Tommy and Devon are gonna be all right."

"Yeah, I guess."

Roberto stared out the window, silently cursing the manicured compound that was designed to look like a university campus when it was nothing but a lousy prison for kids whose parents didn't want them any more. Larkin was here because after his folks got divorced, his mom married some uptight banker dude with a houseful of spoiled brats. Lark hated them all, so he ran away and when the cops picked him up, his family wouldn't take him back.

Dev's situation was pretty much the same, except his dad had a ton of money and coulda bought his kid outta any problem if he'd wanted to, which he obviously didn't. So Dev was stuck here, and so was Larkin and Tommy and Roberto, all because nobody gave a fat rat's tail about any one of them. But they had each other now. In every way that counted, they were true *hermanos,* as close as blood brothers could ever be.

Behind them, the door suddenly opened. Roberto looked over his shoulder as Devon entered the room.

Dev closed the door and sagged against it, still clutching Tommy's inhaler in his limp hand.

Roberto took a hesitant step forward. "What's wrong, man? You look like you seen a ghost or something."

Devon licked his lips, his blank gaze slipping from Larkin to Roberto, then back again. He opened his mouth, but no sound emerged.

"Where's Tommy?" Larkin pushed away from the window, his voice trembling with panic. "He ain't in the Box, is he? Cripes, Dev, you know he can't take that. He's gonna get real sick."

Dev closed his eyes and took a deep breath. "He's not in the Box."

Larkin's shoulders sagged in relief but Roberto remained stiff. He saw something in Devon's face that scared him half to death. "So where is he?"

"He's...gone."

"Gone?" Larkin frowned. "Gone where?"

Devon started to shake all over. "They took him away in an ambulance." He flung the plastic inhaler across the room. "Tommy died, damn it! Those bastards killed him!"

A pall of shocked silence fell over the room. Roberto felt like he was gonna throw up. He stumbled to the cot and sat down, hanging his head between his knees. Tommy couldn't be dead. Devon had to be kidding. It was a joke, that's all. A lousy, rotten joke.

Apparently Larkin thought so, too. His voice was low, deadly. "You're lying."

Devon rubbed his palms over his face, then let his arms drop to his side. "They said it was 'respiratory failure'. They said it happened so quick there wasn't nothing they could do."

Larkin balled his fists. *"You're lying!"*

Devon just stood there, blinking back tears.

Rushing forward, Larkin shoved Devon away from the door then sprinted out of the room, sobbing.

To Roberto, everything seemed to be happening in slow motion. His stomach twisted. He bit his lip, clutched his belly and fought back tears. Reality hit like a fist. Dev wasn't kidding. Tommy was really gone. He wasn't ever coming back.

It was the worst thing that could ever happen.

Beside him, the mattress dipped as Devon sat down and slid a consoling arm around his skinny shoulders. "It's gonna be okay, Bobby. Tommy always hated it here. Now he's gonna be in a better place, right?"

Roberto stared silently at his knees as his churning gut hardened into a fiery knot of rage. All his life, he'd been oppressed and abused by people who were supposed to protect him. In spite of that, he'd done everything a good kid was supposed to do. He'd gotten himself off to school every day and kept a straight A average. At night, he'd cook for himself and if his drunken mother showed up, he'd cook for her, too. As a reward, he'd been "rescued" by the welfare system and deposited in a place where kids were punished just for being alive.

But Tommy wouldn't be punished any more.

Maybe Devon was right. Maybe Tommy was in a better place. As far as Roberto was concerned, any place was better than a world without justice, where nobody cared spit whether or not you followed the rules. It didn't matter if you were good or bad or anything in between. You got what you got because life wasn't fair. People weren't fair. The only thing that mattered was being stronger and more powerful than anyone else so nothing could ever hurt you. And right now Roberto was hurting real bad.

But with the grief came anger, a seething fury that seeped into every fiber of body and mind. Somebody was going to pay for what happened to Tommy. Maybe not today or tomorrow, but someday. Tommy's death wasn't ever gonna be forgotten. Roberto would make sure of it.

Chapter One

Roberto wiped the remnants of shower steam from his bathroom mirror and, more out of habit than necessity, fiddled with the knot in his fashionable silk necktie. After inspecting his starched cuffs, he turned his attention to smoothing an untidy curl of dark hair that constantly annoyed him by coiling over his forehead.

A squirt of spray plastered it in place.

Actually, he'd never paid much attention to his hair until a female attorney he barely knew had suddenly shoved her client's file aside, leaned across the conference table and whispered that she never could resist a man who looked like he'd just rolled out of bed. Then she'd issued a throaty growl and pressed her phone number in his hand.

At the time, Roberto had been too shocked to be embarrassed. Later, he'd been angry that the woman hadn't taken him seriously. Granted, he was younger than his colleagues but he considered that irrelevant. Or at least he had, until that fateful afternoon. That's when he'd realized that in the federal prosecutor's office, image was every bit as important as education and experience. Since then, he'd been scrupulous about maintaining a professional appearance.

Now he gave his reflection a final inspection before responding to the thin whine emanating from beyond the doorway. "Hey there, *mi amigo*. Where have you been?"

Buddy, the mixed-breed mutt Roberto had adopted three years ago, issued an agitated bark and backed into the bedroom.

Roberto followed. "Ready for breakfast, big guy?"

Actually, Buddy wasn't a big dog or a particularly attractive one. Cursed with long, spindly legs and a rangy body coated by prickly, ash gray hair, the animal's saving grace was an inquisitive little face, complete with high-set, slightly tweaked ears, liquid fudge eyes peering from beneath bristled brows and a whiskered muzzle resembling that of a poorly plucked schnauzer. Roberto was nuts about him.

Buddy responded to the breakfast query with an excited yelp and dashed out into the hall.

Roberto paused at the closet, selecting a distinguished gray tweed sport coat before meeting his dog in the kitchen. He draped the jacket over a chair and opened the pantry, which was right next to the kitchen door. Behind him, doggy toenails clicked across polished tile. Roberto absently pulled a can from the cabinet and glanced at the label. "Hmm . . . 'chunks of beef in savory sauce.' How does that sound?"

"Ucky," came the high-pitched reply. "Want Fruity Flakes."

Roberto spun around so fast he nearly dropped the can. There, sitting cross-legged on his kitchen floor, was a grinning, pajama-clad toddler. The child, whom Roberto judged to be about three, was absolutely adorable, with a tiny button nose and silky brown hair arranged into twin sprigs fastened above each ear.

After a stunned moment, he placed the dog food can on the counter and tested his voice. "Well, hi there. Who are you?"

"Caffy," she said.

"Caffy?"

Her tiny brows furrowed. "No, *Caf*-fy."

"Oh . . . Cathy."

She nodded happily. At that moment, Buddy came over to nuzzle her fat little cheek. Giggling, Cathy flung her chubby arms around the animal's neck and hugged him fiercely. "What's doggy's name?"

"His name is Buddy." Roberto crouched down to the child's level and pointed toward a flapped opening in the back door. "Did you by any chance follow Buddy in through there?"

Cathy followed the gesture with her eyes, then pressed both pudgy hands against her mouth and smothered another giggle.

Roberto smiled. "I thought so." He turned to Buddy and forced a stern tone. "And you managed to get the back gate open again, didn't you?"

The animal flattened on his belly, plopped his whiskered chin on the floor and whined pitifully.

"I'll deal with you later," he told the dejected dog. "Meanwhile, we'd better find out where Cathy belongs so she can have her morning Fruity Flakes."

Roberto scooped up the tot, who promptly wrapped her arms around his neck and regarded him somberly. "Are you Bwuddy's daddy?" she asked.

"In a manner of speaking, I suppose. And since we're on the subject of parents, can you tell me where yours are?"

"Mommy's home."

Which, Roberto thought, was exactly where this sweet little girl should be, and would have been if her mother had been watching her properly. "Where do you live, Cathy?"

"In a big white house."

"Ah." Since every third house on the block was white, that information wasn't particularly enlightening. "Could you give me a hint as to where this white house might be located?"

She hunched up her shoulders in an exaggerated shrug and wrinkled her stubby little nose. "Why can't I play wif Bwuddy?"

"Because your mama's probably worried about you." That comment assumed, perhaps charitably, that the woman had actually noticed her daughter was missing. Roberto's own experience had proven that child bearing and child rearing were very different, particularly since physical puberty had no relevance to one's ability to parent. Naturally, he'd have liked to give Cathy's mother the benefit of doubt; unfortunately, allowing a child of this tender age to wander the streets at 6:00 a.m. wasn't a good sign.

At any rate, Cathy made no protest as Roberto carried her out into the sparsely planted backyard. As suspected, the gate was ajar. He paused to inspect the ineffective hook-and-eye closing mechanism that Buddy had somehow managed to nose open, presumably for the benefit of his guest since the clever canine was quite capable of climbing the six-foot wooden fence whenever the mood struck him.

Roberto frowned at the ugly mutt sitting placidly at his feet. "If some gun-toting guy in a ski mask showed up, would you open the gate for him, too? Hospitality has limits, Buddy-boy. The cost of a dog-proof dead bolt is coming out of your chew toy fund."

The chastised animal emitted a yelp of distress and Cathy instantly broke into tears. Startled, Roberto tried to comfort the crying child. "Hey, punkin, it's okay. We'll find your mama."

She wailed even louder. Apparently Buddy was dismayed by his little friend's distress because he leapt up protectively, barking frantically and pawing at his master's hip, ceasing only when Roberto snapped the proper command.

Not that Roberto blamed the dog for being upset. As the little girl's wails grew more intense, Roberto barely suppressed a surge of absolute panic. What he knew about kids could be stuffed in a thimble with room left over. Now he had a hysterical child on his hands and didn't have a clue how to handle what was rapidly deteriorating into a really bad situation.

He awkwardly wiped a thumb across the girl's wet little cheek. "Everything's okay, Cathy. Don't cry…please."

"Doggy…in…trouble," she blurted between pitiful sobs. "Is he gonna—" she hiccuped "—get a spanking?"

The very thought was appalling. "Of course not! Is that what this is all about?"

When she issued a jerky nod, Roberto didn't know whether to be upset or relieved. To a man whose own childhood had be punctuated with violence, the child's fear of physical punishment was an ominous sign. He licked his lips, cleared his throat and posed a carefully worded query. "Cathy, do you get spankings when you're in trouble?"

She sniffed and shook her head. "I'm a good girl."

"Of course you are." Roberto relaxed just a little. "Look, I was just kidding. Buddy can have all the chew toys he wants, okay?"

The sobs stopped. Her lip still quivered, but a shrewd gleam in her soggy blue eyes indicated that she might not have been quite as upset as she'd seemed. It dawned on Roberto that this tiny bundle of innocence had succeeded where a fleet of savvy defense attorneys had consistently failed. She'd manipulated him into a plea bargain.

With a pained sigh, he shifted her weight in his arms. "Have you ever considered becoming a lawyer when you grow up?"

"Uh-uh."

"Trust me. It's your destiny." With that, Roberto swung open the rickety gate and carried his tiny visitor through the narrow side yard to the front sidewalk.

In scanning the neighborhood of neat, ranch style homes, he saw two police cars at the end of the block, parked in front of a house where he'd noticed a moving van a few days earlier. Now several people were gathered in the yard, including at least four uniformed officers, a slightly older version of the girl he held in his arms and a woman who, if body language was any clue, was extremely upset. "By any chance, has your family just moved here, Cathy?"

She nodded somberly. "Car'lyn and me have our very own room."

"That's nice," he murmured as one of the policemen suddenly turned and pointed straight at him.

The woman looked up, touched her throat and would have sprinted up the sidewalk, except for the restraining hand of the only officer who wasn't already moving toward Roberto. The grim look on their faces was unnerving and the fact that their hands were twitching over their holsters wasn't particularly comforting, either.

When one policeman shouted at Roberto to put the child down, he froze. Dear God, they thought he was a kidnapper. For a man who still had nightmares about being unfairly incarcerated, it was the most frightening thing that could happen. And it was about to get worse.

Erica Franklin was dying inside.

The past hour had been the most horrifying of her entire life. Her child was missing; the terror was unimaginable.

"Mrs. Franklin?"

It took a moment for the voice to penetrate her panicked mind. She gazed up at the policeman as though seeing him for the first time.

He regarded her kindly. "I asked if Cathy might have gone to visit one of her friends."

"We don't know anyone," Erica replied numbly. "We've only been here a few days. She doesn't know her way

around—'' Her attention was diverted by an insistent tug on
the hem of her sweater. "Not now, Carolyn."

The soon-to-be-six-year-old would not be dissuaded. "But
Mommy, look!''

Following her eldest daughter's wiggling finger, Erica
squinted into the sun, shading her eyes to focus on a figure
in the distance. For a moment, she saw only a man backlit
by morning sun. He seemed to be carrying something...a
large bag of groceries with...with legs?

She gasped, vaguely aware that the three police officers
who'd been standing beside the second squad car were
moving quickly down the sidewalk. Erica lunged forward,
only to be held back by the officer with whom she'd been
speaking. She struggled against his unrelenting grasp.
"That's my baby. Let go!''

The policeman spoke soothingly but Erica wasn't listening. Every fiber of her being was focused on her child, and
on the unidentified man who held her captive.

There was a shouted command. The man stiffened.
Slowly, he lowered the little girl to the ground, then
straightened and backed away, extending his arms, palms
up. There were more commands. A third policeman suddenly appeared to scoop Cathy up and hustle her back down
the sidewalk. At the same time, the restraining grip on her
own wrist disappeared, allowing Erica to dash forward,
sobbing, and snatch her child from the arms of her uniformed rescuer.

She clutched the warm little body, hugging her fiercely.
"Oh, baby...my sweet girl...Mommy has been so wor-
ried....'' She frantically scanned the beaming child's face.
"Are you all right? Where have you been?''

Cathy grinned. "Playing wif Bwuddy."

Stiffening, Erica glanced at the grim man who was slowly
retrieving a wallet from his hip pocket. Fear kept her from
asking the question which was posed by the closest policeman.

The officer spoke softly, but Erica saw the suspicion in his eyes and it scared her half to death. "Did that man over there promise to be your, ah, buddy?"

Frowning, Cathy shook her head so violently that her ponytailed sprigs bounced. She pointed a chubby finger at the sidewalk. "*That's* Bwuddy."

For the first time Erica noticed the animal sitting at the man's feet. "The dog?"

"Uh-huh." With that, the child launched into an animated explanation, most of which made no sense at all. There was an odd description of the dog having invited her inside by opening first a big gate, then an itsy-bitsy one. After a weird discussion of ucky stuff and Fruity Flakes, the relevance of which was never quite established, Cathy merrily described how Buddy's daddy had promised nobody would get a spanking because Cathy was a lawyer.

After hearing that bizarre pronouncement, the perplexed policeman wandered off to confer with the officers who'd been questioning the man Cathy had called Buddy's daddy.

A few minutes later the policeman returned to relay that strange as it seemed, the man's story actually agreed with Cathy's. Apparently the little girl had followed the dog home, at which time the resident—a Mr. Roberto Arroya—discovered the child in his kitchen and undertook a search to locate her family.

Erica's breath slid out in a massive sigh of relief. There had been no foul play, no harmful intent, just the unpredictable antics of an adventuresome three-year-old. Antics which had, unfortunately, caused inconvenience and embarrassment to a well-meaning neighbor.

Shifting her daughter in her arms, Erica turned to thank the man, who was engaged in somber discussion with one of the officers. With her daughter safely in her grasp and her heart rate returning to normal, she took a moment to really look at "Bwuddy's daddy". Erica's pulse, which had been slowing, leapt through her veins with renewed vigor. This was without doubt the handsomest man she'd ever seen in her life.

His profile was classic, straight and sculpted, set off by dark wavy hair, somewhat civilized with a conservative style that couldn't disguise a natural, untamed wildness that Erica suspected would extend to the man himself. Despite immaculate business attire, a crisp, white dress shirt and sharply creased gray slacks, the man exuded a feral quality that both startled and intrigued her. His movements, fluid and surprisingly graceful, seemed purposeful and controlled, as if some incredible power lurked beneath that veneer of cultured sophisticate. There was a stealthiness to his stance that reminded her of a jungle cat on the prowl.

She found herself wishing he'd turn around so she could see his full face. When he did, the breath backed up in her throat. His eyes were darker than midnight, yet held a glow that defied definition. As his gaze settled on her, his brows lifted slightly and his lips, which had been clamped tightly together, softened.

Erica tried to smile, but feared the attempt had resulted in little more than an odd grimace because his eyes suddenly darkened even more, if that was possible, with a reproachful expression that cut her to the quick. They stood there for a moment, with their gazes locked. She wanted to thank him, but was unnerved by the accusation in his eyes; besides, she could barely breathe, let alone speak.

As she stood there dumbstruck, the man suddenly tucked the wallet back in his pocket, spun on his polished heel and strode away with the whiskered dog loping beside him.

A rush of air escaped her aching lungs. Well, she thought drily, there's one neighbor who won't be putting out a welcome mat. She felt oddly deflated by that, and embarrassed to realize that she hadn't even thanked the man who police had told her was a Federal Prosecutor working in the L.A. office of the U.S. Attorney.

Since Mr. Arroya didn't seem particularly friendly, Erica considered the most prudent way to express her gratitude might be with a note slipped into his mailbox. But even as the thought settled across her mind, she knew perfectly well that she wouldn't be able to resist the opportunity of seeing him again, if for no other reason than to prove that he wasn't the reason her knees had started to shake.

Later, after having answered uncountable questions for the police report, Erica thanked the officers and hustled her daughters into their newly rented house.

Cathy scampered into the kitchen. "Want Fruity Flakes," she announced.

Feeling frazzled, Erica grabbed a box from the pantry. "Okay, sweetie, but you'll have to chew fast because we have a busy day ahead."

Carolyn joined her sister at the table. "Are we going to Gramma and Grampa's house?"

"For a little while." Erica set two filled cereal bowls on the table. "And later on, we're going to see someone else."

Carolyn turned to watch her mother pull a quart of milk from the refrigerator. "Who?"

"You'll see. It's someone really special."

The girl's eyes lit like neon. "Daddy? Are we going to see Daddy?"

Erica took a sharp breath. Since school would start next week, she'd been referring to Carolyn's new teacher, although she should have realized that her daughter, heartbroken by her parents' divorce, considered her father to be the only special person in her young life.

Setting the milk on the table, Erica smoothed Carolyn's sleek honey brown hair. "No, sweetie," she said gently. "We've talked about this. You know that your daddy's still in Seattle."

Her lip quivered. "Can we go see him?"

"Not today, Carolyn. It's much too far."

"Tomorrow?"

Erica turned away, struggling to control the rush of emotion that this subject always evoked. It had been three years since the divorce, three of the longest, most miserable years of her life. The charming and charismatic Carter Franklin was the only man Erica had ever loved. And she *had* loved him, deeply, passionately, with a blind devotion that in retrospect seemed naively foolish. He'd repeatedly been unfaithful, yet she'd always taken him back because she'd believed his accusation that the affairs had actually been her fault. If she'd been a better wife, he'd told her, it wouldn't have been necessary for him to seek pleasure with others.

Erica had accepted the blame because it had been easier than conceding that her husband, the father of her beloved children, was a womanizing scoundrel incapable of loving anyone but himself. Even after shattering Erica by divorcing her, Carter had always nurtured a tiny flame of hope by regularly returning home declaring that he'd changed and things would be different.

Eventually Erica had come to realize that those calculated promises, uttered after the latest love interest had wised up and kicked him out, were consistently broken as soon as a new woman had entered his life.

Even so, Erica might still have been trapped in the unhealthy cycle had it not been for her children—more specifically, Carolyn. As far as Cathy was concerned, Carter was no more than an obscure stranger whose occasional appearance had little effect on her life. But to Carolyn, he was Daddy. She adored him and, Erica suspected, blamed herself for his loss.

Now Carolyn's blue eyes shimmered with sudden tears. "We're never going to see Daddy again, are we?"

"Of course we are, sweetheart. We'll visit him next summer."

She brightened a little. "Promise?"

"Cross my heart." Erica plastered on what she hoped would pass as an enthusiastic grin and gave her daughter a loving hug. "Now, eat your breakfast. Gramma's waiting."

"Okay."

As Carolyn scooped a drippy spoonful of cereal into her mouth, Erica stepped around a stack of unpacked moving cartons and gazed out the window at the cloudless sky. She hadn't realized how much she'd missed California. Seven years ago, she'd left Los Angeles as a starry-eyed newlywed; now she was back—sadder, wiser and hopefully stronger. With the collapse of her marriage, she'd learned a hard lesson about the folly of unequivocal trust.

It was a lesson she wouldn't forget.

"Good morning, Mr. Arroya."

Roberto's reply was little more than a nod and a grunt, but the smiling receptionist, recognizing the chief prosecutor's distraction as a relatively normal state, simply handed him a stack of pink message memos and gestured toward a large glass-enclosed conference room across the lobby. "The briefing has just started."

With mumbled thanks, Roberto glanced over his shoulder and saw his entire staff seated around the table, engrossed in animated discussion. Since none of them had noticed his tardy entrance, he considered a quick detour to his office to hang up his jacket and drop off his bulging valise. At that moment, Edith Layton, his second-in-command, made eye contact through the windowed wall, offered a relieved smile and vacated Roberto's seat at the table, moving to her usual place on the immediate right.

He sighed, stuffed the pink messages in his coat pocket and went to join his colleagues.

After perfunctory greetings had been exchanged, Roberto settled into his chair and accepted the typed agenda Ms. Layton handed him. He scanned it quickly, spotting a new notation that had been added to the department's current case list.

"What the hell is this?" Roberto stared angrily across the table, focusing on a balding, bespectacled young man who was slumped a few seats away. "You're recommending dismissal?"

Michael Burns leaned forward, propped his forearms against the edge of the polished walnut table and spoke without looking up. "I don't have any choice, Rob. There just isn't enough evidence to indict."

"That's garbage. We've got an eyewitness willing to testify that Frank Caricchio ordered the hit. That's conspiracy to murder, a federal offense, and we, ladies and gentlemen, are the eyes and the arms of federal law." When Burns responded by issuing a nervous cough and tugging his collar, Roberto's gaze narrowed. "We *do* have that witness, don't we? Caricchio's bookkeeper is still in our corner, right?"

"Well...yes. But there's, ah, a problem." Burns slid a pleading glance to his left.

Edith rescued him. "We were just discussing this when you came in, Rob. It seems that the bookkeeper, who is now using the name George Mercier, has an outstanding warrant in Maryland as—" She glanced down at her notes, adjusting her reading glasses a bit further down her nose. "Peter George Milhouse."

Roberto's stomach clamped like a fist, but he still wasn't willing to concede. His office had been after Caricchio too long to roll over and play dead at the first sign of trouble. "So Mercier's not a boy scout. The fact remains that he was in the room when Caricchio handed the victim's picture and a fistful of cash to the shooter. Bank records prove the payment came directly out of Caricchio Development's business account."

Edith removed her glasses and met Roberto's eyes directly. When she said nothing, his heart sank even further.

He pinched the bridge of his nose, wishing he could swallow the question now teetering on the tip of his tongue. He couldn't. "What exactly is Mercier wanted for in Maryland?"

"Embezzlement."

"Damn." For Roberto, it was the worst possible news. Caricchio's lawyers would be relentless in using Mercier's past to defend their client. They'd argue that it was the bookkeeper himself who'd embezzled the funds traced to the hired assassin. The fact that it was Caricchio, not Mercier, who'd benefited from the victim's demise would been deemed irrelevant. All the defense had to prove was reasonable doubt, which the Maryland warrant had handed them on a platter.

Frustrated and furious, Roberto slapped his palm on the table, swore in Spanish, then pushed back his chair and went to the window. Ten floors below, traffic nudged its way along a busy boulevard lined by harried pedestrians. Roberto focused on those people, people he was supposed to protect from the bad guys.

And Frank Caricchio was the worst of them, a ruthless and politically connected land developer with a penchant for permanently eliminating business rivals who vexed him with legitimate competition. Two years ago, when county supervisors were considering a zone change that would turn arid foothill land into prime development acreage, Caricchio got wind of the deal and tried to finesse the landowner into a quick sale. The owner refused. Later, they found the guy slumped over his desk with a bullet in his brain. Since the cash box had been taken, investigators had chalked the death up to a robbery-homicide, despite the fact that Caricchio's company picked the coveted land up at auction for a fraction of its worth.

There'd been similar deaths but never any proof that Caricchio himself had been involved. Then last November, after the body of a competing developer was dumped in the desert outside of Victorville, a terrified George Mercier had contacted federal prosecutors looking to trade information for protection. It had been the break Roberto had been hoping for.

Now his entire case was going down the tubes. He wasn't about to stand idly by and allow that to happen.

Crossing his arms against his chest, he turned to face his grim staff. "Then we'll just have to beef up our case."

"With what?" Burns asked. "Now that Mercier's been discredited, we don't have squat."

"I'm afraid that's true," Edith added, much to Roberto's consternation. "It's not like we have the luxury of poking around blind, either. Caricchio's got friends in high places. If there's even the slightest leak that he's under investigation, we'll have half the state legislature on our backs."

Roberto froze her with a look. "I realize this is a quaint notion, but I was under the impression that our job was to mete out justice despite political ramifications."

Edith laid her glasses on the table. "You're right," she said quietly. "It *is* a quaint notion, existing only in textbooks and conjectural, academic debate. In the real world, the one with the most toys wins. At the moment, Caricchio not only has all the toys, he owns the store."

Although several staff members flinched at her blunt appraisal, Roberto took no umbrage. Forthrightness was only one of the qualities he admired in Edith Layton, who was, in his opinion, the sharpest and most capable attorney on staff. Still, this entire Caricchio mess reeked of a sick system in which justice was doled out only to those who couldn't afford to elude it.

It was a painful validation of harsh lessons learned at Blackthorn Hall: with enough power, you could get away with murder.

But not if Roberto had anything to say about it. The law was his sword now and he intended to use it to take whatever slice he could out of crime and corruption. If there was a legal way to bring Caricchio to justice, Roberto was determined to find it.

After dismissing everyone except Edith and Michael Burns, Roberto turned to Burns. "I want phone taps," he told the stunned attorney. "By the end of the day, I want wires on every line Caricchio is likely to touch—home, office, the public booth across the street—everything. And surveillance video," he added. "If he so much as says 'boo' to a cabbie, I want it on film."

Burns mopped his shiny scalp. "We'll need a court order...there's no precedent—"

"Actually, there's a 1987 case we might use," Edith said. "US versus Tyler, et al. If memory serves, probable cause for issuance of a warrant was established on a theory of imminent public danger."

"There's no imminent danger here," Burns countered, blinking frantically.

Edith smiled sweetly. "Tell that to Caricchio's competitors."

If Burns didn't recognize the droll twinkle in Ms. Layton's eyes, Roberto figured it was because the overwrought little man didn't have a humorous bone in his body. Still, he was a damn good lawyer so Roberto decided to let him off the hook. "There's no such case, Mike. I think Edith is pulling your chain."

She leaned back, grinning. "Spoilsport."

Burns didn't seem to know whether to be annoyed or relieved, so he turned his attention to flipping through the fat file in front of him. "I, ah, might be able to come up with something."

"Good. But make sure it'll hold up, Mike. I don't want this thing overturned on appeal."

Indicating that he understood, Burns scooped up the stack of papers and hurried out of the room.

"Alone at last." Stretching lazily, Edith tucked her hands behind her head and focused a bemused expression on her boss. "Let's see, now. The last time you were an hour late, you had double pneumonia. Since you don't seem to be hacking your lungs out, dare I hope that this morning's tardiness was caused by—please, God—an actual female?"

"As a matter of fact it was." He paused long enough for the perennially matchmaking Ms. Layton's eyes to light. "She was a beauty, too, *la más bonita*—with silky brown hair, bright blue eyes and a laugh to make your heart sing. Unfortunately—" he allowed a melodramatic sigh " —she was a bit young for me."

Edith dismissed that with a swish of her hand. "Hey, this is the twentieth century. Besides, a thirty-year-old bachelor can't afford to be picky." She anxiously leaned forward, propping her chin on her hand. "I want details."

"Well, let's see. I offered to prepare breakfast but she didn't find the menu to her liking, so I took her home, where her mother had the police waiting."

Edith's arm collapsed so quickly that her chin nearly hit the table. "Ah... just how young are we talking here?"

He shrugged. "I'm not sure. Two or three."

"Years or decades?" When he responded with a sly smile, Edith leaned back in her chair. "You're putting me on, right? Retaliation for the little joke I pulled on Mike?"

"Why, I'm hurt. You know perfectly well that I haven't a vengeful bone in my body." When she rolled her eyes, Roberto laughed, took pity on her and explained what had happened.

As he recounted the events of the morning, however, he became tense and edgy. There wasn't anything the least bit amusing about the tragic potential of an innocent child stumbling into the wrong hands.

When he'd finished the story, Edith shook her head. "The poor mother must have been frantic."

Remembering the woman's grief-stricken expression, Roberto conceded, albeit grudgingly, that she had seemed upset. Then he added, "None of it would have happened if her children had been properly supervised."

Edith gave him a narrowed stare. "Not even mothers have eyes in back of their heads. Kids do crazy things sometimes. I ought to know. I raised three of the little devils and some of the things they got into... oy! Makes me crazy to think about it." She reached out and gave his arm a chummy shove. "So, what makes you such an expert on the wee ones of our species?"

"Common sense." The gruff reply signaled his fervent wish that the subject be closed to further discussion. But since his colleague wasn't known to be especially observant of such subtleties, he opted for a cue too blatant to be ignored. Pushing back the chair, he stood and snatched up his valise. "Work with Burns on the Caricchio case," he said brusquely. "Keep me apprised."

"Will do," Edith replied, eyeing him warily.

Regretting his snappish tone but too stubborn to retract it, Roberto issued a curt nod and retreated to the relative privacy of his own office.

After shutting the door to discourage unwanted conversation with passersby, he sidled through the narrow space between bulging file cabinets and a desk cluttered by stacks of case files and unread correspondence. Roberto, who was used to the cramped working space, barely noticed the mess. With seven years of federal law practice under his belt, he was well aware that this walled, windowless cave was considered roomy by government standards.

Normally he found that close surroundings aided his concentration. Not today, though. Today his thoughts wandered in an unsettling direction. But the image drifting through his mind wasn't little Cathy; it was her mother.

There'd been something innately appealing about the woman, something that had caused an odd tightening in his chest that he'd originally attributed to anger. Now, however, he realized that his feelings were more complicated, and was curious as to why the fleeting glimpse of a stranger would have such an unnerving effect on him.

Perhaps it was the overt gratitude in eyes that were even brighter and more intensely blue than those of her daughter. Perhaps it was her vulnerability, the bewildered way she'd touched her throat. Or her choked laughter as she'd smothered her child's face with happy kisses. Whatever it was, Roberto couldn't seem to get her lovely face out of his mind. That annoyed the hell out of him.

Chapter Two

"Grampa!"

That was the only intelligible word Cathy spoke as she scampered up the inlaid slate steps and leapt into Kenneth Mallory's waiting arms. Her wild chatter was, Erica presumed, an accelerated version of this morning's adventure compressed into breathless babble that even a devoted mother couldn't comprehend.

Carolyn, who'd ascended the steps with the unhurried grace of royalty, had no such problem. "Cathy got lost and the doggy's daddy didn't have any Fruity Flakes."

Erica responded to her father's bewildered expression with a weary shrug. "I'll explain later. How's Mama?"

"Much better. Just having you and the girls home has made all the difference." Kenneth struggled to maintain a grip on his squirming granddaughter. "Gracious! Aren't you full of vinegar this morning?"

"Wanna see Gramma," Cathy announced.

He smiled tolerantly. "All right, dear. You know where she is."

Cathy dashed into the house the moment her feet hit the ground. Carolyn, who'd patiently been waiting her turn, was rewarded by a loving hug from her grandfather.

"You look very pretty this morning," he told her.

"Thank you," she replied solemnly, then placed a prim kiss on his cheek before following her sister through the expansive foyer and up the sweeping circular stairs.

Kenneth watched wistfully. "They're both so precious. I can't tell you how much it means that they're here." He turned and gently touched Erica's face. "I can hardly believe that you've finally come home. It's been so long—" His voice broke.

As he swallowed hard and looked away, Erica saw the moisture gathering in his eyes. It was a touching sight and a shocking one. To Erica, her father had always been a rock, a man of exceptional strength and unwavering courage. She'd never seen him lose control of a situation, or of himself. He was powerful, physically, politically, and economically, with steely eyes that struck fear in the hearts of those foolish few who dared displease him.

In all her life, Erica had never seen even the merest hint of tears in those eyes—not ten years ago, when his beloved mother had died; not five years ago, when he'd suffered the massive coronary that had nearly killed him; not even five months ago, when the wife he adored had been felled by a stroke. But here and now, the unmistakable glimmer he futilely tried to blink away brought a lump to Erica's throat.

Not wanting to embarrass him, and because she didn't know what else to do, she simply pretended not to notice and went into the house. She set her purse on the antique entry table. "So, Mama's feeling stronger today?"

From behind her, she heard the click of a closing door. "Yes, and that's not all."

There was a tremor to his voice, a tone of thinly veiled excitement that was strangely out of character for him. She glanced warily over her shoulder. "What do you mean?"

Kenneth looked like a man who wanted to giggle and sob at the same time, yet didn't know how to do either. "Your mother finally used the power lift I installed for her wheelchair and has agreed to the therapy."

"Oh, Daddy." Erica bit her lip, overwhelmed by the news. She stumbled forward and fell into his open arms. "That's wonderful."

"Yes, yes it is. She'll get better now." The final phrase, issued as he hugged his daughter with a fervency bordering on desperation, was delivered as an edict.

Erica stepped back, grinning stupidly and wiping her own wet eyes. "After all this time, what changed her mind?"

"You did."

"Me?"

"And the girls, of course. Because she wants to take an active role in your lives, Jacqueline has decided to do whatever it takes to get back on her feet. For the first time since her stroke, your mother has given herself permission for a future." His voice dropped to a whisper. "She has a chance now. She finally has a chance."

After a brief moment, he roughly cleared his throat, struggling to control the final remnants of what he surely considered to be an unseemly display of emotion. Erica, too, averted her gaze, as much to compose herself as to allow her father a private moment.

The awkward silence was broken, however, as a recognizably pungent aroma wafted into the foyer. Kenneth's head snapped up. "Oh, Lord," he murmured. "The bacon."

With that, he spun around and dashed away. Erica followed, entering the spacious kitchen just as her father flipped off the flame and lifted the sizzling skillet from the hot burner. He set the pan on a sculpted iron trivet.

Erica peered around his shoulder. "Blackened bacon, hmm? I didn't know you were into Cajun cooking. I'm impressed."

Not amused, Kenneth cast a harried glance at the wall clock, then snatched up the skillet and poured its contents, charred slivers and bubbling fat, into a grease can beside the range. "I don't understand," he muttered. "This always seemed so easy for your mother."

Normally Erica wouldn't have been able to resist a teasing remark about female superiority, but at the moment her father seemed so forlorn, so utterly lost, that it nearly broke her heart. Suddenly he looked, well, old. His silvery hair was still lush and full, but there were pouches beneath his eyes that Erica had never noticed before, along with ragged new furrows etching fleshless cheeks that seemed oddly hollow.

A lump of incredible sadness wedged in her throat. Less than a year ago, Kenneth Mallory had been more vital and vigorous than men half his age. Years earlier, a heart attack that would have destroyed lesser men had for him been merely a temporary inconvenience. Through sheer grit, he'd fought his way back to health, insisting that changes in his own diet and lifestyle not inconvenience anyone else, which was why Jacqueline, who had the coronary constitution of a twenty-year-old, continued to enjoy the breakfast bacon that her husband had avoided for the past five years.

Now Kenneth appeared to be fifty-eight going on seventy. His shoulders weren't as straight as Erica remembered, his eyes less clear. It was only 7:00 a.m., yet he looked as tired as if he'd just put in a grueling, twelve-hour day. Erica was worried about him, deeply worried; still, she hesitated to ask about his health, knowing that he considered such inquires irksome.

As Kenneth pulled a package of fresh bacon from the refrigerator, an unexpected voice captured his attention and Erica's.

"Gramma wants you," Carolyn said from the doorway. "She wants to come down and eat."

Kenneth went perfectly still. "Gramma hasn't had breakfast in the kitchen since . . . ah . . . for a very long time. Are you sure that's what she said?"

"Uh-huh. What smells funny?"

"Never mind, sweetie," Erica said, stepping forward to take the wrapped bacon from her father's hands. "Go tell Gramma that he'll be right there, okay?"

"Okay." Wrinkling her nose, Carolyn gave the kitchen a sour glance before leaving. A moment later, her footsteps echoed from the stairs.

"She wants to come down," Kenneth whispered, as if assuring himself that he'd heard correctly. He gazed gratefully at his daughter. "You can see now how important it was for you to come home."

Erica wanted to dispute that but couldn't, because the damnable lump had returned to her windpipe and it was all she could do to breathe.

Thankfully the ringing telephone provided a timely distraction. When Kenneth answered it, Erica turned her attention to cooking another batch of bacon. Before the limp strips were warm, she realized that her father's voice had taken on a strained, almost desperate tone. She glanced over her shoulder and saw him looking at his watch.

"I can't possibly make it by then. My wife's nurse won't be here until nine—" He sucked in a breath, turned away from Erica and lowered his voice. "Of course I want it. All I'm asking is that we postpone the, ah, meeting until later this morning. Yes…yes, I understand. Everything has been arranged . . . pardon me?" Sighing, he rested his forehead against the wall. "No, it's impossible. She can't be left alone—"

Erica touched his sleeve, startling him.

"Ah . . . excuse me," he said into the receiver before covering it with his hand.

"You go to your meeting," Erica told him. "I'll stay with Mama."

He frowned. "I thought you had to meet with the Health Department for a final inspection."

The appointment, which was absolutely crucial to opening her new sandwich shop on time, had been rescheduled for the afternoon. After passing that news on to her father, she added, "The meeting with Carolyn's new teacher isn't until ten, so there won't be any conflict there, either. Besides, helping you with Mama was one of the reasons I moved back. Now, tell whoever that is that you'll be there, okay?"

Kenneth hesitated a moment, then did so—rather brusquely, Erica thought—and hung up. He roughly cleared his throat. "I don't want to take advantage of you, Erica. What with opening a new business and caring for the children, you already have quite enough on your plate."

"That's the beauty of running a place that's only open from eleven to three. I'll be able to spend mornings with Mama, which means you won't be missing so many important planning commission meetings, and I'll still be off early enough to pick Carolyn up at school."

He seemed unconvinced but said only, "Are you sure, dear?"

"Absolutely. Now, you bring Mama downstairs and let me take care of breakfast."

"All right, then." He crossed the room with that same purposeful stride Erica remembered, then paused in the doorway to glance gratefully over his shoulder. "Thank you."

She gave him her brightest smile, managing to hold it until he'd left the room. Alone, she slumped over the stove, listlessly poking the shrinking bacon strips with a fork and wishing to heaven that the Health Department and Carolyn's teacher were all that required her attention today.

Unfortunately, she had a potful of crises, not the least of which was that the electric company had lost the shop's work order, which meant an interminable delay before service could be hooked up. Of course, that might not matter since the refrigerated display case had arrived without a chiller motor and there weren't any ceiling lights because the electrician, who'd broken a foot while docking his yacht, had been unable to climb a ladder and install the darned things.

But these were her problems, not her father's, and she was determined to solve them on her own. There'd been a time when the mere thought of having so many responsibilities would have sent her into a tailspin. Divorce, however, had a way of forcing people to take charge of their own lives.

So she'd manage somehow. She'd care for her mother until the day nurse arrived, then sometime between introductions at Carolyn's new school and the Health inspection, she'd figure a way to get the electric company off its duff, threaten the display case manufacturer with a lawsuit and hire a new electrician.

Yet of all the unpleasant duties facing her today, the one she dreaded most would take place later this evening when she went to issue a personal thank you to her daughter's rescuer, that enigmatic neighbor who, if his disdainful expression had been any clue, wasn't planning to nominate Erica as Mother of the Year.

Instead of being annoyed by his judgmental attitude, Erica secretly agreed with it. There was no excuse for not having immediately installed a chain lock on the front door. Because she'd put it off, her daughter had narrowly avoided disaster and a blameless man had been seriously inconvenienced. Along with her heartfelt gratitude, the very least Mr. Arroya deserved was an apology.

The trouble was that Erica just couldn't shake the feeling that things would be considerably less complicated if she went with her first impression and simply tucked a note under his door.

It was after 7:00 p.m. before Erica was finally organized enough to gather her girls and head down the block to the place Cathy referred to as "Bwuddy's house".

They hadn't gone fifty feet before Carolyn tugged on her sleeve and pointed to the ribboned rawhide chew Cathy was carrying. "How come I don't get to bring the doggy a present?"

"That's from all of us, honey."

She eyed the bow-studded cheese basket her mother was holding. "Is that for the doggy, too?"

"No, this is for Mr. Arroya."

"Is it his birthday?"

"Sometimes people get presents when it's not their birthday, especially if they do something really nice."

Carolyn considered that. "It was real nice of Mr. 'Roya to bring Cathy home, huh?"

"It certainly was. So, would you like to give him our gift?"

"Yeah!" Beaming, Carolyn took the basket and proudly carried it all the way to Buddy's front porch.

As the excited girls dashed up the steps, the wooden planks vibrated as if being stomped by a hoofed herd. Erica winced at the noise and tried to quiet her boisterous children before the angry man she remembered flung the door open and confronted them with weapon in hand.

The effort, however, was futile. Carolyn had already glued her finger to the doorbell and Cathy seemed intent on bashing the door down with Buddy's gift-wrapped bone. The final smack bounced off the thigh of the shocked man who finally opened the door and who, thankfully, was holding nothing more lethal than a half-eaten sandwich.

He gaped at them with an expression that would have been comical had Erica not been so mortified. Apologizing profusely, she plucked the rawhide chew from Cathy's hand. Before the understandably startled man could close his mouth, a quivering mass of gray hair lunged onto the porch.

Cathy shrieked with delight and grabbed the ecstatic pooch in a bear hug. "Be careful," Erica admonished, reaching down to loosen the child's grip. "You'll hurt the doggy."

Cathy released the animal, which instantly leapt up and washed her face with a drippy pink tongue. Sputtering, Cathy pulled away from the affectionate lick-fest just as Erica was alerted by a crafty glint in her daughter's eye. She reached out a moment too late. Cathy ducked under her hand and dashed into the house, squealing. The dog followed.

Erica stood there with a handful of air, painfully aware the poor man whose home had just been invaded still hadn't uttered a word. Or closed his mouth, for that matter. Her skittering gaze landed on the sandwich in his hand. "Well," she said brightly. "I'm glad you like cheese."

On that cue, Carolyn stepped forward and held out the brightly wrapped basket. "It's a present," she explained with the exaggerated patience children bestow upon unenlightened adults. "For being a nice man."

An extraordinary thing happened. The dark eyes that had been black with disapproval this morning and numbed by confusion only moments ago suddenly glowed with a softness that took Erica's breath away.

As he bent to accept the basket, Roberto flashed a smile that could have lit a small city. "Thank you."

"You're welcome." She cocked her head, peering up with the unfathomable expression that had been her trademark almost since birth. "Can I come in?"

"Carolyn!"

Ignoring Erica's startled rebuke, Roberto answered the child directly. "Certainly." He straightened, still smiling, and stepped aside. After watching Carolyn glide regally through the doorway, he turned to Erica. The warmth drained from his eyes, replaced by something she hoped was curiosity rather than displeasure.

Feeling silly, she thrust the ribboned bone at him and blurted, "This is for the dog."

The corner of his mouth twitched. "I'm relieved to hear that."

Smiling, Erica relaxed—just a little—as he shifted the basket to the crook of his arm, accepted Buddy's gift and graciously invited her in.

She hesitated. "I don't want to interrupt your eve ning—" A resounding thud echoed from somewhere in side, followed by childish laughter, excited barks and the insistent vibration of scampering feet. Somehow, Erica managed not to moan aloud. Instead, she forced a strained smile. "Then again, I guess we've already interrupted it, haven't we?"

"Not at all," he said smoothly, although Erica knew he was lying through his perfect white teeth. At the moment, it sounded as though the circus had hit town and was train ing elephants in his kitchen.

But she had to give the man credit for maintaining his cool. Despite having been thrust into sudden chaos, he was the consummate host, politely offering her refreshment while unobtrusively placing the remains of his sandwich on a paper plate containing crumbs and a few uneaten potato chips.

After declining his offer, Erica nervously clasped her hands, avoiding eye contact by absently glancing around a room comfortably furnished with distinctly masculine earth tone plaids and chunky oak tables cluttered with over-stuffed file folders and loose paper. And, of course, the remnants of his evening meal. "We've disrupted your din ner as well," she said. "I'm so sorry."

"Dinner is much too elegant a term, Ms.—?"

"Franklin, Erica Franklin." She absently extended her hand, where it dangled briefly while he elbowed a clearing in the mess and set the basket on the coffee table.

"Roberto Arroya." He straightened and took her hand with a smile that was pleasant, though guarded. "I'm pleased to meet you, Ms. Franklin."

"Erica, please." The innocuous words sounded idiotically breathless, as though the tingling sensation in her palm had suddenly glided up to numb her foolish tongue.

Roberto hadn't squeezed her hand in a viselike clench, as was the habit of most businessmen who automatically use handshakes as a signal of strength. Instead his palm embraced hers tenderly, almost intimately, in a gesture that seemed very much like a caress. His surprisingly gentle grip was further softened by the smooth skin of a man who works with his mind instead of his hands.

The intimacy of touch was also reflected in his eyes, eyes that Erica now realized weren't nearly as dark as she'd first thought. They were, instead, a golden brown, almost amber, accentuated with a stubby fringe of coffee-colored lashes that matched both his brows and that luscious mane of softly curled hair.

As she scrutinized him, he was also studying her. Blinking, she realized that they'd been holding hands and staring at each other far longer than a normal how-do-you-do required. Apparently he recognized that as well, because he finally withdrew his hand, glancing down at it as though it felt strange before shoving it into his pocket.

She should have been relieved; instead, she felt a peculiar sense of loss.

Rocking back on his heels, Roberto regarded her with an intensity that was both exciting and unnerving. "So what can I do for you, Erica?"

"Do for me?" she repeated stupidly, with vague but discomfiting awareness that the odd numbing sensation had apparently drifted from her hand to her brain. She tried again. "Oh, you've done too much already."

"Excuse me?"

"I mean, that's why I'm here. To thank you...for giving me Cathy." She cringed, hoping against hope that she hadn't really said that. And if she had, she prayed he hadn't noticed the unintended implication.

A glimmer of amusement in his eyes indicated that he had indeed noticed. "It was my pleasure."

Sighing, she studied her sneakers, ignored the embarrassing innuendo, and cut right to the chase. "My daughter's little adventure this morning could have been tragic. Thanks to you, it wasn't. Words simply can't express my gratitude for that."

When he didn't respond immediately, she skimmed a glance upward and was taken aback by his somber expression. "You needn't thank me. I was happy to help." He paused a moment, as if gathering his thoughts. "I am, however, pleased to know you are aware that a lack of proper supervision for any child, particularly one as young as Cathy, carries a serious and potentially grave consequence."

It took a moment for the crux of that statement to sink in. When it did, Erica was stiff with indignation. "Are you suggesting that my children are not properly supervised?"

"Considering the morning's events, one could logically conclude that more vigilance on your part would have been appropriate."

Although the man wasn't saying anything that Erica hadn't already told herself a mere million times, she was nonetheless irritated that a stranger would take the liberty of insulting her without understanding the facts. Even so, his disapproval stung more deeply than she could have ever imagined. For some reason, she'd wanted him to like her. That weakness on her part made her even angrier, as did the fact that his accusation put a sharper edge on her own guilt.

"Your conclusion is duly noted," she replied coolly.

"I've upset you."

There seemed no reason to confirm the obvious. "Do you live with children, Mr. Arroya?"

"No."

"I thought not."

"But if I did, I can assure you that they wouldn't be wandering the streets alone at six in the morning."

Outraged by his pompous tone, Erica jammed her hands on her hips and would have told him bluntly what she thought of such self-righteous drivel except that a barely audible whimper caught her attention. She looked over her shoulder and saw Carolyn standing in the kitchen doorway with huge tears rolling down her cheeks. "Carolyn...what is it? What's wrong?"

"My...fault," she said tearfully. "I...did it."

Instantly Erica crossed the room and knelt to take the trembling child in her arms. "Did what, sweetie?"

"I l-lost Cathy."

A frisson of fear skittered down Erica's spine, then dissipated as she looked into the kitchen and saw her youngest child sitting placidly on the floor with her arm around Buddy. Returning her attention to Carolyn, she wiped the child's wet face and questioned her calmly. "Cathy's not lost anymore. Everything's just fine."

"But she coulda' got hurt and it woulda' been all my f-fault."

"Oh, Carolyn, that's not true at all. We've already talked about this. You didn't mean to leave the door open. It was an accident. Accidents happen all the time."

"B-but everybody's mad."

"Not at you, darling. No one is mad at you." Erica kissed each of her damp cheeks, then embraced her fiercely. "I love you more than a hot fudge sundae. How much do you love me?"

Clinging to her mother, Carolyn sniffed, wiped her eyes and whispered, "I love you more than, umm, a brand new Barbie doll."

Erica emitted a low whistle. "Wow, that much? Gosh, I'm a lucky mommy."

Smiling now, Carolyn completed her part of the ritual by giving her mother a big kiss and an even bigger hug. When she finally stepped away, she wiped her eyes with the back of her hand and angled a wary glance at their host. "Mommy was taking a shower and I went outside to get the paper and... and... maybe I forgot to shut the door real tight."

Bending to the child's level, Roberto stroked her damp cheek with his knuckle. "It was an accident, punkin. Like your mommy said, nobody's mad at you."

A slight tremble in his voice made Erica look over her shoulder. What she saw amazed her. That expression of aloof superiority had melted into one of compassionate concern and... could it be regret?

If it was, he didn't express it to Erica. Instead, he focused on Carolyn and once again displayed the dazzling smile that did such peculiar things to Erica's pulse rates.

"I've heard that chocolate chip cookies are guaranteed to make sad little girls feel better," he told Carolyn. "What would you say about testing that theory? If it's all right with your mother, of course."

Carolyn's pleading gaze focused on Erica. "Can I, please?"

"We really should be going..." The words evaporated at the disappointment reflected in her daughter's moist eyes. "Well, all right. Just one."

Carolyn's usually solemn face lit in what was, for her, an extremely animated expression. In the kitchen, Cathy gleefully clapped her hands, apparently ascertaining that if Carolyn got a cookie, she'd probably get one, too.

Roberto opened the pantry, laughing as both girls and the yipping dog crowded around him. "Whoa, gang. Give me some elbow room here."

Carolyn instantly stepped back, as did Buddy. Cathy, who didn't seem to believe the request applied to her, grabbed Roberto's belt buckle and hoisted up on her tiptoes to get a better view of the goodies lining the neat shelves. "Want a *big* cookie," she announced.

Erica, embarrassed, hastened to correct her daughter's social blunder. "That's impolite, Cathy."

Inquisitive blue eyes focused on Erica as though seeing her for the first time. "How come?"

"Well...it just is." Her lame reply, which seemed to amuse their host immensely, was even more embarrassing. The man already believed her to be a careless mother; now he probably thought she was a stupid one as well.

Erica wondered why that bothered her. Considering that Roberto Arroya was basically a stranger, his opinion shouldn't matter. The fact that it did was irritating enough to strengthen both her tone and resolve. "Now please let go of Mr. Arroya and move back like he asked you to do."

Fortunately, the child obeyed without displaying the stubborn streak that was the bane of her mother's existence. A sigh of relief lodged in her throat as she glanced up and saw Roberto's smile of approval. Her pulse quickened. Their gazes met and held for a dizzying moment.

Erica forgot to breathe. This man was without doubt the most charismatic human being she'd ever met in her life. There was a sophistication about him, an air of intelligence and genuine style; but at the same time, an underlying aura of raw sexuality which threatened to overwhelm the cultured image Erica suspected he took great pains to maintain.

There was something else, too, something Erica sensed rather than saw. She couldn't quite identify this elusive quality but intuitively felt the heat of it seething somewhere deep inside him. It frightened her a little; fascinated her more.

Just as her lungs began to ache, he blinked and turned away. Erica's breath slid out all at once. Her heart was racing. She felt limp and shaky, causing her to steady herself on the doorjamb. By the time she'd caught her breath, Roberto was calmly distributing the promised treats, including a colorful dog biscuit for Buddy.

Cathy, who'd snagged the first cookie and bitten it in half, now made a belated attempt to emulate her big sister's polite acceptance. Cheeks bulging, she blurted ''Fankoo-o'' through a spray of wet crumbs.

Erica moaned and covered her eyes. Only when she heard a throaty masculine chuckle did she chance a peek between her fingers and saw Roberto, oblivious to the soggy specks clinging to his otherwise spotless shirt, bending to the child's level.

''Slow down, *amiguita*,'' he said, gently wiping her mouth with his thumb. ''Cookies belong in your tummy, not on your face, okay?''

Still chewing madly, Cathy started to speak but caught Carolyn's disapproving look and wisely chose to respond with a tidy nod.

''That's my girl. You're lucky to have a big sister who's such a good teacher.'' Straightening, Roberto patted her head and winked at Carolyn, who puffed with pride at the praise.

It occurred to Erica that the enigmatic Mr. Arroya had paid more attention to her children in the past few minutes than their own father had in the past six years. Although deeply saddened by the observation, Erica was also encouraged to see that Carter's coldness wasn't universal to his gender.

Intellectually, of course, she'd always understood that. Her own father, on those rare occasions when he hadn't been working, had always treated Erica with love and tenderness. Still, she was heartened by the proof that there were other such men in the world, men who treated children kindly and nurtured their feelings. Men like Roberto Arroya.

"...so, can we, Mommy?"

"Hmm?" Disrupted from her thoughts, she realized that Carolyn had been speaking to her. "Can you what, sweetie?"

"Can we go out and play with Buddy?"

"Oh. No, we have to go home."

"But Mommy—"

"I'm sorry, Carolyn, but it'll be bedtime in an hour and you haven't even had your baths yet. Now thank Mr. Arroya for the cookies and wait for me on the front porch, okay?"

Carolyn heaved a sigh then did as she was told, trudging demurely toward the entry while her little sister emitted an earsplitting shriek and raced Buddy through the living room.

"Don't—" the front door slammed "—slam the door," Erica finished lamely. She angled a sheepish glance at their host. "I'm sorry. They're not usually so...ah..."

"Exuberant?"

She relaxed a little. "Actually, they're always exuberant. It's just that they're normally a bit more controllable."

"They're sweet kids," he said. "But while we're in the apology mode, I might as well add mine before you tell your husband what a judgmental jerk I am and he decides to punch my lights out."

The image of Carter confronting anyone more than half his size made her smile. "Since my ex-husband lives two states away, your lights are perfectly safe."

Every trace of amusement drained from his eyes and was instantly replaced by a cool rebuke that sent chills down her spine. "I'm sorry to hear that. Separating children from their father perpetrates a terrible injustice on both."

Taken aback by his abrupt change in attitude, Erica found herself on the defensive. "Apparently you're under the assumption that every man who fathers a child actually wants to be a father. I assure you, nothing could be further from the truth. As for injustice, the world is full of it. I can't change that, Mr. Arroya, and unless you have power beyond the realm of mere mortals, neither can you."

A perplexed frown creased his brow, followed by an expression of incredible sadness. "You're right, of course. I was out of line to comment on something which is quite clearly none of my business. Please accept my apology."

"Of course," she murmured, bewildered by an unpredictability that, somehow, seemed strangely rational. In fact, considering his obvious sensitivity to the subject of father's rights, a thought struck her. "Have you been separated from your children, Mr. Arroya?"

He managed a smile. "I thought we were on a first name basis, particularly since I've given you a daughter." She returned his smile, blushing madly, but made no other reply. After a moment, he glanced away. "I've never been married and I have no children, but a friend of mine recently went through hell when his ex-wife remarried and moved their kids two thousand miles away."

"That must have been very difficult for him."

Roberto nodded. Since Erica could think of nothing else to say, she reminded him that the girls were waiting and the enigmatic Mr. Arroya instantly slipped back into the repose of courteous host, escorting her to the door and bidding them all an unhurried goodbye.

During the short walk home, the girls were all a-chatter about their handsome neighbor and his gregarious, if not so handsome canine companion. Pasting on an agreeable smile, Erica nodded at appropriate intervals but made no comment, lest her perceptive daughters notice that she, too, had been completely entranced. Her mind was filled with images of the enigmatic Mr. Arroya, of the dazzling smile he'd shared only with the children and the desperate despair that had so suddenly appeared in his dark eyes, then vanished without a trace.

No doubt about it, he was a most intriguing man. Of course, the last thing Erica needed at this point in her life was another man, intriguing or otherwise. Experience had taught her that men, particularly the good-looking variety, were about as trustworthy as a congressional lobbyist.

Carter's infidelities had broken Erica's heart. She wasn't about to risk that kind of pain again, nor would she risk subjecting her children to another stinging loss. The decision to avoid emotional entanglements had been a rational one, based on sound logic and concern for her family.

It was also a decision made before she'd met Roberto Arroya.

Chapter Three

At first the dream seemed benign enough. He was surrounded by a feathery fog, cool and pleasant, a refreshing chill on a sultry summer day. There was no urgency to his stroll, none of the intuitive foreboding preceding the nightmares of his youth. He was, in fact, enjoying himself, feeling free, unencumbered by even normal day-to-day tension and stress.

Then the pulsing mist thickened, obscuring his vision, icing his skin. His heart beat faster, harder; adrenaline squirted through his veins. Suddenly he wanted to run, but was blinded by the dense fog and didn't know which way to turn. The hairs on his nape rose, electrified by unseen danger. Something was out there. Something evil.

The mist stirred. At first it was little more than a gentle swirl; then a tornadic wind encircled him, howling like a demon. In the vortex of spinning vapor was a man, squat and ugly, with a skunklike streak striping greasy black hair. His grinning mouth moved without sound. A moment later

Frank Caricchio's words swirled like the whirling haze, coming from nowhere, yet everywhere. "I have the power . . . you can't stop me . . . I have the power . . ."

There was another voice in the background, soft and feminine, husky with indignation. "As for injustice, the world is full of it. I can't change that . . . neither can you."

He spun around, searching for the woman, whom he feared was also trapped in the sinister fog, and tried to call her name but couldn't speak, couldn't warn her of the danger.

Caricchio called into the whirling abyss. "Do it . . . kill him . . . do it . . ." There was a gunshot. Cruel laughter. The acrid smell of death.

A body slumped out of the mist, collapsing at Caricchio's feet. It was a small body, thin and pale, with a tied clump of flaccid brown hair; a white inhaler fell from his pocket. Then Chancellor Ogden Marlow emerged from the fog with a smoking gun in his hand.

Roberto bolted upright, gasping, drenched with sweat. A terrifying paralysis numbed his throat. He couldn't scream. He couldn't utter a sound.

Whipping off the blanket, he dropped his feet to the floor and sat there, slumped forward, until his breathing eased and his pulse slowed.

The mattress vibrated. A fuzzy form settled beside him with a comforting whine. Buddy understood; he'd seen this before. Roberto stroked him, as much to console himself as to reassure the concerned dog.

After a moment, he tested his legs. They were shaky, but they worked.

Once in the bathroom, Roberto turned the faucets on full blast to splash his face with cold water, then shivered, propped his forearms on the counter and sagged over the sink. Snippets of the nightmare continued to flash through his weary mind. Caricchio. Marlow. Tommy Murdock.

But it was the feminine voice that haunted him, husky, soft, like sun-warmed corduroy. Erica Franklin's voice.

Roberto straightened, took a shuddering breath, then went into the kitchen and drank half a quart of orange juice right out of the carton. The rhythmic tap of doggy toenails announced Buddy's arrival. The animal yawned, gazed into the open refrigerator without enthusiasm, then padded away to plop in a favored location beside the water cooler.

Roberto closed the fridge, sat at the table and stared glumly into the darkness. It wasn't enough that thoughts of his beautiful neighbor disturbed his waking hours; now she was invading his private nightmares. Penance, he suspected, for having behaved so abysmally toward her.

Puffing his cheeks, he blew out a breath, closed his eyes and tried to figure out what in the holy hell was wrong with him. The moment he'd laid eyes on Erica Franklin, something inside him had cracked. That had startled and unnerved him.

He didn't want to be attracted to her, but he was. He didn't even want to like her, but he did. He liked her too damned much, despite his unfair criticism and rudeness to which she'd responded with admirable force.

But it was watching Erica comfort her tearful daughter that had touched him most deeply. Since his own experience with maternal tenderness had been limited, to say the least, he'd been fascinated by the depth of her compassion and love. He'd wondered what it must be like to feel such gentleness, such unconditional love. It had been at that very moment when Roberto realized that Erica Franklin and her beautiful children represented all that he'd been denied in life.

And all that he'd ever wanted.

As September mornings went, this was cooler than most. Then again, with the sun barely clear of the horizon, this lazy Saturday was yet to experience the full impact of what would certainly evolve into a real scorcher and send all but the hardiest souls scurrying to whatever air-conditioned space was available.

Meanwhile, Roberto enjoyed the morning's respite with a routine run along the shady sidewalks of the neighborhood park. Without breaking the comfortable rhythm, he spoke to his four-footed jogging partner. "So if you're Caricchio's defense team, facing indisputable evidence that corporation money paid a hired assassin, you'd have to accept the fact that the agreement has been reached, which is all the *actus reus* prosecution needs to prove, right?"

Padding beside him, Buddy replied with what Roberto interpreted as an affirmative yip.

"And you'd have no choice but to imply that someone besides your client, i.e. George Mercier, was involved in that agreement. For the sake of argument, let's say it turns out that old George was involved clear up to his eyeballs. Let's also say George told the shooter that Caricchio was behind the scene giving orders—" Interrupted by a critical growl, Roberto frowned at his canine companion. "Coconspirator exception to the hearsay rule, remember?"

Cocking his prickly head, Buddy peered up with what could be charitably considered a sheepish expression.

Mollified, Roberto continued. "Anyway, would you use the Pinkerton precedent, arguing that Caricchio knew of the conspiracy and was therefore an accessory before the fact? Or would you cut straight to Blumenthal, on the grounds that even if Caricchio had no direct contact, having knowledge of the assassin's existence made him a necessary link in the chain of criminal intent?"

Buddy barked.

"Yeah, that's what I think. In either case, *mens rea* requirements shouldn't be a problem—"

The dog interrupted with a series of even more enthusiastic barks, then veered in front of Roberto, nearly tripping him, and dashed toward the park playground.

"Hey!" he called out, sprinting a few steps onto the grass. "Where the hell are you?—" He stopped abruptly, recognizing the giggling girls who'd dropped from the monkey bars to greet their furry friend. From the corner of his eye, he noticed the armrest of a wrought iron bench that was partially obscured by shrubbery. At the same time, he felt a peculiar tingling along his spine and knew without looking who was there.

The soft corduroy voice held just a hint of amusement. "Do you always argue legal theory with your dog?"

Feeling supremely foolish, Roberto nonetheless managed to face her with a suitably bland expression. "Only if he's studied the proper precedents."

"I see," Erica murmured, her eyes dancing. She looked as if she wanted to say more. Thankfully, she was distracted.

"Mommy, look!" Carolyn hollered from the playground. "Buddy's gonna go down the slide!"

Shading her eyes, Erica followed her daughter's excited gesture. "Well, I'll be," she said, laughing as the dog skillfully climbed the metal ladder. "Is there no end to his talent?"

"If there is, I haven't found it." Smiling with almost paternal pride, Roberto watched Buddy flatten onto his elbows and belly down the polished chute. After plopping into the sand, the animal leapt up and ran circles around the vanquished apparatus, his pink tongue flapping like a victory flag.

Carolyn cheered, clapping madly. Cathy laughed so hard she fell over and was instantly set upon by the worried animal, who transformed his flag back into a tongue and licked every inch of the giggling child's face.

Roberto called out, "Time to go, Buddy-boy. You've shown off enough for one day."

Carolyn whirled as though shot. "Can't he stay…just for a little while?"

God, she was an adorable child. "Well..."

"Please?" Clutching her hands together, she dropped to her knees. "Pretty please?"

Resistance was futile. Shaking his head, he simply turned and walked toward the bench, smiling at the renewed squeals emanating from behind him. "Do you mind if I join you?"

"Of course not."

He paused as Erica hastily moved what appeared to be a stack of flyers from the bench and set them, along with what appeared to be a list of some kind, beside a canvas tote on the ground.

As she scooted over to allow him more room, he realized that the morning's jog had left him sweaty and disheveled; not the most desirable attributes in a bench mate.

She, on the other hand, looked freshly scrubbed, scrupulously groomed and just plain gorgeous. From her immaculate sneakers and crisp knee shorts to the fashionably loose sweater that seemed her only concession to the morning chill, Erica Franklin portrayed the absolute epitome of casual chic.

Self-conscious, he seated himself at the far end of the bench. With the armrest pressing into his ribs, he wiped a fleece-clad forearm across his face to absorb some of the moisture, then furtively removed the terry cloth headband that, although eminently practical, made him look like a first-class dweeb.

Aware that she was scrutinizing him closely, he feigned nonchalance, draped an arm casually over the bench rail, and blurted, "So, how about those Dodgers?"

The corners of her eyes crinkled. "What with another baseball strike, I'm not sure how to answer that."

"Oh, sure. Well, ah, I meant before the walkout."

"Weren't they having their worst season in twenty years?"

"Ah...right. My point exactly." His desperate gaze slipped to the flyers at her feet. "Having a garage sale?"

"Hmm?" She followed his gaze. "Oh. No, I'm having a Grand Opening. Those are the announcements."

"That's a good idea," he replied, without paying much attention to the flyers in question. "I thought about holding an open house when I bought my place, but I never got around to it. It looks like yours will be quite an event," he added, nodding at the impressive stack.

When her lush lips parted in a smile of genuine delight, he relaxed. But not for long.

"I'm afraid I won't be having a housewarming," she said gently. "Setting up a new business takes so much time." With that, she handed him a flyer and to her credit, kept a straight face as he read it. "I used to work in a deli, so when I was looking for a business with short hours, a sandwich shop seemed like a natural way to put my experience to use."

Well, this was great, he thought with no small agitation. The woman had the brains and chutzpah to create her own business, and he'd blithely assumed that she was planning a sweet little house party. Not only had he presented himself as having the IQ of a gnat, she probably thought him sexist as well.

And there seemed no safe way to correct that errant impression. If he'd been in court, he could have pleaded his case with trademark eloquence. Under the current circumstance, however, he was afraid to open his mouth; God only knew what idiocy might fall out.

But if Erica was offended, she was too well-bred to reveal it. Instead, she fiddled with a silky strand of honey brown hair and slid him a shy little smile that made his pulse flutter. "Perhaps you'd like to come."

"Where?" Brilliant question, considering the flyer was still clutched in his clammy hand. "Oh."

"There'll be refreshments," she said quickly. "Nothing fancy, I'm afraid. Just punch and cookies and...and..."

Looking pained, she studied her knees. "It was just a thought. You'll probably be busy."

"Not necessarily. I mean, I'd have to check my schedule but, ah . . ." He angled another look at the printed sheet, frowned and inspected the details more carefully. The business in question, appropriately christened The Sandwich Shoppe, was less than two blocks from his office. "Spring Street is a good location. The city hall annex, courthouse and downtown library are all in walking distance."

"That's the idea. My father knows a lot of people at city hall and he's been nudging every one of them to try our specialty lunch menu."

"Which includes?"

"Lots of good things. The Conservative, for example, is a grilled tuna melt served with potato salad, and The Flaming Liberal consists of ham on a jalapeño roll and spicy bean salad." She grinned at his incredulous expression. "Since the shop is situated in the political heart of the city, a bipartisan menu seemed to make sense. I've also developed a turkey club called The Watergate—complete with secret sauce, of course—and my Iran-Contra BLT is to die for."

She spoke with such good-humored pride, Roberto couldn't help but laugh. "And if I were to study the shop's menu in the proper frame of mind, would I be able to decipher the hidden political agenda of its owner?"

"That depends. If I were to examine your caseload, would I be able to deduce your opinion on, say, the U.S. military's role as the world's police force?"

"*¡Ay, caramba!* That's deep. You're not just a pretty face, are you?"

She smiled sweetly and repeated the question, to which Roberto responded with acute candor, thus launching a lively political debate. Over the next hour they discussed, argued, disputed and occasionally agreed upon a vast array of complex and diverse ideology, from the theory of global warming to constitutional implications of prayer in public schools.

The good-natured wrangling was both enjoyable and intriguing. Roberto discovered, for example, that the lovely Erica Franklin was an avowed fiscal conservative, who paradoxically supported public assistance and firmly believed rehabilitation more effective than punishment. Since Roberto's convictions were just as contradictory—a social liberal with traditional family values and a hard-nosed, throwaway-the-key attitude on crime—their discussions were spirited, to say the least.

Despite obvious differences, the debate never drifted into rancor or disrespect. In fact, Roberto found Erica's opinions to be refreshingly thoughtful and based on sound logic and insightful intellect. She was highly informed, able to cite source material in support of, or to dispute, any particular view on a wide variety of topics.

Her impressive memory tripped him up more than once, especially when she tossed back his own words, quoting him verbatim, then dissecting the precise semantics of what he'd said versus what he'd meant to say. He was chagrined to realize that prevailing in a definition dispute was damned near impossible when one's learned opponent could recite *Webster's Dictionary* chapter and verse.

Not that he hadn't held his own. In fact, he'd just backed her into a figurative corner on the mathematical merits of the Pythagorean theorem when she suddenly tossed up her hands.

"All right, already. If you insist that Euclid came up with the formula, then I'll take your word for it. But I could have sworn that Babylonian tradition says otherwise."

"Oh, it does," he assured her. "First proof has always been attributed to Pythagoras, but the commoner proof was given by Euclid three centuries later."

She shook her head. "You must have been a very precocious child."

The comment startled him, as did the blatant admiration in her eyes. He looked away, feeling phony. If she knew that his childhood had been one of degradation and poverty, those beautiful eyes would be filled with pity instead of respect. So he simply shrugged without comment and was relieved when Carolyn appeared beside the bench.

"It's too hot," she said, yanking off her sweater and dropping it, along with her sister's, in a wad at her mother's feet. Then she turned to Roberto. "Will you push us on the swings?"

"Now, Carolyn, it's not nice to put people on the spot like that," Erica told her.

"But if I don't ask, how will he know what I want?"

"She has a point," Roberto said. "Besides, everyone knows that swings are twice as much fun with a good pusher."

Carolyn let out a whoop and dashed toward the playground. "He's gonna push us!" she shouted at her sister, who instantly crawled off the corrugated merry-go-round and scurried to the swing set.

"Now you've done it," Erica told him. "When it comes to swings, they each have the constitution of an astronaut. You could push them for a week and they'd still be crying for more."

"I don't know about a week, but it won't hurt me to give them a few minutes."

"Still, it's nice of you." She gave him a grateful smile, then retrieved the rumpled sweaters.

He found himself fascinated by the way she folded the garments before tucking them neatly into the canvas tote. In point of fact, everything about Erica Franklin was fascinating, from the prim way she crossed her slender ankles to the funny twitch at the corner of her mouth that conveyed amusement. He would have been perfectly content to stay there all day.

As Carolyn hollered an impatient reminder, however, he realized each girl had claimed a swing and was eyeing him expectantly. So he reluctantly stood, flexing his stiff muscles, and sloughed through the sand, past Buddy, who was resting in the shade of a seesaw, to where the girls were waiting.

"Real high," Cathy said the moment he arrived. "I wanna go re-e-al high."

Carolyn cupped her mouth and whispered loudly enough for anyone in the park to hear, "She can't go real high. She's just a baby."

To which her sister indignantly insisted, "Am not!"

"Are, too."

"Am *not!*" Cathy shrieked, causing Carolyn to roll her eyes and, much to Roberto's relief, drop the matter entirely.

"Hang on," he counseled, waiting for Cathy to wrap her fingers around the fat chain before the first tentative push.

"Higher," she chortled. "Wanna go higher."

"Pump your legs," Carolyn suggested helpfully. "Watch me."

She demonstrated the technique, emitting a delighted giggle when Roberto caught her on the backswing and propelled her to even greater heights.

It took a few minutes for Roberto to establish a synchronized rhythm of sidestepping the backward momentum of one swing to propel the next one forward. The process was a bit more complex than first calculated, although he soon got the hang of it and was having almost as much fun as the girls.

As his confidence increased, he chanced a glance at the bench and caught Erica watching him with an oddly pensive expression. When their eyes met, she quickly looked away and began fiddling with what appeared to be the same list that she'd been reviewing earlier.

Roberto also discovered that with only a bit more concentration, he could vary the rhythm to sneak more frequent glances in Erica's direction, thereby enjoying the ethereal radiance of sunlight reflecting from her shiny hair. There was something about her that gave distinction to commonplace events. Sunlight, for example. A cyclical emanation of solar energy which, upon touching this beguiling woman, metamorphosized into a mysterious, mesmerizing aura. Amazing, he decided. And certainly worth a second look. For purely scientific reasons, of course, which justified his interest and required no further search for a deeper motive.

That is, until Erica suddenly dabbed her forehead, then seized the hem of her sweater and yanked the garment over her head to expose a cutoff T-shirt and a startling expanse of bare skin.

Roberto froze, gawking like a schoolboy. That's when Carolyn's swing slammed into his ribs.

Through a crimson fog, Roberto was vaguely aware of being flat on his back, gasping to refill traumatically deflated lungs. For a disoriented moment, he wondered if there was an elephant sitting on his chest because the effort to breathe wasn't going well at all. In fact the only sound he heard, aside from a peculiar rushing behind his ears, was an unpleasant wheezing that reminded him of air being sucked through a flat straw.

Something patted his cheek, something small and cool. A child's hand, perhaps. Muffled words seemed to be circling him, too, words which would have been audible if not for that ungodly death rattle.

Roberto had just about given up hope of ever drawing another breath when his rib cage convulsed and air exploded into his starving lungs. With every subsequent gasp, the annoying tinnitus dissipated and his mind started to clear.

"Mr. Arroya...Roberto...can you hear me? Are you all right?"

He tried to reassure Erica that he was fine, but all that came out of his mouth was that damned flat straw sound. Then something wet and cold poked into his ear—a less than thrilling sensation—followed by the drippy warmth of a wet tongue dragged across his face.

Roberto reared up, sputtering, and found his voice. "*¡Quitate!*"

Whining, Buddy responded to his master's choked command by moving back a few inches and executing a "sit" that was shaky at best. With his squirming little butt bouncing on the ground, the agitated animal was obviously prepared to spring into licking mode at the slightest provocation.

Since that was a situation Roberto preferred to avoid, he managed a limp but reassuring pat between the dog's prickly-pert ears. "Good—" pause for breath "—boy."

As Buddy woofed happily, Roberto realized that Erica was kneeling beside him. Not only that, she was actually holding him up.

"Are you hurt?" she asked, scrutinizing him anxiously. "Should I call a doctor?"

"No. I'm fine . . . really."

Since the assurance was punctuated by a wince of pain, Erica framed his face with hands that were incredibly soft and urged him to look up. She studied his eyes—probably checking the evenness of his pupils. But despite that Samaritan motive, Roberto found himself hypnotized by the intensity of her gaze.

To his surprise, he realized that her eyes weren't your normal, everyday run-of-the-mill blue. They were a smoky cobalt with flecks of vivid emerald. Extraordinary, he thought, as distinctive as the sweet fragrance wafting from her hair. Honeysuckle, with a citrusy tang. Exotic. Alluring.

Seductive.

"Mr. Arroya?"

He blinked, realizing that she'd been speaking to him. "Excuse me?"

"I asked if you were in pain."

Absolutely, but not the kind she meant. "No."

"Are you sure? That was a terrible blow." Her gentle hands moved down to delicately probe his rib cage. "Any soreness here? Or here?"

Roberto hadn't known that a touch could be so tender. Not trusting his voice, he shook his head.

Her hand lingered a moment, her fingertips grazing his chest with a feathery stroke that seemed more like a caress than an inspection. Then she sat back on her heels, allowing him a full view of the cropped top that had distracted him in the first place. It seemed oddly proper now, extending nearly to her waist. But with her arms raised...well, that had been an entirely different matter. Still, he was unnerved by his reaction. He was, after all, thirty years old and hadn't hyperventilated over a flash of feminine skin since his days as a hormone-pickled adolescent.

As he mulled that over, a muffled sob caught his attention and Erica's. When he looked up, Cathy was standing a few feet away, sucking on her index finger, watching him with eyes as round as lunch plates. Behind her was Carolyn, mouth contorted, shoulders quivering, tears streaming down her face. "I-I didn't mean to," she wailed.

In less than a heartbeat, Erica was on her feet, consoling the distraught child. "Of course you didn't." But Carolyn was inconsolable. Clutching her mother, she continued to sob violently while Erica stroked her hair, murmuring. "There, there, sweetness. It's all right. Mr. Arroya isn't hurt and everything is going to be just fine."

Finally, Carolyn's red eyes focused on Roberto. "Are y-you mad at m-me?"

The girl's distress raised a lump the size of Montana in Roberto's throat. "I could never be mad at you, punkin." Instinctively, he opened his arms. Without hesitation, Carolyn released her mother and fell into Roberto's waiting embrace. He hugged the quivering child, soothing her with consoling whispers that felt strangely comfortable on his tongue. "It wasn't your fault, Carolyn. I zigged when I should have zagged, that's all. If anyone has a right to be angry, it's you."

Sniffing, she straightened and wiped a pudgy fist across her face. "Me? Why?"

"Because there you were, having a great old time and I messed it up." He heaved a dejected sigh and deliberately hung his head. "The worst part is that you'll probably never let me push you again."

"Yes, I will. Honest." Using both of her small hands, she lifted Roberto's head. "You're a real good pusher."

"And you're a real good swinger, too." Grinning, he tweaked her tummy. "So, can we have another date sometime?"

"Uh-huh." Carolyn climbed off his lap, giggling. "How 'bout tomorrow?"

"That's fine with me." He stood slowly, testing his legs and dusting sand off his sweatpants.

Carolyn beamed.

Her mother, however, seemed less enthused. "We're going to be with Gramma tomorrow, remember?"

"Oh." The child considered that for a moment, then turned to Roberto. "You can come, too. Gramma and Grampa have a real big swimming pool."

Erica did a double take that would have been comical if she'd not been so obviously dismayed. She blinked rapidly, eyes darting from Roberto to her grinning daughter. "Ah . . . I'm sure Mr. Arroya has made other plans, dear."

Desperation just naturally brought out the devil in him. "Nope, not a one."

The look she gave him was a peculiar blend of shock and annoyance that made him regret the smart-aleck remark. Returning her attention to the children, she gestured toward the bench. "We have to be leaving now. Would you girls put Mommy's things back into the bag? Neatly, please."

"Okay."

Erica waited until the children had scampered out of hearing range before turning to Roberto. She regarded him warily. "I'm sorry, but my mother has been ill—"

Roberto held up a palm. "I'm the one who should be apologizing. You were so startled by Carolyn's suggestion that my warped sense of humor got the best of me and for some inane reason, I thought you'd be amused."

"Oh." Her relief was softened by a smile. "Ordinarily I would have been. I guess I've just been a bit preoccupied lately."

"About your mother's illness?" He was too courteous to request details, although he hoped she'd provide them.

She didn't. "Partly. Of course, the move has been stressful and trying to get all the loose ends tied up before the shop opens next week—" She gasped and looked at her watch. "Good Lord, how can it possibly be that late? I've got a half dozen interviews this afternoon and the first one is in less than an hour."

Alerted by his perplexed expression, she explained. "My father has finally convinced me that I won't be able to handle everything at the shop by myself, so I'm trying to hire a counter person." She spread her hands apologetically. "I really am late."

"I should be going, too," he said, although at the moment, he couldn't remember why. He did, however, follow Erica back to the bench, where she hastily gathered her things. When his gaze fell on a flyer peeking out of the canvas tote, he pointed to it. "May I?"

"Of course." She flashed a grateful smile and handed him one. After a flurry of goodbyes, she hurried toward the sidewalk, glanced over her shoulder and mouthed the words, "Hope you can make it," just before she disappeared from sight.

Roberto folded the flyer, tucking it in the breast pocket of his sweatshirt. He glanced down at Buddy, who'd quietly padded over and was now sitting beside him. "You understand, of course, that the tall one is mine."

Buddy barked.

Chapter Four

"So, Miss Drake, tell me about yourself." Receiving no reply, Erica glanced up from the sparsely completed application form and noted that the college student to whom she'd been speaking seemed more interested in a workman installing the new chiller motor than the interview itself. She spoke more forcefully. "Exactly what experience do you have?"

"Huh?" Miss Drake reluctantly refocused across the table. "Experience? Hmm. That's a toughie. My boyfriend works for a video store. He lets me help sort tapes and stuff. Does that, like, count?"

Erica winced as the girl snapped her gum. "It's, ah, not exactly what I was looking for, but thank you for coming in."

"Huh? Oh. Yeah, well, if my dad calls, would you tell him I was here? He says if I don't look for work, he's going to, like, disinherit me or something."

When Erica assured the girl that she'd, *like,* be happy to confirm the interview, Miss Drake grinned, snapped her gum and with a final admiring glance at the shirtless workman, sashayed out the door.

"Mommy!" Carolyn called. "Cathy took my very best Barbie doll and won't give it back."

Erica turned her attention to the corner table, which was cluttered with tiny outfits and bosomy dolls. "You know the rules, Cathy. You mustn't take your sister's things without asking permission. Besides, you have your own dolls to play with."

Cathy frowned so hard that her eyebrows crunched over the bridge of her nose. "Mine are ugly."

"That's because you don't take care of them," Carolyn told her. "Their hair is all matted."

"Is not!"

"Is too."

"Girls, please—"

"Hey, lady. You want to sign this?"

"Is *not!*"

Moaning, Erica turned and looked at the clipboard the workman was holding out. "Are you finished already?"

"Yeah. Bottom line . . . by the X."

After reading the work order, she scrawled her signature. "I appreciate you coming out on the weekend. You're a real lifesaver."

"No problem."

Carolyn suddenly squealed, "Give it *back!*"

"No."

"Mom!"

Erica sighed and, noting that the workman had hiked a brow at the bickering youngsters, responded with a sheepish, what-can-you-do smile.

"Best of luck, lady." With that, he hoisted his tool case and strode out so quickly that he nearly flattened a thin, skittish woman who was hovering in the doorway.

As the man brushed by her, the woman hunched her shoulders like a frightened cat. Her muted print dress, clean and crisply pressed, was a size too large, as was the crocheted lace cardigan that draped her gaunt frame like an oversize curtain. Along with a worn pocketbook, she was clutching a completed application form.

Erica vaguely recognized her as one of those who'd picked up the form in response to a Help Wanted sign in the shop window. "Hello," Erica said pleasantly. "Are you here about the counter job?"

The woman's darting gaze settled on Erica. "Yes'm, if you have time."

"Of course I do." Because she seemed so very nervous, Erica made an effort to be especially cordial, inviting her inside and ushering her to the table with exaggerated courtesy. The woman managed a weak smile, but remained apprehensive and flinched as a new argument erupted from the girls' corner table. Erica excused herself and hurried over to where the girls were engaged in a tug-of-war over a colorful swatch of fabric.

"That's mine," Carolyn insisted, trying to pry her sister's clenched fingers from the tiny outfit. "Gramma gave it to me for Christmas."

Cathy stuck out her chin. "Uh-uh. Mine."

Both girls fell silent as their mother's shadow loomed across the table. "I know you're tired," Erica told them quietly. "But I need for you both to play quietly for a few more minutes so that I can talk to that lady over there."

"Then do we get ice cream?" Carolyn asked.

"Yes, then we get ice cream."

"Goody!" Cathy released the disputed item to clap her hands, so her sister furtively retrieved the little garment and tucked it into a plastic carrying case.

With peace restored, at least for the moment, Erica returned to the interview table. "I'm sorry for the interruption," she said. "It's been a long day and they're getting cranky. You know how kids are."

The woman gazed wistfully at the now angelic children. "Yes," she whispered. "I know."

Erica regarded her for a moment, struck by her remarkable transformation as she watched the girls play. "Do you have children, Ms., ah . . . ?"

As the woman tore her gaze from the children, the wariness returned to her eyes. "Rettig," she said, laying the application on the table. "Sara Rettig."

Erica introduced herself, then scanned the completed form. "So you have children?" she repeated.

"Yes." She hesitated, avoiding Erica's gaze. "Frankie is nine now and Katie, my baby, is almost seven."

"They must keep you on your toes."

Sara's tongue darted out to moisten her lips. "They . . . don't live with me."

"Oh." Flustered by the unintended blunder, Erica stared back down at the form. Since it was inconceivable to her that a mother, any mother, would willingly give up custody of her children, she presumed that Sara Rettig must have been the victim of some tragic twist of fate.

Unwilling to add to the woman's misery, Erica opted for a quick change of subject. "According to the application, your experience as a part-time waitress was nearly ten years ago. Apparently you were most recently employed as assistant manager of a hardware store, a position which terminated two years ago. What have you been doing since then?"

The question was posed pleasantly and innocently intended. Erica assumed—that word again—that before the divorce mentioned on the application, Sara Rettig had been supported by her husband.

But Sara Rettig didn't confirm that. In fact, she said nothing at all, and when Erica glanced up, she saw the woman staring silently at the table, wringing her hands.

"Ms. Rettig? Did you not understand the question?"

"I knew this would happen. I'm sorry, ma'am, for wasting your time."

When she started to stand, Erica stopped her. "Wait. Please. I didn't mean to offend you."

She hesitated, then reseated herself without looking up. "You didn't offend me. It's just that when you find out where I was during those two years, you won't hire me. Nobody will."

Acting on impulse, Erica reached across the table and touched the despondent woman's hand. "I can't make a decision if you won't give me the facts, can I?"

Sara bit her lower lip, blinking back tears. After a moment, she began to speak in a halting voice, which trailed off occasionally, but was certainly audible enough for Erica to be first horrified, then deeply empathetic.

Apparently Sara had dealt with the devastation of her husband's abandonment with an abuse of prescription drugs that had evolved into a hard-core street addiction. To support her habit, she'd engaged in a series of petty crimes for which she'd eventually been convicted and imprisoned. Having been released less than two weeks ago, Sara was now desperate to get her life back on track in order to reclaim her children from foster care.

At the moment, however, all Erica saw in the woman's eyes was hopelessness and utter despair. "I figured once I got a job, I'd be able to prove to those welfare people that I could be a good mama to my kids. I didn't think no farther than that, didn't realize that no one was going to hire a woman like... like me."

"You made a mistake," Erica said softly. "Granted, it was a whopper but you've paid for it and learned from it. I can't believe there aren't people out there willing to give you another chance."

Sara shrugged. "I've put in twenty applications. Every time folks find out about my past, that's the end of it. When I came here today, I was going to lie."

"Why didn't you?"

"I don't know. Maybe I just figured I'd get caught."

"Or maybe you're basically a decent person who wants to build a future based on honesty and truth."

Sara pushed back her chair, her grateful smile quivering at the corners. "Thank you. You've been very kind."

"You understand that the job doesn't pay much more than minimum wage." Ignoring Sara's startled expression, Erica rushed on. "Initially, we'll only be open about five hours a day. If things go well, we might be able to increase our hours but for the moment, I'm afraid the position is part-time at best. Your primary duties will be at the counter, although I'll expect you to help out in the kitchen if necessary. Since there'll only be two of us, we'll both have to pitch in and take care of anything that needs to be done. I'd like to spend some time with you before we open on Wednesday, so can you be here Tuesday around noon?"

"You mean . . . you want to hire me?"

"If the terms are agreeable."

Sara looked as if she might faint. "Well, sure, of course they are."

"Good." Standing, Erica extended her hand. "See you Tuesday, then."

Grasping the proffered hand with both of her own, Sara squeezed so tightly that it was all Erica could do not to yelp in pain. "God bless you," Sara whispered. "You won't be sorry."

"I know that."

But as Sara left the shop, Erica was left to wonder if this was yet another case of her heart overruling her mind. She could only pray that this time, her heart was right.

* * *

Roberto had just stepped out of the shower when the phone rang. He draped a small towel over his neck, wrapped a large one around his waist, and picked up the bedroom extension.

Devon Monroe's raspy voice filtered over the line. "Hey, Bobby. I've been calling all morning. Where've you been?"

"Jogging." Roberto sat on the bed, drying his face with the hem of the small towel. "What's up?"

After a brief but telling pause, Devon asked if tomorrow's game was still on.

"Tomorrow's Sunday, isn't it?" After Devon acknowledged that it was, Roberto said, "Then the game is on. Unless you want to chicken out. I know how it galls you to lose."

"You wish," Devon replied, laughing. "I'm ready to kick butt, Bobby-boy. You might as well concede now and save yourself some grief."

"Dream on." Roberto scoured the terry cloth over his damp hair, then tossed it aside and waited for Devon to broach the real reason for his call.

It didn't take long. "By the way, word in the newsroom is that your office has a bead on Frank Caricchio. Got a statement? As an anonymous informed source, naturally."

Smiling to himself, Roberto shook his head. "You know better than that, Dev. I don't do leaks."

"Aw, hell, Bobby, my job's on the line here. My editor will have my hide if I don't get a jump on the competition."

"Oh, play me another one, Dev. No editor worth spit is going to can a Pulitzer prize winning reporter because he can't tap an exclusive." Roberto rolled his neck, feeling neither frustrated nor threatened by the request. It was Devon's job to use every available source to get the story, just as it was Roberto's responsibility to maintain the integrity of his office. Both men understood that.

A long-suffering sigh from the other end of the line indicated that Devon was well aware that his quest was futile. "Well, if you change your mind, you've got my number."

"Don't hold your breath," Roberto said cheerfully. "We wouldn't want to turn your bride into a widow."

"I'm sure Jessica would be touched by your concern."

The two men chatted briefly then, after exchanging mutual bluster about who would do what to whom during tomorrow's game, the conversation ended.

Roberto hung up, still smiling. Over the years, Devon had repeatedly tried to wring information out of him, particularly when his office was involved with high-profile cases; he'd never succeeded, of course, nor had anyone else. It was a matter of principle, on values etched in stone and ethics which had guided Roberto's life. Without those standards, he wouldn't be any better than the mobsters and drug dealers he prosecuted every day. He would, in fact, turn into that which he despised most—a legitimized hypocrite, bastardizing justice for personal gain. He'd turn into Ogden Marlow. And that was Roberto's worst nightmare.

"Mommy, Mommy! Watch me!" Drippy and shivering, Cathy posed on the edge of the pool with puffy plastic floatees encircling her upper arms. "I can dive, Mommy. Watch me!"

"I'm watching, sweetie." Erica shifted in the lounge chair, shading her eyes as her youngest bellied into the water with a ferocious splash. The child surfaced, sputtering, and waved happily. "That was very good, Cathy."

A soft chuckle wafted from the adjoining chair. "My lands, if that was a good dive, I'd hate to see a poor one."

"Now, Mother, you have to admit it's a big improvement over last summer, when she wouldn't even poke her big toe in the water."

Jacqueline Mallory smiled at the memory. "That was such a lovely visit, but much too short. I remember wishing that you could have stayed longer."

"You always used to tell me to be careful what I wished for because I might get it. Now that we're underfoot almost every day, do you think you should have taken your own advice?"

"On the contrary, dear. It's the very best wish I ever made." Since her left side hadn't been affected by the stroke, she had no difficulty spanning the short distance between chairs to pat her daughter's arm. "I'm so happy that you and the girls have come home."

As Jacqueline turned her attention to the splashing children, Erica inspected her mother's profile, noting new evidence of strain and age that hadn't been apparent during past visits. Her mother, although not vain, had always prided herself on her appearance. She'd been an active, attractive woman, who'd taken great pains to maintain a healthy body and youthful outlook on life. Since the stroke, her once shiny chestnut hair had faded, becoming brittle and streaked with gray. According to her father, Jacqueline had initially been so depressed by her helplessness that he feared she'd lost the will to live.

That seemed to be changing now, slowly. Jacqueline was making an effort, as evidenced by the rubber exercise ball nested in her right hand. For the past week, the squeeze ball had been her constant companion. That, along with a willingness to begin therapy on her paralyzed leg, signaled a renewal of the trademark optimism that Erica remembered.

But Jacqueline was still emotionally fragile, and the motorized wheelchair parked by the patio door was a continual reminder of her physical limitations, subjects Erica was determined to avoid. "Daddy seemed to be in an exceptionally good mood this morning."

"Yes," Jacqueline replied with a surprising lack of enthusiasm. "His Sunday golf games used to be the highlight

of his week. He never complained, of course, but I knew
how much he missed them. He's been so tense lately and he
always seems overly tired. I've been worried about him. And
ashamed, of course, to know that I'm the cause.''

"You're not the cause of anything, Mama.'' Erica deliberately avoided confirming that she, too, had been concerned about her father's noticeable fatigue. "Daddy has
been spending Sundays with you because he wanted to.''

"No, he felt compelled to. I told him to go and have fun
with his friends, but he wouldn't. Now that you're back,
things will be different. Kenneth feels comfortable doing
what he enjoys and I—'' Jacqueline gave the ball a purposeful squeeze. "I'll be back on my feet by Christmas and
your job as Mama's baby-sitter will be over.''

"I'm not your baby-sitter,'' she insisted, despite the sad
fact that it was partially true. "I'm here because I love you
and because we have a lot of catching up to do. I've missed
you, Mama, so very much.''

Jacqueline glanced away for a moment. When she faced
Erica again, the old sparkle had returned to her eyes.
"Enough of this maudlin behavior,'' she said firmly. "Tell
me about your hunky neighbor.''

"Mama!''

"Carolyn says he's an excellent pusher...I assume she was
referring to swings rather than the, ah, drug kind?''

Erica responded with a stunned stare.

Accepting that as an affirmative, Jacqueline flicked her
good wrist and hurried on. "I thought so. At any rate, when
Carolyn described him as being 'way cute', I got the impression that she was quite smitten. How about you, dear?
Are you smitten as well?''

"Oh, good grief. I can't believe I'm having this conversation with my own mother.''

"Then with whose mother would you prefer to have it?''

"You know what I mean.''

Jacqueline sighed. "Unfortunately, I do. We've never really had a serious talk about this type of thing, have we? My fault, of course. I was never terribly comfortable discussing—" she cleared her throat, partially obscuring the word "—sex."

"Sex?" Erica spun in her chair.

Cringing, Jacqueline motioned toward the pool. "Lower your voice, dear. The children—"

"What on earth does having a handsome neighbor have to do with—" she dutifully lowered her voice "—sex?"

"Having never met the man, I really couldn't say. I thought you might enlighten me."

Now Erica really *was* shocked. "Good Lord, Mother, I barely know him."

"He sounds very nice."

"He is, but that doesn't mean I've gone to bed with him."

Jacqueline flushed a bit, but remained otherwise staid. "Of course it doesn't. But things have changed since I was a girl. I understand that in these modern times when a young, attractive woman meets a likewise young and attractive man, the relationship can move rather quickly toward certain, ah, intimacies, which in my day, weren't spoken of in polite company. If you should experience such . . . well, urges—"

Moaning, Erica covered her face with her hands.

Jacqueline struggled on without missing a beat. "—I want you to feel free to discuss them with me. You do have a supply of condoms, don't you?"

"Oh, dear God."

"Safe—" cough "—sex is very important nowadays. Just last month, *Cosmopolitan* had quite a lengthy article on the subject."

The entire situation would have been laughable, if Jacqueline herself hadn't been so stiffly serious. Since the subject was obviously painful for her mother, it occurred to

Erica that there must be a very good reason why she'd felt compelled to broach it.

"Mama, please. I'm a twenty-eight-year-old divorcée with two children. Obviously, I understand both the process and consequence of sexual activity, so could you please explain to me why we're having this discussion now?"

"Because we haven't had it before," her mother said miserably. "If I'd been a proper parent, you'd have felt comfortable sharing your feelings years ago, before you ran off with what's-his-name and ruined your life."

Erica's breath slid out in a sigh. "So that's it."

Jacqueline stared at the numb arm folded in her lap and said nothing.

"Look at me, Mama." When she reluctantly complied, Erica continued. "The fact that you never actually sat me down and showed full-color slides of human procreation had absolutely nothing to do with my decision to marry Carter. I was young, yes, but I wasn't—and you'll have to trust me on this—I wasn't stupid and I wasn't uninformed, all right?"

Unconvinced, Jacqueline shook her head. "I was too strict, wasn't I? Your father always told me that I didn't allow you enough freedom but I just wouldn't listen. I was so afraid you'd do something foolish...like I did at that age."

Erica's chest tightened as if caught in a vice. "What are you saying, Mama? That you regret marrying Daddy?"

"Regret...your father?" She looked up, horrified. "Heavens, no!"

"Then I don't understand."

Jacqueline sighed, chewed her lower lip for a moment, then sighed again. "It was my first husband I regret, the man I married to get away from *my* mother."

A mule kick in the heart would have been less traumatic. "You were married to someone else...before Daddy?"

Her mother nodded grimly. "Because I was underage and had lied on the marriage license, my parents had it annulled immediately."

"Well. Goodness." Erica sat there, struggling for something to say and finally blurted, "Why didn't you ever tell me?"

"I was ashamed, I suppose, and so very afraid that you'd think less of me."

"That wouldn't have happened," Erica said softly. She tried to picture her mother with someone else, but couldn't. Since the image refused to form in her brain, it wasn't real to her. She understood what her mother had just told her; she simply couldn't find a way to make it matter. "I've always loved you, Mama. I never wanted to get away from you. How could you have thought that?"

She shrugged awkwardly. "I couldn't come up with any other reason you'd marry such an awful man."

"There was one."

"Really? What was it?"

"I was truly in love with him." Erica fidgeted with her fingers, realizing that the words sounded hollow even to her. "Or at least, I thought I was. The truth is that I might have simply been in lust. Whatever Carter's faults, you have to admit that the man had sex appeal to die for."

Jacqueline considered that. "I suppose one might even describe him as 'way cute'."

Erica flushed to her roots. "So that's it. You're afraid that I, foolish, naive and sexually uncontrollable dupe that I am, haven't learned a darn thing from the past seven years and will throw myself into the arms of the first attractive man who crosses my path."

"That's not at all what I meant, dear."

"All right, I admit Roberto Arroya is 'way cute'. I'll even go so far as to confess that he's every bit as sexy—make that *twice* as sexy—as Carter ever was. And yes, I'm slightly attracted to him. Maybe more than slightly. But let me tell you, there's a lot more to Roberto Arroya than a pretty face and a tight behind.''

"Really, Erica—"

"Mr. Arroya is probably the wittiest, most interesting and intellectually stimulating person I've ever met."

"Stimulating," Jacqueline murmured, fanning herself with her hand. "Oh, my."

"Yes, stimulating. In fact, he's positively brilliant. Of course, he does have this odd habit of debating with his dog but then again, everyone has at least one little glitch in the gray matter, don't you think?''

Jacqueline fanned faster. "If you say so, dear."

"I do say so and what's more, having a sexual encounter with Roberto Arroya has never, *ever* so much as crossed my mind." With that, she folded her arms and glared sullenly across the yard.

"Erica?"

"Yes, Mama?"

"Your nose is growing."

Erica sighed. "I know, Mama."

Larkin McKay pump-faked the opposing guard and reversed a rush to the end of the driveway. He spun around, aimed, and just as he lobbed a shot at the hoop fastened over Roberto's garage door, the same guard jostled his elbow. The ball nicked the rim and veered into the front yard.

"Foul!" Larkin shouted, pointing at his hairy, four-footed opponent. "He hacked me."

Devon Monroe, Larkin's teammate for these routine Sunday games, wiped a forearm across his sweaty brow. "That should be good for at least three penalty shots."

"No way," Roberto argued as he loped to retrieve the ball. "A hacking foul is defined as 'hitting an opponent's arm with the hand'."

"So?"

"So—" Roberto nodded at Buddy, who was happily wagging his tail. "No hands. Therefore, no foul."

"A minor technicality," Larkin mumbled, wiping his glasses on the hem of his T-shirt. "He deliberately obstructed my shot."

"That's his job, Lark. It's called defense."

Buddy barked.

"On the other hand," Devon interjected thoughtfully, "Lark clearly had established position."

Larkin nodded. "It was a charging foul, no doubt about it."

Blowing out a breath, Roberto spoke to his fuzzy teammate. "They've got us there, Bud."

The dog's ears drooped.

"One free throw," Roberto said, flipping the ball to the broad shouldered blond who was displaying a triumphant grin.

Larkin, concentrating on the shot, absently bounced the basketball on the driveway. On the third bounce, however, Buddy bounded onto the makeshift court and head-butted the ball into the next yard, a clever but ill-timed move resulting in a flurry of protests from the opposition.

With a pained sigh, Roberto explained the situation to his overzealous teammate. "It's a penalty shot, Buddy. We're not allowed to block it."

The animal cocked his head, angled a sorry-about-that look at Larkin, then ambled to the sideline and sat placidly beside his master.

Larkin gave the dog a slitty-eyed stare, then gently lofted the ball through the hoop.

"He swished it," Devon crowed. "A perfect shot."

Roberto swore. Buddy bared his teeth.

Smirking, Larkin spread his hands and bowed. "Thank you, thank you. What can I say? It's a gift."

Roberto bluntly compared that statement to bovine pasture paddies, then added, "Hell, I could do that, too, if I spent half my life practicing. Unfortunately, some of us have to work for a living.''

A pale eyebrow arched above his wire-rimmed spectacles. ''Are you implying that I, who have devoted myself to counseling those less fortunate than ourselves, am not contributing to society? I have a PhD, you know.''

''Beer break,'' Devon announced, bending over the cooler.

''Forgive me, *Doctor* McKay,'' Roberto said with a good-natured grin. ''It's just that most shrinks don't hold court in a gymnasium and impose upon friends to chaperon their clients three nights a week.''

''The youth program is a vital part of working with troubled families,'' Larkin replied. ''I don't think a few hours of volunteer effort from my blood brothers is too much to expect, particularly considering the undisputed fact that I'm better educated than either of you.''

Roberto chuckled. ''Apparently a mere master's degree and license to practice law pales in the light of your sterling accomplishments.''

''Of course.'' Larkin regally held out his hand. ''You may kiss my class ring.''

''Gee, thanks,'' Roberto replied, laughing. ''And you can kiss my—''

''Beer?'' Devon tossed a bottle in the air.

Roberto snagged it handily. ''So, Dev, who do you vote for as The Brotherhood's best and brightest?''

Devon flipped the cap from his beer. ''Don't ask me. Having barely made it through college, I'm practically illiterate.''

''You're a journalist,'' Roberto replied. ''You're not supposed to be literate.''

''True.'' Devon took a deep swig, then smacked his lips. ''Guess I'll just have to settle for being the best looking.''

''In your dreams,'' Larkin answered with a snort.

Shrugging, Devon stepped aside so the husky blond could avail himself of the cooler contents. "My wife thinks I am. That's good enough for me."

"Ah, newlywed bliss," Larkin mumbled, wiping crushed ice from a bottle of beer. "I remember it well."

Having completed the task of filling Buddy's water dish with a garden hose, Roberto stretched out on the grass. The subject of Larkin's bitter divorce and subsequent custody battle for the children he adored was, Roberto decided, best avoided. He turned to Devon. "So, how's Jessica doing?"

Devon's eyes lit up at the mention of his wife's name. "Great, really great. There's no sign of recurrence and she's had so much energy lately, it's as if she'd never had cancer at all."

"That's good news, man," Larkin said, lowering himself onto the lawn. "I'm happy for you both."

Beaming, Devon joined his friends.

The three men sat silently, cooling their bodies and sipping their beer. Buddy strolled over, whiskers dripping from his own liquid refreshment. He plopped down, laying his soggy chin on Larkin's lap. Ignoring a wet stain soaking through his sweatpants, Larkin lazily scratched the dog's head.

Contented, Roberto rolled his beer bottle between his hands and regarded his *hermanos*. Mutual ribbing aside, they'd all done well since their days at Blackthorn Hall. Larkin was a respected psychologist; Devon, now an acclaimed investigative journalist for the *L.A. Times,* had a Pulitzer Prize under his belt from his stint as a foreign correspondent; and Roberto was fulfilling a silent promise by avenging Tommy Murdock's death the best way he knew how. Only fighting injustice wasn't all it was cracked up to be. The good guys didn't always win.

And the Blackthorn legacy continued.

Chapter Five

"I should have known a lunch invitation from you was too good to be true." Edith Layton stared beyond the patio of bright umbrella-topped tables to a garish banner stretched over the shop's sparkling windows. "Free Samples," she read aloud. "Bite Before You Buy. Oh, gag me. That's just too cute, isn't it?"

Roberto gave her a withering look. "I think it's rather catchy."

"That's what I meant. Cute and, ah, catchy." She cleared her throat, lowering her glasses to peer over the clear plastic rims. "Well, since we're here, we might as well check it out. Who knows, the stuff might even be edible."

Ignoring his colleague's lack of enthusiasm, Roberto wound his way around the tables feeling strangely relieved that Erica's Grand Opening had garnered such a good turnout. And the clientele was as impressive as the crowd. In the first thirty seconds, he'd recognized two council members, the senior staff advisor of a local congressman and half of city hall. Unless Erica had hired a top-notch publicist, those flyers of hers must have had a bigger circulation than the *Wall Street Journal.*

The crowd inside was even more densely packed than on the patio. He scanned the chattering throng, disappointed that he didn't immediately spot Erica. There was, however, a pinch-faced woman in a bibbed Sandwich Shoppe apron sidling between tightly clustered bodies toward a row of well-stocked buffet tables.

Edith saw her, too. More to the point, Edith saw food. She grabbed Roberto's hand and yanked him toward the tables, which were loaded with serving vats of variety salads and platters of sandwiches cut into finger-size bites.

Without taking her eyes from the sumptuous repast, Edith thrust a plate into Roberto's ribs. "Chow down, boss. I have the feeling this'll have to last us awhile."

Roberto took the plate, but continued to gaze expectantly around the room. He spoke to the aproned woman, who appeared to be taking inventory of the buffet. "Is Ms. Franklin here?"

Startled, the woman stepped back as though shocked to have been noticed. "Ah...sure...she's, ah..." Her wary gaze darted toward the counter area, settling on the back of a tall, silver-haired man in a banker gray suit. "She's over there."

Roberto followed her gesture and saw a flash of familiar honey brown hair. When he turned to thank the woman, she'd already melted back into the crowd.

"You know," Edith said, chewing on a sliver of turkey on rye. "She looks familiar to me."

"Who?"

"That waitress. I'm sure I've seen her somewhere."

"Could be," Roberto muttered, less interested in Edith's observation than retaining a visual bead on the elusive Ms. Franklin. When he spied her again, he left the empty plate on the table and begin the tedious chore of muscling his way through the packed room.

Edith called after him. "Hey, Rob, aren't you going to eat? We've got a meeting in forty-five minutes."

Not wanting to take his eyes off Erica, Roberto raised a hand, signaling that he understood, and continued to squeeze between human barriers until he'd positioned himself right beside her. A sweet-tart scent of citron honeysuckle wafted a dizzying cloud around his head. He inhaled deeply, his gaze riveted on those elegant cobalt blue eyes.

She was smiling pleasantly, listening to the ruminations of a portly chap who was dawdling on about permit fees and the high cost of redevelopment. Unlike the silver-haired, banker-suited man, Erica seemed less fascinated by the conversation than resigned to it.

As Roberto moved slightly closer, noting that Erica, too, was wearing a "Sandwich Shoppe" apron, she absently glanced up with that same politic smile, blinking in surprise before her features lit with genuine delight. "I'm so pleased you could come," she said, seeming both flabbergasted and thrilled by his presence.

"I wouldn't miss it." Although the polite platitude rang a bit hollow, Roberto realized with no small surprise that he meant every word of it.

"I'm glad." Her dazzling smile made his chest quiver strangely.

Meanwhile the portly chap, now ignored, repeatedly cleared his throat and in fact, damned near choked himself in a bid to reclaim Erica's attention. For reasons best unexplored, Roberto found a perverse satisfaction in knowing that she was more interested in him than a fat codger with a shiny scalp and a nose the size of Boston.

"Have you tried the Iran-Contra?" Erica asked.

"Not yet. I just arrived."

"Oh." She still hadn't taken her eyes off him. "I think you'll like it."

"I'm sure I will."

With a disgusted snort, the peeved old goat finally gave up and burrowed into the crowd, grumbling, with the silver-haired banker suit hot on his heels.

"Erica, dear. Aren't you going to introduce us?"

Perplexed, Roberto glanced around, then down and finally noticed the attractive, stylishly chic woman who, along with her wheelchair, had been obscured by the two men who'd just left. The woman, immaculately attired in ivory linen, occupied the chair with a majesty that drew attention from her right arm, which was folded awkwardly in her lap, to the deep blue eyes sparkling from a proud and stately face.

"Oh, Mama, I'm sorry." As Erica performed a rushed introduction, she seemed a bit flustered.

Jacqueline Mallory, however, was the epitome of patrician grace, smiling pleasantly as she tilted her head to get a good look at the man towering above her. "Carolyn was right," she said finally. "He certainly is."

Erica's smile froze. She bent to whisper something in the woman's ear, then straightened. "Mama has heard all about you," she said, then quickly added, "From Carolyn. And, ah, Cathy, of course. Both of them."

"You've made quite an impression on the girls." Jacqueline spoke eloquently, but there was an odd twinkle in her eyes, as if she were enjoying a private joke.

Roberto liked her instantly. "The girls think I'm a good pusher."

Her genteel smile widened into a grin. "So they've told me. Carolyn is somewhat concerned about your inability to distinguish between a zig and a zag, but assures me that the problem is one you'll probably outgrow."

Erica pointedly rested a hand on her mother's shoulder. "Mama, you promised."

"Hmm?" The woman's eyes widened into the picture of innocence. "Oh, of course, dear. You can count on me."

Although whatever obscure communication transpiring between mother and daughter was well beyond Roberto's grasp, it didn't take a student of human behavior to observe that while Jacqueline Mallory was enjoying herself immensely, Erica was visibly unnerved.

She gave her mother a significant look and spoke through clenched teeth. "You look hungry, Mama. Perhaps you'd like another opportunity to sample the buffet."

"No, thank you, dear. I'm quite comfortable."

Erica seemed prepared to argue the point, except that the silver-haired banker-suit reappeared. "Mr. Josakian is quite perturbed, Erica. Insulting a man who's running for county supervisor is not the wisest course of action."

"Hmm? Oh, well, I'll talk to him in a few minutes. Daddy, I'd like you to meet—"

Jacqueline interrupted. "This is Erica's neighbor, Kenneth. Her *neighbor*." The last word was emphasized with a wink, which confused Roberto nearly as much as the silver-haired man's reaction.

"Ah, I see. Her neighbor." Kenneth's worried frown melted into an expression of instant comprehension mingled with abject curiosity. "Well, I'm certainly pleased to meet you."

As the men shook hands, Roberto noted with some confusion that Erica had covered her eyes and, he thought, uttered a low moan.

Roberto returned his attention to the man who was heartily pumping his entire arm. "We've heard a lot about you, young man."

"Daddy, please."

The whispered entreaty immediately caught Kenneth's attention. He released his grip. "That is, I, ah, owe you a debt of gratitude for keeping my adventurous granddaughter out of harm's way."

Erica seemed oddly relieved by something that appeared to be little more than unnecessary clarification. Apparently, there was a clandestine communication between Erica and her parents that Roberto wasn't meant to understand. Whatever it was, however, couldn't disguise their bond of mutual respect and affection. Since Roberto had never been part of a real family, he was both intrigued and a bit envious of the familial closeness Erica shared with her parents. But he was also confused by the telling looks they exchanged, looks that he deduced had something to do with him.

Perplexed, Roberto offered a perfunctory reply, then studied the tall man's face. "Kenneth Mallory," he repeated, absently stroking his chin and digging deeply into his memory. In a moment, it came to him. "Of course, the county planning commissioner."

Conceding that he was, Mallory dug into his breast pocket and pressed a business card into Roberto's hand. "I understand you're an attorney. If any of your clients need a little grease on the bureaucratic wheels, give me a call and I'll see what I can do."

"He's not that kind of attorney," Erica explained. "Mr. Arroya is a federal prosecutor for the Department of Justice."

"Federal prosecutor...Arroya?" Mallory stiffened as if slapped; his eyes darkened suspiciously. "As a matter of fact, your name rings a bell, too. Were you by any chance involved in that capital sting a few years back?"

Alerted by the man's sudden change of demeanor, Roberto replied with caution. "Our office handles dozens of cases each year. I believe that was one of them."

In point of fact, he knew that it was because he'd been the lead prosecutor. Six members of the state legislature had been convicted on charges ranging from bribery to racketeering. It had been a major coup, and one of the main reasons Roberto had been promoted into his present supervisory position.

Judging from the hard glint in Mallory's eyes, Roberto seriously doubted the commissioner was impressed and wisely chose to keep the details to himself. He did, however, wonder why Erica's father seemed so disturbed by the case, and was pondering that very question when Edith Layton pushed into the circle.

"I finally figured it out," Edith whispered as softly as her raucous voice would allow. "I remember where I saw that waitress."

Fortunately, Edith caught Roberto's warning glance and blinked around the group. Recovering quickly, she offered the curious group a bright smile and introduced herself, then added, "I'm sorry to interrupt, but we have a meeting and if we don't hoof it out of here in the next thirty seconds, we're going to be unfashionably late."

Roberto would have preferred a few moments to get a handle on Mallory's peculiar mood change, but a glance at his watch confirmed Edith's prediction.

"Do you really have to leave?" Erica asked.

"I'm afraid so." He offered an encouraging smile. "Thanks for the invitation. I've enjoyed it."

"I'm glad."

Their eyes locked for a moment, a long one, then Roberto felt an insistent tug on his sleeve. Reluctantly, he turned away and followed his colleague outside.

Erica watched until he'd disappeared from view, then confronted her father. "What in the world was that all about? You treated Roberto as if he were some kind of murderer."

"He might as well be," Kenneth replied sadly. "He's killed enough careers."

The startling announcement left Erica speechless. Fortunately, her mother had no such impediment. "That's an odd thing to say, Kenneth, and extremely unkind."

Unmoved by his wife's rebuke, Kenneth Mallory dug in his heels. "The man is ruthless, with a reputation for being so damned ambitious that he'd step on his own mother's face to get an inch up on the competition."

Erica touched her chest, stunned. "I can't believe that. Roberto is the kindest, most gentle person I've ever met."

"He's a human piranha." Breathing hard now, Kenneth loosened the knot in his tie. "That man will do anything, and I mean *anything,* to win. Arroya goes after good people who, because of a crisis in their lives, may have made a mistake. Then he persecutes them without mercy and—" Kenneth ripped open his collar "—he destroys them."

Although Erica was disturbed by the dire warning, she was more concerned about her father's sudden pallor. "Daddy, are you all right?"

Jacqueline touched her husband's arm. "Kenneth . . . ?"

"I'm...fine." He dabbed his moist forehead. "Some air, perhaps. It's quite close in here." With a strained smile, he patted his wife's shoulder, then spun around and was swallowed up by the milling crowd.

Erica would have followed, except for her mother's restraining hand. "He'll be all right, dear. He just wants to be alone."

"But why?"

"It happened long ago, Erica, while you were still in Seattle." Jacqueline sighed. "A friend of your father's was involved in that legislative investigation he mentioned. I didn't know the man myself, but apparently he and Kenneth had been university classmates and they'd remained close over the years."

Erica was beginning to get the picture. "So this, ah, friend of Daddy's was convicted of some wrongdoing?"

"Yes, but I'm not certain of the particulars, nor did I realize that your Mr. Arroya was involved." Jacqueline gazed into space, absently tapping her jaw. "Although Kenneth was surprised and saddened by the incident, I don't recall that he ever commented on the authorities being at fault. In fact, I remember quite clearly that he was disappointed in his friend for having become involved in such a sordid affair.''

"Then why would he blame Roberto, particularly now, after all these years?"

"I don't know," Jacqueline murmured, frowning. "I truly don't know."

Erica certainly didn't know either. She did, however, have a theory. A disturbing one. Of the myriad reasons a usually composed man would be thrown into such an agitated state, sheer exhaustion seemed the most logical. There'd been several signals that her father was under a lot of strain, not the least of which was that he just didn't look good. Sometimes he was pale to the point of ashen, and he'd lost weight. Too much weight, Erica thought, although her father insisted that he'd simply honed his body into "fighting weight".

Unconvinced, Erica had continued to fret about his health, assuming that her mother's illness had taken a toll on both of her parents. This latest bout of sudden fatigue, however, had been particularly unnerving. The raw panic in her father's eyes had scared her to death.

Balancing one foot on the step stool and one on the kitchen counter, Erica clamped a pencil between her teeth and struggled to hold the curtain rod level. Her hand slipped. The rod tilted.

It occurred to her, as blue gingham bunched at her knuckles, that the process might have been easier had the curtains not been strung along the rod, but she'd wanted to make sure the flounced hem was even with the window ledge before installing that last critical piece of hardware. Unfortunately, since she'd had to climb halfway up the wall simply to hold the rod in place, she couldn't even see the stupid hem, let alone measure it.

"Mommy," Carolyn called from the living room. "Cathy's standing in front of the TV and she won't move."

"Am *not!*"

Before Erica could juggle the dipping curtain rod long enough to free a hand and pull the pencil out of her mouth, the doorbell was buzzing.

"I'll get it," Carolyn hollered.

"No, me."

"Cathy... let go of the knob. You're not s'posed to open the door."

"Am too."

Erica called out, "*I'll* answer the door," then tried to unhook the portion of rod that was fastened several feet from her precarious perch. With a deft twist, the rod popped free.

She'd just started backing down the step stool when she heard the front door open. Instantly, a series of excited giggles emanated from the living room, along with a familiar canine woof. Erica froze. Unless Buddy had learned how to ring a doorbell, the dog was probably not alone, an assumption quickly confirmed by a smooth masculine voice. Erica couldn't hear what was being said but she darn well knew who was saying it.

And here she was, wearing a paint-spattered sweatshirt and a pair of jeans so thrashed that the knees were little more than bare threads. She could only imagine what her hair must look like. As for her makeup, well she hadn't so much as glanced in a mirror since this morning, so the possibilities were chilling.

Shuddering, she skimmed a glance at the back door. Maybe she could escape.

Both girls burst into the room at once. "I got Baby Simba!" Cathy chortled, waving a plastic lion cub over her head.

Carolyn was clutching a slightly larger version. "And I got Big Simba. Look, Mommy, he's got a grown-up mane, just like his daddy."

So much for escape.

It wasn't until Roberto's lean frame filled the doorway that Erica realized how silly she must look, standing on a splintered stool while peering through a gap in curtains that for some unknown reason, she'd felt compelled to hoist over her head. "Hi," she said, hoping he wouldn't notice anything absurd about her predicament.

He smiled. "Let's see, you're either hanging curtains or giving a puppet show."

"Take your choice," she mumbled, stepping down and tossing rod and curtains onto the kitchen table in a single fluid motion.

Brushing her hands together, she pasted on her brightest smile and concentrated on the chattering children, both of whom were absolutely fried with excitement over their new toys. Erica admired the gifts, giving each little figurine equal praise while Buddy circled impatiently. When the girls dashed off to play, the dog followed.

"That was very thoughtful of you," Erica said, avoiding Roberto's gaze.

"Carolyn mentioned that she and Cathy were big fans of *The Lion King*."

"They've seen it four times." Erica finally looked at him and saw to her shock that he was holding a magnum of champagne and a long-stemmed yellow rose.

In response to her unspoken question, he set the bottle on the counter. "To toast the success of your Grand Opening. And this—" he held out the rose "—well, I, ah, just thought you might like it."

She cradled the flower in her palm, thinking that she'd never seen anything so lovely in her life. "It's beautiful," she whispered. "Thank you."

"You're welcome." Suddenly bashful, he looked away, cleared his throat and gestured toward the window. "Can I give you a hand with that?"

"Hmm? Oh, no, thanks. It's bad manners to put guests to work, particularly guests bearing gifts."

"I'm not a guest, I'm a neighbor. Neighbors are supposed to be helpful."

She laughed, feeling oddly giddy. "In that case, I could use a little assistance. Just let me put this in water."

As she retrieved a bud vase from the cupboard, Roberto inspected the rod hardware, then glanced up at the side she'd already installed. "Looks like you've got it half done."

"Only the easy half. I was trying to adjust the level and not having much luck when—"

The phone rang.

"Darn." She slipped the bud into the filled vase, wiped her hands on her jeans and grabbed the wall phone receiver. Her heart sank as a nasally voice announced yet another collect call from her ex-husband. Talk about rotten timing. Turning toward the wall, Erica ducked her head and lowered her voice. "Yes, I'll accept the charges."

In a moment, an all-too-familiar voice crackled over the line. "Ricki? Hey, kid, how're you doing?"

"Fine, Carter. We're doing fine."

"That's great. Listen, I've got two words that are going to change your life—virtual reality."

"Virtual what?"

"Reality, babe, virtual reality. It's the video wave of the future."

"Video…you mean like a computer game of some kind?"

"Not a game, Ricki. We're talking business here, big business and we've got the chance to get in on the ground floor."

Erica massaged the bridge of her nose. "Sorry, but I'm not in the position to invest in one of your, ah—" A glance across the room confirmed that Roberto appeared to be listening, so she changed the phrase *harebrained schemes*, which was hovering on the tip of her tongue, to a more socially acceptable description. "One of your business ventures."

"I'm not asking you to risk a penny," Carter insisted.

"Then what, exactly, are you asking?"

"A small loan, that's all, just enough to get my foot in the door."

Erica nearly dropped the phone. "You want me to give you money?"

"A few thousand. It's no big deal."

"It's a very big deal to me. I don't have that kind of money. In fact, I don't have any money at all. I just drained my account with a two-month advance to the girls' day care center because you promised you'd start making child support payments this month—"

"So talk to your old man," Carter said, cutting off the unpleasant subject of his own financial responsibility. "He's got more money than he knows what to do with."

"My father has already paid to move us down here and I haven't even made the first payment on the loan he gave me to open the shop."

Momentarily forgetting that she was not alone in the room, Erica was suddenly agitated to the point of panic. Not only was her ex-husband asking for money when he should have been putting the check in the mail, but she had the sinking sensation that he had no intention of honoring their original agreement which was that she wouldn't bring the court into this if he'd straighten out his finances and send regular payments.

When he resumed the sales pitch, she interrupted. "You're not going back on our deal, are you?" The silence that followed was the longest moment of Erica's life.

"We didn't really have a deal," Carter said slowly. "I told you I'd start making payments if I could. Thing is, I can't. Not yet, anyway. Now when this virtual reality thing gets going—"

"You can't be serious. Less than two months ago, you were begging me to forgive your past-due support in return for a promise that you'd never miss another payment. I kept my end of the bargain." When he replied with an irritable growl, her panic surged. "You promised, Carter. You *promised.*"

"Is that Daddy?" Carolyn appeared at Erica's side, wringing her hands in excitement. "I wanna talk to Daddy."

As Carolyn tugged on Erica's sleeve, Carter's fury resonated through the line. "Don't be giving me that 'promise' crap. You promised to be my wife, remember? One broken promise deserves another, I always say."

"Mommy... I wanna tell Daddy about my new teacher and my Simba toy and Gramma's pool. Ple-e-ase."

Forcing a smile, Erica held up her palm. "You can talk to Daddy in a minute, sweetie. Just wait in the other room and I'll call you, okay?"

The child hesitated, waiting for her mother's reassuring nod before reluctantly backing out of the kitchen. Across the room, Roberto, who'd been screwing the final piece of hardware into the wall, had interrupted the chore to watch the proceedings. His eyes were darker than midnight; he'd definitely been angered by what he'd overheard. She managed what she hoped was a combination smile—reassurance that this wasn't as bad as it sounded, even though it was worse, along with an apology that the conversation was taking so long. Upon returning her attention to the telephone, she wasn't surprised to realize that her ex-husband's tirade had continued without pause.

Aware now that she was being monitored, Erica interrupted with a voice so light and airy, so deliberately pleasant that Carter went silent, presumably from shock. "I'll think about what you said and we'll talk about it later, okay? Besides, Carolyn is dying to talk to you. But before I put her on the line, I wanted to remind you about her birthday."

"Hmm? Her what?"

Erica's stretched smile barely moved. "Your daughter's birthday is next month, on the tenth."

"Oh. Yeah, sure. So, about the money—"

With light laugh that was as much for Roberto's benefit as for any tiny ears lurking outside the door, Erica cooed, "This really isn't a good time to discuss that. Now, I'll just call Carolyn to the phone—"

"I'm running late, Ricki. I'll talk to her next time, okay?"

Erica went stiff. "It'll just take a minute, Carter. Please, she's waiting. Don't disappoint her again—"

The muffled click was followed by a dial tone.

For what seemed a small eternity, Erica simply stood there, numb, unable to believe that even a narcissistic jerk like Carter Franklin could be so cold to his own child. She wanted to scream, to dial his number and deafen him with her indignation. But that would only make things worse.

And she couldn't cry, because Roberto Arroya was still gazing across the room, eyes black with anger.

So Erica did the only thing she could think of, which was diffusing the situation by ignoring it. After hanging up the telephone, she clasped her trembling hands and turned to the stunned man who'd just finished hanging her curtains. "My, don't they look nice. And perfectly even, too. Thank you so much."

He laid the screwdriver on the table. "Erica—"

"Mommy?" Carolyn sneaked an impatient peek around the door, looked from her mother's empty hand to the cradled receiver and emitted a sharp wail.

Erica knelt quickly to embrace her distressed child. "Oh, sweetie, I'm so sorry. Daddy wanted to talk to you, too, but he got another call—a business call—that he just had to take. He told me to give you something."

The girl's lip quivered. "What?"

"This." Erica gave her a fierce hug and covered both little cheeks with kisses, stopping only when Carolyn started to giggle. "There. Daddy told me to tell you that he loves you this much." She demonstrated by spreading her arms as wide as possible, then added, "And he's going to call you back just as soon as he can."

"Really?"

"Cross my heart." Hoping God would forgive this lie, and all the others Erica had told to protect her children's feelings, she gave Carolyn a final squeeze. "Now go tell your sister it's bath time, okay?"

"Okay." Carolyn cast a longing glance at the telephone before leaving the room.

To Roberto, the entire scene he'd just witnessed seemed surreal. He'd heard every word of Erica's conversation, and was fairly certain that her ex-husband had sent no hugs or kisses to his daughter. In fact, assuming one could make an accurate assessment from half a conversation, Roberto would bet money that the guy hadn't even mentioned the child's name. The very concept of a father so detached, so emotionally unavailable to his children was... was...

Was too damned common.

Roberto remembered when Erica had come to thank him for bringing Cathy home and he'd made some self-righteous comment about the cruelty of separating children from their father. *Apparently you're under the assumption that every man who fathers a child actually wants to be a father,* Erica had told him. *I assure you, nothing could be further from the truth.*

She'd been right, of course. Despite a secret need to believe that all men viewed fatherhood with Larkin McKay's passion, Roberto knew that wasn't true. He'd never laid eyes on his own father, and seriously doubted that his mother could even identify the lucky fellow. If she'd even known the guy's name, she'd never shared that information with her son. In fact, Roberto had considered himself the product of immaculate conception until a red-haired bully in the second grade had revealed the human mating process in crass detail.

Roberto had, of course, run home crying and would have begged his mother to dispute such an unsavory story had she not been passed out on the sofa. By the time that particular bender ended, Roberto had already chosen to believe that he'd been left on her doorstop, a fantasy that continued to comfort him through most of his childhood.

He wondered what fantasy little Carolyn used for consolation.

Of course, Carolyn and Cathy had one thing going for them—a mother who loved them with all her heart. Even now, as Erica knelt on the floor, head bowed, shoulders quivering, love of her children radiated from every pore in her body. His heart went out to her; the rest of him followed.

He crossed the room and laid a hand on her shoulder. "The bastard should be shot," he said quietly.

She lifted her head, momentarily turning to wipe her face before rising to her feet. "Carter isn't as bad as he seems. He's just . . . immature."

"That's probably his best quality."

"Carter has a lot of good qualities. He's enthusiastic, ambitious and, ah, he can be very charming."

"Sounds like a profile of a scam artist."

Horrified, Erica spun to face him. "That's a terrible thing to say! Regardless of his faults, he is the father of my children."

With a pained sigh, Roberto gave her shoulders a soothing squeeze. "I'm sorry. I was trying to be a smart aleck."

"Why?"

He smiled. "Because the alternative was to display an anger that I thought you'd find unattractive."

She cocked her head, studying him as if trying to see beyond the glib words into the essence of his very soul. "Anger is a normal emotion," she finally said. "It's how one deals with it that counts."

"And how do you deal with it, Erica?" He slipped his index finger beneath her chin, urging her to look up. "By making excuses for a man who clearly doesn't deserve them?"

"I'm not making excuses for him." The words were delivered numbly, without emphasis. And her gaze slipped as she said them.

Clearly, she was lying. Although the original lie had most certainly been geared to protect her daughter's feelings, Roberto could only think of one reason why she'd continue the deception now that Carolyn had left the room. Considering what that reason might be struck a surprisingly raw chord.

"Erica?"

Her lashes fluttered down for a moment, then she took a deep breath and met his focused gaze. "Yes?"

"Do you still love him?" Having posed the question, Roberto gathered his courage for the response he feared.

She was silent for a long time. Finally, she shook her head. "No," she whispered. "I don't."

His relief was so massive it frightened him. "I'm glad."

"Why?"

"Because you deserve someone better."

A sensual curiosity darkened her eyes. "Someone like you?"

"Maybe." His gaze was riveted on her lips. They looked so soft, so moist. So inviting. Yet there was an appealing naiveté about her, a sense a guileless optimism that contradicted the hardship she'd endured. It was an endearing quality, and unbelievably sexy. In fact, everything about her fairly oozed sexuality, from the smoldering desire in those gorgeous eyes to her subtle scent, a heady mixture of honeysuckle and innocence that was more arousing than anything he'd ever experienced.

He caressed the silky skin along her throat, guided the tip of his finger upward to trace her firm jaw. When her lips parted in a silent sigh, it was all the invitation he needed. Lowering his head, he brushed his mouth gently across her lips and felt her body tremble in response. His own body was reacting oddly, too. His lips tingled from the brief touch and there was a strange rushing in his ears. Like running water. Bath water.

"Mommy," Carolyn hollered from the bathroom. "Cathy's trying to get in the tub by herself!"

Erica blinked twice, as if awakening from a dream. She stared up in shock, then took an unsteady backward step. "I, ah . . . The girls are waiting."

"Sure. Of course." Roberto cleared his throat to cover the sound of his pounding heart.

She paused at the doorway. "Would you mind doing me one more favor?"

At the moment, he'd have agreed to reroof her house with toothpicks if she'd asked him to. "Name it."

"Could you open the champagne?" Apparently his stunned expression indicated that to be the last thing he'd expected to hear, because she hastened to clarify the request. "It's just that I'm not very good with corks and, well, this was supposed to be a celebration, right?"

An invisible vise suddenly tightened around his chest. Then, after slipping him a tentative smile, Erica blushed prettily and disappeared down the hall.

Roberto stood there until the sounds of splashing and happy laughter filled the house. He felt like a first-class heel. The champagne and rose had been an afterthought, a way to soften the real reason for his visit. The truth was that Erica would have more bad news tonight, and Roberto was here to deliver it.

Chapter Six

"Hmm, the sweet sound of silence." Erica sank wearily onto the sofa, accepting a bubbling wineglass from Roberto, who then poured himself a glass, set the bottle on the coffee table and settled down beside her.

Erica noticed how fragile the crystal stemware seemed in his hand, an intricate contrast between strength and daintiness that was strangely alluring. But then everything about Roberto was alluring, from the muscular ripple of his forearms, bared by a white knit polo shirt that did wonderful things for his dark complexion, to the sexy way his wild hair had escaped its gel prison to flip over his forehead and curl around his brow.

Looking away, she dabbed at her own forehead. It was exceptionally warm tonight, although admittedly she hadn't noticed the heat until Roberto sat close enough for her to feel the radiant warmth of his body. Erica found herself exquisitely aware of him, and of his scent—a subtle blend of spices that was unique and incredibly erotic.

She pursed her lips, blowing a slow breath. The attraction was natural, of course. He was an appealing man and she, well, she hadn't been with any man, appealing or otherwise, in a very long time. Still, she reminded herself that they were just neighbors. Close neighbors. Friends, actually. But whatever they were, this damnable silence was allowing her mind to wander into inappropriate territory.

"I think Cathy was asleep before her head hit the pillow," she said suddenly.

"Hmm?" Roberto glanced up as if surprised to see her. "Oh. Yes, she was fairly well out of it, but I suspect that her sister could have lasted a while longer."

Erica relaxed a little. Talk was good. Kept the mind busy. "Ah, yes, my little night owl. If left to her own devices, Carolyn would stay up for the 3:00 a.m. movie, then sleep until noon."

"A girl after my own heart," Roberto murmured, balancing the champagne glass on his knee. "Sunrise is for roosters."

"I'm surprised to hear that from a man who chugs around the park at dawn." Although he smiled, Erica thought he seemed a bit distracted.

"Unfortunately, even the most nocturnal of our species must conform to societal timetables," he said. "But Carolyn and I don't have to like it."

Erica's laughter ended in a nervous squeak that made her wince. She cleared her throat and tried for an airy, unaffected tone. "The girls really enjoyed your bedtime story. I don't think they've ever heard the one about three bears suing Goldilocks for breaking and entering."

He responded with a pained shrug. "I did the best I could on short notice. Bedtime stories are kind of new to me."

"You did fine. They loved it." *And so did I*, Erica thought. It was, in fact, one of the sweetest stories she'd ever heard because it revealed a side of this enigmatic man that she hadn't seen before. Upon describing how Goldilocks struck a plea bargain, exchanging maid service for room and board, only to become the newest member of the loving bear family, Roberto had betrayed a secret optimism that had touched Erica to the core.

She wanted to tell him that, but the sudden distance in his eyes gave her pause. So they sat quietly for a moment, with Roberto staring into his goblet as if it contained universal secrets and Erica sneaking furtive glances at the man whose exceptional good looks still left her breathless.

There was no denying that Roberto had an exquisite profile, well angled and perfectly proportioned. When Erica's gaze slipped to his mouth, her own lips tingled in remembrance. It hadn't really been a kiss, of course. It had been, well, a caress, a feathery touch so brief that she'd been amazed by the power it evoked. Shocking. Quite literally shocking, a jolt that had buckled her knees. Afterward, her heart had pounded for half an hour and she'd scolded herself for indulging what was quite certainly nothing more than an adolescent crush.

As crushes went, however, this was a real doozy. God, he was handsome, even more gorgeous than Carter had ever been. Erica wondered what inner weakness consistently drew her to such beautiful men. But Roberto seemed different than most men of his ilk. Carter, for instance, was unendingly self-absorbed and emotionally vacuous, while Roberto honestly seemed more concerned with others than with himself.

He also appeared completely oblivious to his own appeal, although the fact that he couldn't enter a room without turning heads had been proven earlier at the shop. Roberto may not have noticed that he'd held the gaze of every woman there, but Erica certainly had. Her ex-husband had drawn the same kind of attention; and he'd repeatedly taken advantage of his appeal by selecting the most attractive women with whom to share his extramarital antics.

Of course Erica realized that Roberto was very different from Carter. Still, the similarities, external though they were, gave small credence to her deepest fears. Carter had broken her heart, damaged her self-esteem and destroyed her faith in marital fidelity. Yet here she sat, making goo-goo eyes at the first handsome man to cross her path. Go figure.

Sighing, Erica reached to set her untouched champagne on the coffee table. The movement apparently broke Roberto's concentration, because he suddenly spoke.

"A toast," he said, lifting his glass. "May your new venture be the Spago's of sandwiches."

"I'll settle for profitable enough to pay bills." When he nodded approval of the amended toast, they touched rims and took an obligatory sip. The champagne was smooth and deliciously dry. "Hmm. This isn't the $3.99 stuff from the supermarket, is it?"

He feigned shock. "For a celebration of this magnitude? Surely you jest."

"Is this where I'm supposed to say, 'Don't call me Shirley'?"

"You mock me, madam. I'm deeply hurt."

Although she couldn't suppress a chuckle at his indignant expression, she silently chided herself for enjoying his company—not to mention the lush view he provided—entirely too much. Looks. Brains. Personality. The guy had it all. Somewhere on earth was a bland, homely idiot, devoid of attractive attributes because Roberto had quite obviously received more than his share. Erica lifted her glass for another sip and, peering unobtrusively over the rim, noticed his expression had become somber again.

He pursed his lips, took a deep breath, and spoke without taking his gaze off the glass he was twirling between his palms. "Your mother is a lovely woman."

"Yes, she is."

"The other day, you mentioned that she'd been ill. I hope it's nothing serious."

"Well, actually it was. She had a stroke about six months ago."

"I'm sorry."

"She's doing much better. She's even getting her sense of humor back."

"I noticed." Roberto gave the glass a wry smile. "Your father didn't seem particularly amused though."

Erica sobered at the reminder of her father's foul mood, and the dire warning he'd issued about Roberto. She started to speak, hesitated, then decisively issued the question. "Have you and my father met before?"

"Hmm?" He finally looked up. "No, I don't think so. Why?"

"I just wondered. He, ah, seemed to know who you were."

"I know who your father is, too, but purely by reputation."

"What do you mean by that?"

Apparently the question was more defensive than she'd intended, because Roberto immediately qualified his response. "After six terms on the planning commission, Kenneth Mallory is a powerful man. There aren't many people in the county who haven't heard of him. I suspect that he might even have been partially responsible for the excellent turnout today."

Erica flushed. "You mean you don't think my famous Watergate lunch was enough to drag out the mayor, the county supervisors and half the city council?"

"It might have been, I suppose. Your flyer was very convincing."

"Well, you were right the first time. Daddy called in every political favor he'd ever earned and then some." Feeling somewhat nonplussed by the admission, Erica avoided his gaze by tidying a stack of children's books that had been strewn across the coffee table. As she did so, she astounded herself by revealing even more personal details. "I'd like to tell you that he did that without consulting me, but it would be a lie. The fact is that if the shop fails, I'm bankrupt. I need every advantage I can get to make a go of it, and if using my father's name will pull in a few more customers, I'll darn well use it."

"I don't blame you."

She pushed the neat stack of books aside and glanced over her shoulder. "You don't?"

"Of course not. Since you're partners, it only makes sense that he'd be involved—"

"Whoa." Leaning back, she held up a palm. "What makes you think that we're partners?"

He seemed a bit startled. "I, ah, thought I overheard you say something to that effect a few moments ago, when you were on the phone."

"Ah. You must have overheard me mention the loan." She waited for his assenting nod, then explained. "After seven years of marriage, I didn't have a dime's worth of credit in my own name. There wasn't a bank in town who'd talk to me about the kind of money I needed, so Daddy had his lawyer draw up the papers for a start-up loan with interest at current rates."

Roberto hiked a brow. "Your own father is charging you interest?"

"It's a business deal. I insisted."

"Somehow that doesn't surprise me." His smile faded. He tapped a finger on his thigh, seeming preoccupied with his thoughts. After a moment, he spoke carefully. "Since the shop is obviously important to you, I assume that you'd want to be apprised if anything—or anyone—jeopardized its success."

"Excuse me?"

He pulled up one knee and turned sideways on the sofa, facing her. "How many employees do you have?"

Erica wasn't sure what she was expecting, but that question definitely wasn't it. "Only one."

"And that would be Sara Rettig?"

"Yes." Erica didn't recall having introduced Sara to anyone; but then again, Roberto was the type who could very well have introduced himself, so the mere fact that he knew the woman's name didn't set off any mental alarms.

"How much do you know about her?"

Now the alarms went off. Her gaze narrowed. "I know she's a hard worker. I couldn't have gotten through today without her."

He considered that for a moment. "She's a prostitute."

"What?"

"She turns tricks to support her addiction. Heroine, according to her rap sheet, but she could be using anything by now."

"How in the world can you possibly know that?"

"A colleague who once worked for the district attorney's office recognized Ms. Rettig, so I took the liberty of pulling her records. It's all there, Erica, every sordid detail."

Furious that he'd been investigating her employee, Erica could barely stammer, "I—don't...believe this."

Misunderstanding her indignation, Roberto laid a consoling hand on her knee. "I know this must come as a shock—"

"Oh, it's shocking all right." She pushed his hand away and angrily confronted him. "How dare you violate that poor woman's privacy?"

"How dare...*I?*"

"Yes, how dare you? Sara is trying to build a new life for herself. What gives you the right to try and destroy that?"

Roberto stiffened, eyeing Erica as if she'd just confessed to some kind of heinous crime. "You *knew?*"

"Of course I did. Sara told me all about her past." Erica's gaze skittered away for a moment, realizing that Sara had left out the prostitution part, but no matter. The woman had been basically honest and Erica couldn't fault her for an inadvertent omission here or there. "But even if she'd lied to me, you had no right to investigate someone just because you felt like it. Isn't that a violation of her constitutional rights or something? Never mind. Even if it isn't illegal, it should be."

Roberto raked his hair, shook his head, and shifted sideways. "I don't get it. The woman is a whore, a junkie and a thief, but you hire her anyway, giving her carte blanche access to your cash register because...because... Now, that's the part that escapes me."

Erica eyed him coldly. "I don't like the word *whore*."

Frustrated, he covered his face with his palms, peered over his fingertips and apologized for the offensive terminology. After a long moment, he laid one hand in his lap and stretched the other arm along the back of the sofa. "Perhaps we could discuss this rationally."

"Of course we could, assuming there was something to discuss. Sara Rettig is my employee. I'm happy with her and that's that."

"Do you know about her children?"

An unpleasant coldness slid down Erica's spine. "I know that they were put in foster care when she went to jail. But that was two years ago. She's working hard to get them back." When Roberto didn't respond, Erica angled a wary glance in his direction. A muscle above his jaw was twitching. "That's right, isn't it?"

"Partly." Roberto's eyes were nearly black with anger. "The kids went into foster care five years ago, not two. A neighbor called welfare to complain that the children had been left alone for nearly a week. By the time authorities showed up, Sara had returned, so they had no case for abandonment but since there wasn't any food in the house—which, by the way, was in deplorable condition—they took the kids anyway. If it had been up to me, she'd have been charged with neglect but for some reason, the powers that be chose not to. Over the next three years, however, she was arrested a dozen times on shoplifting, possession and prostitution charges.''

Erica's heart sank to the bottom of her rib cage. Sara's omissions, it seemed, were considerably more alarming than she'd first presumed. Although to be fair, the woman had never specifically said when she'd lost custody of her children. Erica had merely assumed it had been the result of her imprisonment. ''Sara mentioned that she'd been in jail for the past two years on burglary charges. It that much correct?''

''Yes. She pleaded guilty to having emptied a minimart cash register while the owner was in the back room.''

Somewhat relieved, Erica considered that a small vindication of a trust that may had been offered a bit too freely. ''And she served the full sentence?''

''Yes.''

''So, having paid for her mistakes, Sara now has the same rights as any other citizen.''

His jaw muscle continued to twitch violently. ''For the moment.''

''Oh, please. You make it sound as if people aren't capable of changing their lives.''

''Some people aren't.''

His judgmental attitude was beginning to grate on Erica's nerves. ''People like Sara, I suppose?''

''Yes, people like Sara. A woman who'd abandon helpless children to pursue her own selfish pleasure isn't capable of changing, Erica. If you weren't so damned naive, you'd see that.''

''Naive? Me?'' She was naive, of course, but coming from Roberto the accusation seemed remarkably sinister. ''All I see at the moment, Mr. Arroya, is a self-righteous man who doesn't seem to have a clue about having to struggle for crumbs. Not everyone was blessed by the privilege you and I enjoy. Some people have to claw their way through a life that hasn't been particularly kind.''

The defiant lift of her chin wilted beneath the intensity of his dark stare. ''Are you quite through?''

Acutely uncomfortable, she responded with a nonchalant shrug.

''First of all, I'm not certain where you've gleaned your information that I've been 'blessed by privilege,' but I can assure you that the rat-infested apartment where Sara Rettig's kids fended for themselves was a veritable palace compared to the dump I grew up in. I 'have a clue' about crumbs, Ms. Franklin. In fact, that's about all I had to eat for the first ten years of my life.''

Erica felt herself shrinking into the cushions. It had never occurred to her that a man as sophisticated, educated and successful as Roberto Arroya hadn't been raised in the same socioeconomic lifestyle that she'd enjoyed. ''I'm sorry,'' she whispered. ''I didn't know. God, I'm so embarrassed.''

Suddenly the fury drained from his eyes and was replaced by a touching softness. ''Don't be. You can't understand what you haven't experienced. In a sense, that purity is part of your charm.''

Roberto lifted her fist from her lap, gently unfurled her balled fingers and sandwiched her hand between his warm palms. ''Look, Erica, I'm not particularly proud of my less than auspicious beginning and there's no reason for you to feel guilty because you were raised in a clean, wholesome environment. Good fortune is nothing to be ashamed of.''

The words struck a chord. ''I do feel guilty sometimes. I've always had so much more than most people. It never seemed quite fair.''

''Fair is a relative term. Children have little control over their lives, but I believe excuses have to end where adulthood begins. Regardless of our point of origin, where we choose to go and how we choose to get there is up to each of us. It's called personal responsibility and some people—a lot of them, actually—reject the entire concept because it's so much easier to blame someone or something else.''

''And you believe that Sara is one of those people?''

''Yes, I do.''

''But you don't even know her, Roberto. How can you judge a person by a stack of old records?''

''Because those records reflect the choices she's made, choices that consistently avoid responsibility no matter what the cost to others.''

''People change.... ''

''Not people like Sara.'' There was a hardness to his voice, and in his gaze, that was frightening. Before she could study the revelation in his eyes, he turned away, releasing her hand as he abruptly stood. He crossed the room, stepping over the sleeping dog without so much as a downward glance, and paused to stare absently out the window. ''Don't give her your trust, Erica. She'll only betray it.''

There was more than a warning in Roberto's voice. There was the pain of experience, the disillusionment of one who knew firsthand what it felt like to have one's trust violated and betrayed.

Instinctively, Erica rose and went to him, then laid a comforting hand on his arm. ''Who was it?'' she asked softly. ''Who does Sara remind you of?''

For a moment, she didn't believe he was going to respond at all. He simply clenched his jaw, continuing to stare out at the darkness as if he hadn't even heard the question. Just as she decided that he simply wasn't going to answer, his muscles shuddered, then relaxed in resignation.

He spoke so softly that she could barely hear. ''My mother.''

Erica should have guessed as much, but hadn't. She was speechless, able to do little more than caress his biceps and offer a consoling squeeze.

Apparently, it was enough. His free hand came around to cover hers and, although he was still staring out the window, he spoke again. "I hadn't made a conscious connection, but the fact is that my mother really was a lot like Sara. The primary difference was their drug of choice. *Mamacita* preferred alcohol, although she supported her addiction in the same tired old ways—thievery and men."

"I'm so sorry," Erica whispered, having finally found her voice. "That must have been indescribably horrible."

He shrugged. "Initially, I didn't realize anything was wrong because I'd never known anything different. As I grew older, of course, I began to notice that my friends weren't expected to put drunken parents to bed at 3:00 a.m., nor were they locked out of their homes so that certain, ah, profitable entertainment could be conducted inside."

The mental image of the bewildered child he'd once been just about broke Erica's heart. "Did your mother ever get any help? I mean, is she still? . . . you know . . ."

"I haven't the vaguest idea." His biceps contracted and the muscle beneath his jaw began to twitch rapidly. "The last time I saw her, she was passed out on the floor while three burly welfare officers hauled my ten-year-old butt into what was laughingly referred to as 'protective custody.'"

"Oh, Lord. You were put into foster care?"

"Not right away." His smile wasn't particularly pleasant. "At that time there were precious few foster parents willing to take a grimy little Hispanic out of the city's most notorious *barrio.* I guess they figured that at the onset of puberty, I'd suddenly tie on a bandanna, yank an AK-47 gun out of my backpack and murder them in their sleep."

"I've never heard anything so utterly ridiculous," Erica said, nearly sputtering with indignation.

"Not really. Considering where I came from, I can't say that those fears were totally unjustified."

"You were a child, for heaven sake. *A child.*"

"There are no children in the *barrio.* Just small people."

Before she could fully absorb the impact of that statement, Roberto was speaking again. "Anyway, the authorities who'd effected my benevolent 'rescue' were faced with the quandary of where to put me. They decided on Black-thorn Hall.''

The name meant nothing to Erica. ''Is that some kind of private school?''

''In a sense, I suppose. Originally, it was established as a juvenile detention facility for hard-core offenders. It ended up being a long-term boot camp for unwanted children.''

Both hands flew up to muffle her gasp. ''They put an innocent ten-year-old in *reform school?* That's outrageous!''

''Yes,'' he mused. ''I suppose it is. But I have to admit that for better or worse, those years at Blackthorn Hall became the driving force of my life.''

As he stared absently into his past, Erica watched his expression change to one of wistfulness and of sorrow. She realized that now, at this very moment, he'd opened a small window to his soul. All she had to do was look inside and glimpse what was there; the strength and weakness, the complexities he concealed from the world, all that he was now and had ever been was laid bare to her. She had only to take the next step. To look. To ask. To understand.

And she did.

They talked for hours, sharing secrets, describing innermost passions that had guided the choices they'd made. Roberto revealed snippets of life at Blackthorn Hall, including the administrative gestapo that had instilled an intense loathing of injustice and in doing so, had shaped his destiny. His eyes softened as he spoke of the friendships forged from adversity, a brotherhood of unity and strength that he drew on to this very day. And his eyes filled with incredible sadness as he told of the tragedy that had forever altered the course of their young lives.

Afterward, a profoundly shaken Erica regarded the man beside her with a new awareness and immeasurable respect. ''How did you ever get out of there?''

"One of the facility's teachers took an interest in me. More precisely, he was fascinated by my IQ and continually petitioned the welfare system until a foster family was found."

"Were they nice people?"

"Yes, they were. Because they were usually caring for ten to fifteen kids at any given time, there wasn't much personalized attention, but to me it was heaven. I stayed there for three years, until I got a scholarship to USC. Then I moved on campus and the rest, as they say, is history."

A bit of quick math indicated that Roberto couldn't have been much older than fifteen when he'd entered the university. And with a scholarship no less. "When I teased you about having been a precocious child, I had no idea that you were a certified genius."

He coughed into his hand, seeming unsettled by a discussion of his mental acumen. "Actually, I was just a determined little bookworm."

"Now don't be modest. Why, I'll bet you were so bright, you probably breezed through law school in a year and were still in your teens when you passed the bar." Although he neither confirmed nor denied her assumption, Erica noticed a patch of crimson staining the side of his neck. "Are you blushing?"

"Of course not."

"Yes, you are."

"Latinos don't blush," he insisted. "It's not macho."

"Well macho or not, you're pink as peony." Erica laughed, delighted by the unexpected vulnerability. "But don't be embarrassed. The shade becomes you."

Sighing, Roberto gave up and angled a shy glance in her direction. "I don't suppose you'd be willing to make this our little secret."

"I don't know. Some things are just too good not to share."

"I'll pay."

Erica snapped her fingers. "Say, I wonder if that colleague of yours—Ms. Layton, isn't it?—would be interested to know that a well-placed comment about gifted intellect will make you glow in the dark."

Roberto moaned. "I'll pay *big*."

Enjoying herself immensely, she dismissed the offer with a flippant wave of her hand. "I don't want money."

"What then, my house? It's yours. My car?" He dug into his pocket. "Here, take the keys."

She touched his wrist to stop him from retrieving said keys. "I don't want your house or your car."

Roberto frowned, then glanced at the hairy gray lump curled beside the sofa. "Not my dog?"

"Heavens, no!"

"Then what is it you want?"

Erica's smile faded. She looked up at him, nearly drowning in the intensity of his dark eyes. Something came over her, a desperate need coupled with startling boldness. Without a second thought, the words slipped softly to the tip of her tongue and fell off. "I want you to finish what you started in the kitchen."

The moment she saw his shocked expression, she wanted to snatch the words back and swallow them whole. It was too late, of course. She'd already made a complete idiot of herself and the worst part was that she was less disappointed in what she'd asked of him than the fact that he hadn't immediately responded.

Then a strange thing happened. The corner of his mouth lifted in an odd little smile and a peculiar illumination radiated from his eyes. His palms slid up her arms, over her shoulders to rest briefly at the base of her throat. One hand remained there, caressing the sensitive pulse point. The other glided up to cup her chin, tilting her head back.

She forgot to breathe.

His scent drifted around her in a tangible embrace. She was dizzied by his nearness and the subtle spice of his cologne. Her knees weakened. She touched her palms to his chest, balancing herself and praying her legs wouldn't give way. For all she knew, they already had. She couldn't feel them anymore. Perhaps she was levitating, held upright by the magical touch of his thumb caressing her cheek. She didn't know. She didn't care, because his lips were moving closer. And closer.

Then, when his mouth was so near she could feel the sweet warmth of his breath, she trembled once, parted her lips and was swept away by the power of his kiss.

She melted bonelessly against him, her fingers tangled in his knit shirt as if her frantic clutching could stop the room from reeling. Colors poured in her mind, a swirl of images spinning out of control until she was utterly lost, completely absorbed. It was the most incredible experience of her life.

Too soon, Roberto stepped away, seeming as awed and shaken as she was. He gazed at her for a long moment, then took a deep breath, whispered good-night and went out the front door.

Erica stood there as if rooted in place. Behind her, she heard a soft yawn and the gentle padding of paws on carpet. Buddy brushed by her leg to seat himself directly in front of the door. After a moment, it opened and Buddy ambled outside. With a sheepish shrug, Roberto closed the door and was gone.

But Erica knew that he'd be back; and her life would never be the same.

Chapter Seven

"Do you want the cucumber sliced or cubed?" Roberto paused, paring knife at the ready, awaiting profound guidance from the salad guru who was now converting a carrot into incredibly precise slivers.

Erica didn't bother to glance up from her chore. "It doesn't matter to me, but slices don't have to be peeled."

That sounded reasonable. "Slices, then." He whacked at the hapless vegetable with a technique that was moderately effective, if somewhat crude.

When the chore was complete, he dumped the fat rounds into a bowl of greens and raw broccoli florets, then wiped his hands on a tea towel and checked the steaks that Erica had set aside to marinade. "Maybe I should put these on the grill."

"The potatoes won't be finished for another half hour."

"Oh." His stomach grumbled in disappointment.

Erica chuckled softly, a melodic sound that never failed

to make his pulse race. "If you're really starving, there's a bag of cookies in the cupboard."

Roberto knew exactly where the cookies were. Over the past two weeks, he'd spent enough time in Erica's kitchen to know it as well as he knew his own—and vice versa. Erica, who'd been appalled by his normal sandwich and potato chip supper, had taken it upon herself to remedy what she considered a serious nutritional deficiency. Since then, the only meal they hadn't shared was last Sunday, when Erica and the girls had dined with her parents. It had been the quietest evening Roberto had spent in ages. And the loneliest.

He'd missed the constant dinner table chatter. He'd missed Carolyn's lively school updates. He'd even missed the constant cajoling over Cathy's stubborn refusal to eat anything green. Most of all, he'd missed the comfort of being part of a loving family, a delicious sense of belonging that he hadn't experienced since his time at Blackthorn Hall.

Day by day, Roberto was becoming more emotionally connected to Erica and the girls, a situation which both delighted and dismayed him. Happiness, he'd discovered, is a fleeting thing. He'd long ago learned never to trust it, never to expose himself to the emotional abandonment that experience had proven inevitable.

Yet somewhere deep inside, Roberto realized that he must harbor some faint flicker of hope. Why else, Larkin had once asked, had he chosen a house in the suburbs over the standard, noncommittal bachelor pad?

At the time, it hadn't been a question Roberto was ready to answer. He still wasn't. But he'd spent a hell of a lot of time thinking about it.

"Roberto?"

"Hmm?" He glanced over his shoulder, instantly recognizing Erica's tolerant smile.

"I won't tell the girls you sneaked a cookie before dinner. Cross my heart."

Since his stomach felt like a withered grape, the offer was tempting. He gazed outside, to where the girls were playing in the front yard. "I'd better pass," he said finally. "The rustle of cellophane would bring them flying through the door with their hands out."

"You can always say no."

Roberto smiled. He knew without looking that Erica's eyes would be twinkling. Where the girls were concerned, the *N* word just wasn't part of his vocabulary. He'd tried a few times, but after weighing options, their requests had always seemed reasonable enough so he'd acquiesced.

And what was the harm? Life was tough, filled with disappointments. If an extra cookie or staying up to watch a Disney video could bring a little more joy into their lives, Roberto couldn't bring himself to deny it. He left that to Erica.

Now he slid a longing glance at the cookie cupboard, then sighed. "I can make it a half hour. After that, all bets are off."

"Such a stoic man," Erica said, laughing. As she started to speak again, there was a high-pitched squeal outside. In the blink of an eye, she was out the door with Roberto right on her heels.

They spotted Cathy squatting at the edge of a thick shrub row, peering into the foliage. She shrieked again, then dissolved into delighted giggles as the adults tore across the yard. "Fuzzy bug!" she hollered, pointing into the bush.

Panting, Erica touched her chest as if trying to slow her racing heart. "What on earth—?"

Roberto peered over Cathy's shoulder and spotted the hairy creature inching its way along a spindly twig. "It's just a caterpillar."

"Catty-pillar!" Cathy repeated, practically bouncing with excitement.

"There are hundreds of them around at this time of year," Roberto said, bewildered by the child's enthusiasm over a common insect. "Look, there's another one under that leaf."

The sight of two such magnificent creatures elicited a renewed series of joyful shrieks, which finally caught her sister's attention. Across the yard, Carolyn dropped Buddy's ball in the grass and ambled over to check things out.

"It's nothing but an ol' woolly worm," Carolyn said, obviously disappointed that the subject of such excitement wasn't something more exotic. Like, say, a boa constrictor.

Buddy didn't seem particularly enthused either. After a quick sniff of the wriggling insect, he padded over to a patch of shade and flopped down, visibly bored.

But Cathy's glee could not be daunted. "Woolly worm," she repeated, clapping her hands. "Catty-pillar."

"She's never seen one before," Erica explained.

"I gathered as much," Roberto murmured, still taken aback by the child's reaction. "But it's just a common caterpillar."

"To you, maybe. To Cathy, it's a small miracle." Erica carefully removed the fuzzy insect from the twig and held it out to her curious daughter. "Someday this little guy will take off his fur coat and become a beautiful butterfly," she told Cathy, whose eyes rounded in astonishment.

"Can I pet him?" she asked.

"Yes, but be very gentle."

"Don't squish him," Carolyn warned. "Or he'll poop in Mommy's hand."

Erica didn't seem particularly pleased by that possibility, but made no comment as Cathy, with a solemn expression befitting such a hallowed moment, slowly reached out and brushed a fingertip across the hairy nap.

"He's all tickly!" she yelped, yanking her hand away and tucking it safely under her chin. "Can you take his coat off?"

Erica straightened. "Well, no, sweetie. He has to do that by himself."

"How come?"

It was Carolyn who answered. "Don't be silly, Cathy. Mommy doesn't know where the zipper is."

Roberto nearly choked. Cathy, however, accepted the explanation with a solemn nod while Carolyn slid the adults a look of sage tolerance for a little sister who was too immature to understand something as obvious as worm coat fasteners.

Strangely enough, Roberto was not only amused by the girl's skewed rationale, but on some odd level he actually understood it. Over the past weeks, his life had taken on a new radiance. Viewing everyday events through the children's eyes had allowed him to rediscover small wonders that he'd always taken for granted. In a sense, he felt as if his own stolen childhood had been returned to him. It had been the most precious gift he'd ever received.

The sentimental musing was interrupted by an excited voice from the street. "Hey, Carrie, look what I got!"

All eyes turned to the pigtailed girl who was straddling a shiny red bicycle. Carolyn sucked in a sharp breath. "Wow," she murmured, awestruck. "Peggy's got a brand new bike. Can I go see it, Mommy?"

Erica, who'd been biting her lip in a staid attempt to keep from laughing at the zipper comment, managed to answer in a voice that only shook a little. "Sure, sweetie. Just stay in front of the house. Dinner will be ready soon."

Before she'd finished speaking, both girls were dashing across the yard. As Erica bent to return the caterpillar to its bushy home, Roberto watched Carolyn reverently stroke the gleaming metal, her eyes shining. "Carolyn doesn't have a bike, does she?" he asked.

Erica straightened, brushing her palms together. "No. I was hoping to get one for her birthday but I don't think that's going to be possible."

Roberto considered that to mean that since her ex-husband had reneged on their child support agreement, she couldn't afford the bicycle. Now, as Carolyn expressed oohs and áhhs of admiration for an object she couldn't have, Erica swallowed hard. He saw disappointment in her eyes, the pang of a mother unable to provide something that her daughter deeply wanted.

Roberto's first reaction was one of sympathy for both Erica and Carolyn, because as far as he was concerned, they deserved the best of everything. It didn't take long for the rage to form, a searing pain in his gut at the injustice that any man could callously abandon a family that Roberto would give his life to nurture and protect.

It was at that very moment that he remembered Larkin's question. And he finally knew the answer.

After counting the day's receipts, Erica closed the cash register and glanced over at Sara, who was supposed to be wiping down the tables. The woman was listlessly staring past the Closed sign in the front window while twisting a cloth into a damp spear. "Sara, is everything all right?" When there was no response, Erica repeated the question, a bit louder this time.

Sara spun around, eyes huge. "Yes'm?"

"I asked if everything was all right."

"Oh. Sure." Her gaze skittered along the floor. "Just fine."

"You looked a million miles away."

With a mumbled apology, Sara immediately set to work scrubbing the nearest table with such force, Erica feared she might wear off the laminate. Sara had been jittery lately, causing Erica to wonder if the woman's quest to regain custody of her children had taken a sour turn, although Erica was reluctant to broach the subject. Sara was, after all, quite a solitary person, so Erica had respected her privacy and refrained from asking personal questions.

Thanks to Roberto, Erica already knew more about the poor woman's humiliating history than she'd ever wanted to know. Since Sara would be mortified to learn that her past had become grist for public discussion, Erica had kept quiet about everything Roberto had revealed and had sworn him to secrecy as well. He hadn't been happy about that—his trust of convicted felons was only slightly higher than his respect for government bureaucrats—but he'd nonetheless complied. During routine lunchtime visits to the shop, Roberto treated Sara with customary courtesy along with an unobtrusive scrutiny which, in all probability, was noticeable only to Erica.

At the moment, however, there was a desperation in poor Sara's eyes that was worrisome and the poor woman looked absolutely exhausted. "It's a gorgeous afternoon," Erica said suddenly. "Why don't you leave early and enjoy the day."

Sara looked up, startled. "I haven't swept yet."

"I can do that."

"But it's my job."

Despite Erica's good intentions, Sara appeared so stricken that it seemed prudent not to press the point. "All right, then. I'll be in the office if you need me."

With a bland nod, Sara went back to scouring the spotless tables while Erica gathered up the cash receipts and daily order slips. As always, she left the office door open.

The reconciliation went smoothly, balancing to the penny. After three weeks in business, shop profits were increasing every day. Take-out orders were booming and by noon, there was a line at the counter that stretched nearly to the front door. Not in her wildest dreams could Erica have envisioned such success. She was thrilled and relieved. Unless the place burned down, she'd be able to make the first loan payment to her father by the end of next week. It would be one of the proudest moments of her life, a life that became more joyous with each passing day.

And Roberto Arroya was a big part of that newfound joy.

There were twinges of doubt, of course, remnants of Carter's betrayal that crept into her mind at the most inopportune times. But she pushed them away. Roberto wasn't Carter, and making one mistake didn't mean that she'd lost the ability to judge people fairly. So she'd been fooled once. It happens, right?

"Right," Erica murmured aloud. Thus fortified, she wrapped a rubber band around the stack of counted cash, added a deposit slip, then knelt in front of the safe. More out of habit than conscious thought, she rotated the cylinder right, left, then right again, pressed the lever down and pulled open the door. Ignoring the documents she kept inside, insurance papers and the like, she added the bundled cash to a canvas bag which contained three similar bundles. Friday's bank deposit would be the largest yet. Smiling to herself, she closed the safe and spun the cylinder.

Erica stood, rubbed the back of her neck, then turned and gasped at the backlit figure standing in the open doorway. She froze, her heart pounding. "Sara...?"

When the woman's head snapped up, a shaft of light illuminated her face. She looked, well, strange, with vacant eyes and a chilling, trancelike expression. "Yes'm?"

Erica's breath slid out all at once. "Is something wrong?"

"No, ma'am." Sara gestured back into the shop. "That friend of yours is at the front door. You want I should let him in?" As the woman turned completely into the light, the odd expression dissipated.

A trick of shadows, Erica assumed. "Roberto's here?" When Sara nodded, Erica suddenly felt ridiculously frenzied. Hurrying to a small mirror on the far wall, her hands flew up to pat and finger-comb her hair. "Yes, please, let him in. I'll be right there."

Erica was too busy fussing with a shadowy smudge under her eye to notice when Sara left the office, but in less

NO COST! NO OBLIGATION TO BUY!
NO PURCHASE NECESSARY!

PLAY "LUCKY 7"
AND GET AS MANY AS SIX FREE GIFTS...

HOW TO PLAY:

1 With a coin, carefully scratch away the silver panel opposite. Then check the claim chart to see what we have for you - FREE BOOKS and gifts - ALL YOURS! ALL FREE!

2 When you return this card we'll send you specially selected Silhouette Special Editions and the gifts you qualify for, absolutely FREE. There's no catch. You're under no obligation to buy anything. We charge nothing for your first shipment. And you don't have to make any minimum number of purchases.

3 After you've received your FREE books, if we don't hear from you, we will send you six brand new Silhouette Special Editions to read and enjoy every month for just £2.20* each - the same price as the books in the shops. There is no extra charge for postage and packing and no hidden extras.

4 The fact is thousands of readers enjoy receiving books through the post from the Reader Service. They like the convenience of home delivery… they like getting the best new novels at least a month before they're available in the shops… and they love their subscriber Newsletter, featuring author news, horoscopes, penfriends, competitions and much more.

5 We hope that after receiving your free books you'll want to remain a subscriber. But the choice is yours - to continue or cancel, anytime at all! So why not take up our invitation - you'll be glad you did!

*Prices subject to change without notice.

You'll look like a million dollars when you wear this lovely necklace! Its cobra-link chain is a generous 18" long, and the multi-faceted Austrian crystal sparkles like a diamond!

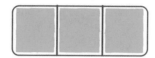

Play "Lucky 7"

2S6SE

Just scratch away the silver panel with a coin.
Then check below to see how many FREE GIFTS will be yours.

YES! I have scratched away the silver panel. Please send me all the gifts for which I qualify. I understand that I am under no obligation to purchase any books, as explained on the opposite page. I am over 18 years of age.

BLOCK CAPITALS PLEASE

MS/MRS/MISS/MR

ADDRESS

POSTCODE

 WORTH FOUR FREE BOOKS
PLUS A NECKLACE AND MYSTERY GIFT

 WORTH FOUR FREE BOOKS
PLUS A MYSTERY GIFT

 WORTH FOUR FREE BOOKS

 WORTH TWO FREE BOOKS

READER SERVICE 'NO RISK' GUARANTEE

- You're not required to buy a single book!
- You must be completely satisfied or you may cancel at any time simply by writing to us. You will receive no more books; you'll have no further obligation.
- The free books and gifts you receive from this offer remain yours to keep no matter what you decide.

SILHOUETTE READER SERVICE
FREEPOST
Croydon
Surrey
CR9 3WZ

NO
STAMP
NEEDED

than a heartbeat, she heard the click of the front door lock, followed by a deliciously familiar masculine voice.

She took a step back, gave a final glance at her reflection and saw a flushed woman with shining eyes staring back at her. It occurred to Erica that the person in the mirror bore more resemblance to a love-struck adolescent than a twenty-eight-year-old mother of two.

"Erica?" It was Roberto.

"I'll be right out." Tearing her gaze from the mirror, she took a deep breath and hurried into the shop. "Hi," she gushed, wincing at the throaty sound of her own voice. "What brings you here in the middle of the afternoon?"

Instead of answering her question, he posed one of his own. "Are you through locking up for the day?"

"Not quite," Erica said, noticing for the first time that there was a definite excitement in his eyes, kind of like a child on Christmas morning. "Why?"

Again he ignored the question. "How soon before you can leave?"

"Fifteen or twenty minutes."

"That long?" Disappointed, he glanced at his watch. "It's almost three-thirty and the store closes at four."

"What store?"

He gave her a smug grin. "That's the surprise."

"Surprise? What kind of surprise?"

"If I told you, it wouldn't be a surprise, would it?" He frowned at his watch again. "Are you sure you can't leave now?"

"Well, ah..." She absently glanced around the shop. "I have to wash the salad pans and mop the floor—"

Sara blurted, "I'll do it."

Roberto looked at the woman as if just reminded that she was there. He said nothing, although his expression hardened a bit.

Erica was torn. "I don't know, Sara. You seem so tired this afternoon anyway and it doesn't seem fair to make you do my work along with your own."

"It won't take long, ma'am, and I don't mind, truly I don't." Sara spun around, went into the office and returned with Erica's purse. "You go on now," she said, handing Erica the pocketbook. "Have a nice time, hear?"

"Well..." Guilt gave way to anticipation. Erica was positively dying to know what Roberto had up his sleeve. "If you're sure."

Roberto started to say something but Sara interrupted. "I'll check the back door and make sure everything's locked tight, just like you showed me."

Since the doors locked automatically, Erica wouldn't have to relinquish her key, a consideration that offered an embarrassing sense of relief. Determined that Roberto not notice her brief lapse of faith, Erica squared her shoulders and gave her employee a confident smile. "Then I'll see you tomorrow."

With a mumbled "yes'm", Sara went behind the counter and began removing salad pans from the cooler.

When Roberto hesitated, Erica boldly opened the front door. "Shall we go?"

"Hmm? Oh. Sure." He cast a final glance over his shoulder, then escorted Erica to his car, which was parked outside.

A moment later, as they pulled away from the curb, Roberto asked, "What time do you normally pick up the girls from day care?"

"Between four and four-thirty."

He pulled a fold-up cellular phone out of his pocket. "You may want to let them know you'll be a little late."

She took the phone. "How late?"

"That depends," he said, with that same secretive grin. "On how long you make me beg."

The implication of that statement struck her speechless. At the same moment, Roberto apparently realized what he'd said because his head swiveled around and he gave her the most horrified look. "That's not what I meant! I mean, I have no intention of...ah..." A red stain crept up his throat as he refocused on the road.

"Are you trying to assure me that this surprise of yours won't take place at a local motel?"

Shaking his head, he moaned something that sounded like *Madre de Dios* before roughly clearing his throat. "Of course not. In fact—" He turned into a strip mall parking lot. "We're here."

Erica lifted the sun visor and peered out the windshield. "A toy store?"

"Not just any toy store. Wait until you see..." The rest of the sentence floated out of earshot when he exited the car and shut the door. Twisting in her seat, Erica watched him through the back window. His mouth was still moving when he opened the passenger door "—different styles, but there's one in particular that I think you'll really love."

Laying the cellular phone on the seat—there was plenty of time to call the day care center—Erica stepped outside but before she could question what in the world Roberto was talking about, he grasped her elbow and propelled her into the store, where a chunky, mustachioed clerk greeted him like a long-lost brother.

"Bienvenido, Senor Arroya," the man said, then launched into a barrage of Spanish which far exceeded Erica's limited knowledge of the language. She did, however, understand the approval in the clerk's dark eyes as he nodded in her direction. *"¿Ésta tu bonita esposa?"*

Roberto's response apparently clarified that Erica was not his lovely wife, because the jovial clerk shrugged and uttered something that caused an exchange of just-between-us-menfolks grins.

Erica, who was beginning to feel like a slab of corned beef at a picnic, managed a polite smile. "I'm sorry, I don't understand enough Spanish to carry my part of the conversation."

Roberto's apology was immediate and sincere. "Manuel doesn't speak English," he explained after the clerk had disappeared into the back of the store. "He owns this place and has a reputation for carrying only the finest merchandise at prices that can't be beat."

"And what, exactly, are we pricing here?"

"Well…" Roberto hesitated, then issued a crow of delight as Manuel rolled a sparkling bicycle up the aisle. "That! Isn't it terrific?"

It was, of course, although Erica was too stunned to reply aloud. All she could do was stare while Manuel set the kickstand, then stood back like a proud grampa. He said something in Spanish, to which Roberto responded in kind, but Erica wasn't paying attention. She was overwhelmed by the sheer beauty of the bicycle. It was absolutely gorgeous, with its muted lavender-and-rose frame set off by a plush, white seat and matching handgrips.

"What do you think?" Roberto asked anxiously. "Would Carolyn like it?"

"Oh…" Erica absently massaged a sudden lump in her throat. "I…that is, she would love it, of course, but…I couldn't possibly afford it. Not right now, anyway."

He looked as if he'd been struck. "I was hoping you'd allow me to buy it."

At first, Erica thought he was offering a loan. She looked up with the refusal teetering on her tongue and saw the warmth in his eyes. That's when it hit her. "You want to give this to Carolyn, as a birthday gift?"

"If it's all right with you."

"But it's…it's too much." Erica knew she was stammering but couldn't help herself. It was a magnificent gift, but much too expensive and besides, she'd been plagued by the recurrent thought that the convenient appearance of Peggy's new bike in Roberto's presence smacked of a setup.

On the other hand, the situation may have been pure happenstance. As far as Erica knew, Carolyn didn't have a devious bone in her little body. Still, Roberto had repeatedly proven himself a generous man; Erica couldn't bring herself to take advantage of that, even for the sake of her children. "I'm sorry," she said finally.

Roberto regarded her thoughtfully for a moment, then spoke to Manuel. *"Un momento, por favor."*

"Sí, ciertamente, señor." The man issued a polite nod before discreetly disappearing between toy-stacked shelves.

When they were alone, Roberto spoke quietly. "I understand your reluctance. If I were in your place, I'd probably feel the same way."

"How do you think I feel?"

"Disappointed, I imagine, that you're not currently in a position to give your daughter something that she wants."

The observation was accurate enough to make her cheeks heat. "It's not just that. Carolyn has to understand that she can't always have everything her friends have." A furtive glance indicated that he was nodding in agreement. Erica looked back at the gleaming bicycle and sighed. "The thing is that Carolyn has never even asked for a bike. I think she realizes that it's something we can't afford right now." When he still made no comment, Erica squared her shoulders and faced him. "You don't need to spend money on Carolyn to make her like you. She already thinks the sun rises on your shoulders. It doesn't matter what you get for her birthday, or whether you get her anything at all. Her feelings won't change."

Roberto stared at her, as if he couldn't quite believe his ears. "You think I'm trying to buy her affection?"

"I'm just saying that if you were, it wouldn't help because she's absolutely crazy about you. We all are, of course…ah…I mean…that is…" Frustrated, she scoured a palm across her forehead and was wondering why she was suddenly incapable of spitting out a coherent sentence when an odd sound caught her attention.

It was a low vibration at first, but after a moment it rumbled into a soft chuckle. Roberto was laughing at her. Erica didn't know whether to be chagrined or indignant.

After noting her less than pleased expression, Roberto coughed away all trace of amusement. "I've got an idea," he said. "The bike can be from both of us. Or just from you. It doesn't matter to me whose name is on the card." He slid his hands into his slacks pockets, hesitated, then looked directly at Erica with an intensity that took her breath away. "I never had a bike when I was a kid. I've never forgotten what that felt like. Let me do this for Carolyn. Please."

The request, issued in a soft, matter-of-fact voice, was so profoundly poignant that it brought tears to Erica's eyes. She could picture Roberto as a lonely young boy, his nose pressed on a smeared window, watching other children play and knowing that he was different, that he'd never truly belong. It wouldn't have mattered if the other boys rode shiny new dirt bikes or rusted relics; they'd been interacting, sharing experiences and camaraderie in which young Roberto had never been included.

Erica was deeply touched by the plight of that lost little boy, who had, perhaps by divine intervention, evolved into a man of unique strength and infinite compassion.

"Erica?" The quiet question, tinged with concern, was followed by the gentle caress of his thumb across her moist cheek. "Have I upset you? God, I never meant to—"

She shook her head. "No. I'm just so…so…touched."

He seemed bewildered by that. "It's just an ordinary birthday gift. I'd hoped you'd be pleased."

"I am. Very pleased. But there's nothing ordinary about the gift," she whispered. "Or about the man who is giving it."

It took a moment for his eyes to reflect her meaning. When they did, their joyful glow warmed her to her toes. "Does that mean we can buy Carolyn the bike?"

"Not we. You." Because she couldn't help herself, she laid her palm against his cheek. "And I can't wait to see her face when you give it to her."

As his hand slid down to stroke her throat, an electrical warmth tingled through her body to settle in her liquid core. Anticipation of his kiss made her wild inside. They'd kissed before, more than once, and the encounters had always been extraordinary. But this time was different. This time, a white heat was boiling in her belly; this time, she felt a need, a sizzling desire that went beyond lips, beyond skin, beyond soul.

And when their mouths met, locking in a union so intensely intimate that the earth jarred beneath their feet, she felt something even deeper, something so far beyond the realm of her experience that it boggled the mind. It beguiled her; it frightened her; it shook the foundation of all she'd ever believed about human emotion. And about love. Because this was new. This was different. This was something she'd never felt before. And she didn't have a clue what it all meant.

Roberto lifted his head, breaking the kiss. He was breathing hard, looking as stunned and awestruck as Erica felt. She was still clinging to him like a drugged tick, but her legs had gone completely limp and if he hadn't been holding her up, she'd have certainly collapsed into a quivering puddle on the toy store floor.

Before she'd completely gotten her bearings, Manuel peeked around a stack of computer games, grinning madly. "*¿Está todo bien?*"

Roberto laughed and slipped a supporting arm around Erica's waist. "*Sí, mi amigo.* Everything is fine."

Erica rested her head on Roberto's firm chest, listening to the soothing rhythm of his heart, and told herself that everything was more than merely fine. Everything was, in fact, magnificent, even more magnificent than Carolyn's beautiful new bike. Life was wonderful. For the first time in more years than she could remember, Erica was truly happy.

The next morning, Erica unlocked the shop at the usual time, which was about 9:45 a.m. As always, she left the blinds down and the Closed sign in place to prevent early birds from entering before the shop opened at eleven.

As she passed through the kitchen, she noticed that the salad pans were gleaming, the counter was shining like a new dime and the floor had been mopped within an inch of its life. Sara, it seemed, had outdone herself.

Smiling, Erica went into the tiny office and tucked her purse in the desk drawer. Everything was as she'd left it, including the open checkbook and pile of invoices waiting to be paid. They'd have to wait a few hours longer. There was a ton of work to be done to prepare the shop for its first customer of the day.

During the next half hour, Erica filled stainless steel containers with fresh sliced vegetables, prepared three batches of special potato salads—mayo, mustard and German— then turned the iced tea machine to brew cycle. She was in the process of tearing lettuce for the green salad when she noticed the time and realized that for the first time, Sara was late.

Initially, Erica chided herself for worrying. After all, it was only 10:15 and the poor woman had worked well beyond her scheduled hours last night.

By 10:30, Erica had convinced herself that Sara had probably missed her bus.

By 10:45, Erica had retrieved Sara's employment application and was dialing her number, whereupon an automated voice replied that the phone was no longer in service.

It was at that point that the cold chill slid down her spine. Her gaze was drawn to the floor safe. In that instant, she intuitively knew that it would be empty.

And it was.

Chapter Eight

"Hi." Roberto stepped inside and glanced around the too-quiet living room. "Are the kids asleep?"

"Yes." Erica held the front door open for another moment before peeking out at the empty porch. "Where's Buddy?"

"Curled up at the foot of my bed. He must have had a big day."

"Didn't we all?" Erica mumbled, closing the door. "Would you like some coffee?"

"No, thanks." He folded his arms, studying the floor. After a moment, he looked up. "How are you doing?"

"Terrific, just terrific," she said without bothering to disguise her sarcasm. "I've just spent half the evening trying to convince my creditors to accept tuna sandwiches in lieu of cash. Oddly enough, they weren't particularly receptive."

"Maybe I can help—"

She held up her hand, silencing him. It took a moment before she could control the sudden quiver in her throat and respond. "I'm not taking your money, Roberto. This is my problem. I'll solve it."

Although he seemed prepared to argue the point, thankfully he didn't. Instead, he respected her wishes by changing to a subject that was, unfortunately, almost as distressing. "Does your father know what happened?"

Erica flinched at the thought. For some unfathomable reason, she'd called Roberto before she'd even called the police. But telling her father was another matter. "No. I can't bear to tell him that when it comes to being a gullible fool, I still haven't learned my lesson."

"I doubt he'd see it that way. I certainly don't."

"Why not? You're the one who warned me about Sara. The fact that you're too polite to rub it in doesn't change the fact that you were right."

Before Roberto could reply, Carolyn dashed into the room with a ruffle-hemmed nightie frantically swirling around her bare feet. "Guess what!" she chortled, skidding to a stop in front of Roberto. "My daddy got me a birthday present!"

"That's great," Roberto said, bending to stroke her bobbing head. "What is it?"

"I don't know 'cause it didn't come yet. But it's gonna be real special. He promised."

When Roberto slid Erica a questioning glance, she managed a weak smile. "Carolyn's been leaving messages on Carter's machine all week, asking him to come down for her birthday. Last night, she finally got through to him."

"Daddy can't come see me," Carolyn explained. "On account of him being real busy and stuff. When I open my present tomorrow, I'm gonna pretend like he's here and it'll be almost as good."

"I'm sure it will." Roberto gave the child an encouraging hug. "I can see why you're so excited."

Erica gazed down at her beaming daughter and prayed that this time, Carter wouldn't let her down. "Scoot back to bed, sweetie. Tomorrow's going to be a big day, remember? Cake and ice cream and—"

"Daddy's present!" Carolyn took advantage of Roberto's bent position to hug his neck and plant a wet kiss on his cheek. "'Night, Mr. 'Roya."

"Good night, punkin." He straightened, waved, and waited until the child had scampered from the room before returning to the original subject. "The shop is too busy for one person to handle. Have you decided what you're going to do?"

"Hmm? Oh, yes. My mother has a friend who owns an employment agency. They have a lady with similar experience who's willing to start Monday." Erica saw the silent question in Roberto's eyes and answered it. "I told my mother that Sara had a personal emergency."

He hiked a brow. "Not completely untrue, I suppose."

"Yes, well…" She cleared her throat. "Anyway, I spoke to this lady on the phone and she seems quite, uh, knowledgeable. We're meeting at the shop on Sunday to go over a few things."

"Would you like me to watch the girls?"

The unexpected offer startled her. "You don't have to do that. I can take them with me."

"It would be easier if you didn't have to keep them occupied. Besides, I imagine the birthday girl will be looking forward to, ah…" He angled a glance toward the hall and lowered his voice. "Playing with a certain wheeled object."

His smug grin tickled her. Lord, he was excited about that bike. She knew he could barely wait for Saturday, but was uncomfortable about interrupting the rest of his weekend. "I thought you always kept Sunday afternoons free for basketball with your friends."

"They could use a day off. Buddy and I always beat their pants off anyway." He suddenly sobered, as if struck by an unpleasant thought. "Then again, I've never claimed to be an expert on kids. You'd probably be more comfortable with an experienced baby-sitter."

"There is no one I'd be more comfortable leaving my children with than you," she said, and was rewarded by one of his dazzling smiles.

"Then it's settled." Roberto's smile slowly faded into the preoccupied expression Erica had learned to recognize during their weeks together.

Having deduced that he was struggling with yet another jolt of unfortunate information, she decided to make it easy on him. "You might as well tell me. Whatever it is, I'll find out sooner or later."

"All right," he said, clearly unhappy about the impending revelation. "LAPD checked out the address on Sara's application. It's a rooming house, but no one matching her description has lived there during the past six months."

Somehow, that didn't surprise Erica. She simply nodded, numb to the snowballing mountain of bad news.

After a silent moment, Robert added, "The police lab also confirmed that Sara's fingerprints were all over the safe. I don't want to be critical, Erica, but under the circumstances, I really don't understand why you gave her the combination."

"I didn't." Sighing, Erica turned away and rubbed a sudden chill from her upper arms. "She must have watched me open it, then memorized the combination. At the time, it didn't occur to me that she'd be able to do that." She felt Roberto's warmth against her back a moment before he embraced her. Closing her eyes, she rested the back of her head against his chest and tried a more optimistic speculation. "Maybe after we left last night, a burglar broke in and forced Sara to open the safe."

"Then why wouldn't she have called the police?"

"Maybe she was afraid. I mean, with her record, they might not have believed her."

"So she just scurried off into the night, without even leaving you a note telling you what happened?"

Erica felt like she'd swallowed a brick. "It's possible."

Roberto turned her around to face him and gave her shoulders a gentle shake. "Face it, Erica. The woman is a thief. She robbed you."

"I can't believe it's that simple. Sara has done some bad things in her life, but basically she's a good person—"

"No, she's *not*." This time, he shook her shoulders with a bit more force. "Good people don't do bad things, Erica. Bad people do bad things."

"That's not true, Roberto. People can't be categorized as either good or evil."

"They can and they are," he insisted. "Life has a big fat line down the middle. Once a person chooses which side to stand on, that's where they stay. Sara Rettig made that choice a long time ago."

The anger in his voice was startling. Again, Erica was haunted by her father's admonition about Roberto. *Ruthless,* he'd said. *A man who goes after good people who, because of a crisis in their lives, may have made a mistake.*

Slowly it dawned on her that there might be a modicum of truth in her father's warning. Roberto *was* ruthless, but not out of sinister ambition. He simply saw life and everything in it in terms of black or white, good or evil, heaven or hell. To him, there were no shades of gray. He categorized people, perhaps unfairly, based on an indisputably high moral ground. Those who fell from favor were summarily dismissed as untrustworthy, unsympathetic.

Unredeemable.

Erica wondered what kind of mistake it would take to turn this compassionate, sensitive man into a relentless avenger. And what would happen if she were ever to make such a mistake.

The thought made her shudder.

Roberto's arms tightened protectively. He kissed the top of her head. "Are you cold?"

Yes, she was cold. Cold inside, frozen by the fear that someday she might make that fatal error and the warmth in his eyes would turn to black ice. Then she would lose his friendship. Lose him. And she wouldn't be able to bear it.

A weak chirping sound suddenly startled her. Roberto loosened his grasp at the same moment that she pulled away, her head swiveling to locate the source of the strange noise. As she spun around, she saw Roberto dig into his slacks pocket and retrieve a tiny black case. "It's my beeper," he explained, inspecting the number displayed on the digital readout. "May I use your phone?"

"Of course." She gestured toward the nearest telephone, which was on an end table beside the sofa.

As he headed toward it without comment, Erica went into the kitchen to give him—and herself—a moment of privacy. She was trembling, emotionally drained and physically exhausted. Sara's betrayal had been another spike driven in her heart, another chip torn out of her own self-confidence. Like Carter, Sara Rettig had again proven that Erica's ability to judge people, to see beneath their superficial facades, was imminently flawed.

She'd never considered optimism as a character defect, but perhaps it was. Perhaps trusting people, believing in basic human decency, was nothing more than the wishful thinking of an intellectual simpleton.

The consideration was chilling. Erica didn't want to raise her children in a world where people were figuratively herded to opposite sides of an imaginary line. But she didn't want them to be repeatedly disillusioned, either.

With a pained sigh, she rubbed her head as if to scour away the unwelcome thoughts, the silent questions to which there seemed no acceptable response. And since there were no answers, at least none that she could find at the moment, she shook the entire matter out of her mind, turned the oven to pre-heat and opened the box of cake mix that she'd set out on the counter.

By the time she'd gathered the remaining ingredients for Carolyn's birthday cake, Roberto was standing in the doorway looking drawn and shaken. Erica laid the wooden spoon beside the mixing bowl. "What is it, Roberto? What's wrong?"

Raking his fingers through his hair, Roberto avoided her eyes. "They've found Sara."

Erica steadied herself on the counter. "Where?"

"At County General. Witnesses said that a car rolled up and shoved her out in the emergency room parking lot." He paused for a breath before finally looking up to meet Erica's horrified gaze. "She suffered a drug overdose. Most likely heroin, but we can't verify that until the toxicology report is complete."

"Oh, my God." The room started to spin. "I-I've got to go see her."

"It's too late." Roberto emerged from the doorway and slid a bracing arm around her waist. "She's gone, Erica. Sara is dead."

Roberto dragged himself into the darkened bedroom to find a snoring lump of fur on his pillow. He patted the animal's bony rump. "Move it."

Buddy blinked up and yawned. After a luxurious stretch, he ambled across the mattress, circled twice and flopped at the foot of the bed, laying his prickly chin on neatly crossed paws.

Sitting on the vacated spot, Roberto bent to pull off his shoes. "It's a good thing you stayed home," he told the dog. "I know how bummed out you get when people cry."

Buddy whined.

"Yeah. It's the pits." The shoes Roberto tossed in a corner were soon joined by a knit polo shirt unceremoniously yanked over his head. He slumped forward, resting his forearms on his thighs. "Erica cried tonight," he whispered. "She cried for someone who'd lied, cheated, stolen her money and betrayed her trust. The woman wasn't worth spit, but that didn't matter to Erica. She just stood there, sobbing as if her heart had been ripped out, and there wasn't a damned thing I could do about it."

The mattress vibrated. In a moment, a hairy head was tucked beneath his master's arm. Roberto absently stroked the contented animal. "Do you believe in angels, Bud? I'm not talking about the heavenly kind, with wings and all. I mean real human angels, saints on earth who can look at a pile of cow dung and imagine a field of flowers."

Buddy issued a loud sigh.

"I can't figure it. First of all, she married the jerk of all times, a world-class cretin who walks out on her when she's *pregnant,* for God's sake—" He glanced down at the dog. "Did you know that? I found out last week, when I wondered out loud why Cathy wasn't as upset about the divorce as Carolyn. That's when Erica calmly mentioned—calmly, mind you—that her idiot husband left a month before Cathy was born. That's why the poor little kid isn't bothered that her father isn't around. She barely knows who the devil he is."

Roberto nodded in response to Buddy's low growl. "Yeah, I think so, too. Unfortunately, castration is considered cruel and unusual punishment for humans. Hmm? Oh, well, it's different for animals. Hell, no, I don't know why. It just is, that's all. And don't give me that look. It was for your own good."

Apparently miffed by the reminder, Buddy returned to the foot of the bed, presenting his back to Roberto, who continued the monologue as if he still had an audience. "Don't get me wrong. I don't really want Erica to change—God knows, she's perfect the way she is—I just don't want her to be hurt any more, you know? I want to protect her, keep her happy and safe forever. I've never felt this way before. What do you think it means, Bud?''

The question was answered by a rhythmic, vibrating rumble. Roberto glanced over his shoulder and realized the dog was snoring again. With a pained sigh, he stretched out with his hands tucked beneath his head. At least someone would get some sleep tonight. But it sure as hell wasn't going to be him.

The back yard was alive with giggling youngsters. From his vantage point at the kitchen window, Roberto watched the gaggle of excited kids dashing between small tables adorned with colorful balloons, whacking those unfortunates who ran slower than they and squeaking "You're it!" at the top of their well-honed lungs. One athletically inclined youngster was flinging a Frisbee for Buddy. The determined dog, decked out in his spiffiest party bandanna, leapt to bite the thing out of mid-air, and received a chorus of appreciative cheers for the effort.

In the center of the freshly cropped lawn, beside a round table impaled by a huge, striped umbrella and heaped with brightly bowed packages, Jacqueline Mallory watched the happy melee from her wheelchair. Her husband hovered nearby, bending occasionally to pat his wife's hand or whisper something that she apparently found amusing.

Roberto's gaze was drawn to the older couple. He was fascinated by the warmth in their eyes when they looked at each other, and the subtle poignancy of each small touch. That they were very much in love was obvious; yet there was something even deeper going on there, an intimacy that transcended the routine comfort of people who'd spent decades together. Roberto had never seen a couple so psychically attuned. A minuscule dip at the corner of Mallory's mouth and his wife automatically laid a consoling hand on his arm. A hint of perspiration on Jacqueline's brow and her husband instantly responded, wheeling her into the umbrella's cooling shade.

"What's going on out there?"

"Hmm?" Roberto glanced over his shoulder at Erica, who was arranging candles on a freshly iced cake. "Oh. The kids are running wild and your parents seem to be getting quite a kick out of watching them."

"Is Carolyn in the yard?"

Roberto refocused his gaze through the window. "I don't see her."

Sighing, Erica laid the unused candles aside. "She probably went out front to wait for the mailman."

"Probably." He propped a hip against the counter and folded his arms, fretting about Carolyn's obsession with her father's present. It wasn't that the child was materialistic. Carolyn didn't give a flying fig whether she got a fifty-dollar computer game or a package of bubble gum. She simply wanted her father to remember her birthday—to remember *her*. Not an unreasonable expectation for a just-turned six-year-old. And Roberto couldn't figure why he had such a bad feeling about this. The guy *had* promised, after all; not even a lowlife like Carter Franklin would break a promise to his own flesh and blood.

But if the tight strain lines around Erica's mouth were any clue, Roberto wasn't the only one who was worried. Then again, she'd had more than her share of grief in the past twenty-four hours. "Did you get any sleep last night?"

She glanced up and managed a thin smile. "Some. You?"

"Some," he lied. "So, how're you doing?"

They both knew what he meant. "I'm all right," Erica said. "It's just that I can't stop thinking about Sara. I should have seen that she was faltering and done something to help her."

With two steps, Roberto was standing across the table from her. "There's nothing you could have done."

"I don't know that because I didn't even try."

"It wasn't your responsibility to save Sara," he insisted. "People who want help will ask for it. She didn't."

Biting her lower lip, Erica stared down at the cake, although he doubted she actually saw it. "Maybe she didn't know how."

He wanted to refute that, but knew anything he said would simply keep Sara Rettig's tragedy fresh in Erica's mind. That was the last thing he wanted. In truth, he wished to hell that he could take Erica in his arms and kiss her pain away. With a yard full of youngsters, not to mention her own parents right outside the door, that didn't seem a prudent course of action. At least, not at the moment.

Erica heaved a resigned sigh. "This is Carolyn's day," she said. "I don't want to spoil it." Using a butter knife, she smoothed a few uneven splotches in the chocolate frosting. When she was finally satisfied, she set the knife down and gave the cake a last, critical inspection.

"It looks great," Roberto assured her.

"You don't think it's a little crooked?"

"Trust me. It's perfect." His finger inched toward a blob of icing clinging to the edge of the plate.

"Uh-uh." Erica gave his hand a gentle shove. "No tasting."

"But it's dribbling. It looks, well, messy."

"So you were going to tidy it up, hmm?"

"I was hoping to."

She chuckled, shook her head and was, Roberto sensed, just about to give in when the back door opened.

Kenneth Mallory strode inside, holding an empty glass. After dismissing Roberto with a cool glance, he spoke to his daughter. "Is there any lemonade left, Erica? Mother is thirsty."

"In the refrigerator," she murmured. As Mallory crossed the kitchen, Erica fidgeted with the knife as if trying to avoid both her father's gaze and Roberto's.

When the Mallorys had arrived this afternoon, Kenneth had been clearly displeased to find Roberto in his daughter's house, although Roberto wasn't at all certain why. The man had been civil, of course, but his eyes had demanded a certain social distance. He'd gone so far as to avoid using Roberto's name, relying on the impersonal title of "counselor" when decorum required specificity.

Picking up the hint—no one could accuse Roberto of being deliberately obtuse—he'd returned the favor by referring to Mallory as "commissioner", which seemed to suit the older man just fine.

From the outset, Erica and Jacqueline had exchanged telling glances indicating that they, at least, understood what was happening even if Roberto did not.

At the moment, however, Mallory's appearance in the kitchen elicited a tension that Roberto found irritating and completely unreasonable. Since earlier attempts at small talk with the commissioner had been unsuccessful, he continued to ignore the man's silent hostility by turning his attention to Erica. "So, when can Carolyn open her presents?"

"Why, are you anxious?" She fairly purred the question and slipped him a knowing smile.

"You're going to torment me, aren't you?"

"For a while, I think. After all, anticipation is half the fun."

Apparently Mallory, who'd just finished filling his wife's glass and replacing the lemonade pitcher, was annoyed by any conversation which didn't include him. He ahemed roughly, a not so subtle reminder that he didn't appreciate being ignored.

"I'm just teasing Roberto," she explained to her father. "He's gotten Carolyn a very special present and can hardly wait to give it to her."

"Oh?" For once Mallory regarded Roberto without giving the impression that he'd like to slit his throat. "Well, whatever it is, I'm sure Carolyn will be pleased."

"I hope so," Roberto said.

Erica brightened. "Would you like to see it, Daddy? It's in the garage and I know Roberto would love to show it off."

The two men exchanged glances that quite clearly revealed that they'd rather chew glass and wash it down with battery acid.

"Great! It's settled. I'll take this out to Mama." Erica plucked the lemonade glass from her reluctant father and hustled out the door, leaving the confused men to either glower at each other or go ahead and get the unpleasantry over with.

After an indecisive moment, they mutually chose the latter. Mallory stepped into the hall, opened the door to the adjoining garage. "Shall we, counselor?"

"After you, commissioner."

Accepting the lead, Mallory flipped on the light and stepped down into a space cluttered by lawn mowers, unpacked moving cartons and, oddly enough, Erica's car. The older man glanced around, vaguely curious. "Where is this, ah, thing?"

"Over here, under the tarp." Roberto sidestepped a scuffed red wagon and moved toward the plastic-covered lump in the corner. He waited a moment, until Mallory was in position, then carefully held up the canopy to expose the gleaming lavender-and-rose-colored bike. A matching helmet dangled from the handlebars.

"Oh, my," Mallory murmured, moving in for a closer look. "That really is exquisite, isn't it?"

Roberto could barely contain his excitement. "You don't think it's too small, do you? I looked at bigger ones, but I was afraid she might hurt herself. The shop owner said that most accidents were caused by kids riding the wrong size bike."

"Really? Well, I suppose that makes sense. When Erica was little, she borrowed her cousin's bike, although she could barely reach the pedals. If I recall, she took a nasty spill." Mallory hastened to reassure Roberto that the incident described was the only time in all her years of bike riding that Erica had ever so much as skinned a knee. "The helmet and training wheels will help Carolyn learn to ride safely," he added.

Still unnerved by the thought of nasty spills and skinned knees, Roberto regarded the beautiful bicycle with new concern. "Do you think so? I mean, if there's any chance she might hurt herself—"

"Nonsense. She'll be absolutely delighted. Besides, all children should have a bicycle. I'm simply annoyed that I didn't think to get her one myself." Then Mallory slapped Roberto on the back, completing the ageless ritual of male bonding to confirm a common objective, which was, in this particular instance, Carolyn's happiness.

Relaxed and confident, Roberto re-covered the bike. He knew he was grinning like a damned fool, but what the hell? So was Mallory.

They left the garage and emerged from the house engrossed in conspiratorial whispers about their shared secret. Erica and Jacqueline looked up from their own discussion, noted the intimate conversation between the two men and responded with identical expressions of stunned disbelief. Before either woman could speak, a joyful squeal caught everyone's attention.

"Mommy!" Carolyn hollered from the front of the house. "Daddy's present is coming!"

Erica, looking massively relieved, hurried toward the front porch. As Mallory went to assist his wife, Roberto followed Erica, rounding the corner of the house just as the mailman turned into the walk. Carolyn dashed to meet him, bouncing around the perplexed man as if she had springs on her feet. The carrier placed a few loose envelopes in Carolyn's outstretched hands, tipped his hat to the gathering crowd and headed back down the sidewalk.

Bewildered, Carolyn handed the mail to her mother. "Which one is from Daddy?"

Although Roberto was some distance away, he knew from the look on Erica's face that none of the envelopes was from Carolyn's father. She said something—he couldn't hear what. Carolyn's lip quivered. Tears slid down her cheeks.

Mallory pushed his wife's wheelchair around the corner and stopped beside Roberto. "What's going on?"

"Carter blew it again," Roberto said.

Mallory swore. Jacqueline stared at her lap.

Across the yard, Erica was trying to coax Carolyn to rejoin the party, but the sobbing child refused. Ignoring her mother's suggestion that the gift had simply been delayed in the mail, the child stubbornly insisted that it was coming special delivery and she wasn't leaving until it arrived.

Finally Erica straightened, gave Roberto a gut-wrenching look of despair, then rushed up the front steps and into the house, presumably to telephone her cold-hearted ex-husband.

Mallory wheeled his wife over to the heartbroken child, who crawled into her grandmother's lap and sobbed pitifully. Roberto simply stood there, too stunned to believe what had happened and too furious to trust his own voice. He finally returned to the back yard, where the other children continued to party, oblivious to the distress of their little hostess. He went into the kitchen just as Erica was hanging up the phone. Her shoulders slumped forward. She pressed her forehead against the wall.

Roberto knew that she'd just called Carter. "He didn't send anything, did he?"

She shuddered once, then turned to face him. "He didn't have time," she said bitterly. "But he'll get around to it. He promised."

Roberto crossed the room and gathered her in his arms. "It'll be okay," he whispered.

Erica didn't believe that for a minute. "It won't be okay. Do you know what this is going to do to Carolyn?"

"Yes."

She bit her lip, trying not to cry. "It didn't have to be anything big or expensive. All he had to do was stuff a cheap necklace in an envelope and stick a stamp on the damned thing."

"I know."

Erica laid her cheek against his chest, absorbing courage from his warmth and wondering why her ex-husband couldn't be as kind and compassionate as Roberto. As soon as she'd asked the silent question, she answered it. Because if Carter had been like Roberto, he'd still have been her husband. All her life she'd been searching for a man like this, a sensitive man who cared about the needs of a child. And of a woman.

All her life she'd been searching, and here he was.

The thought was both startling and, given the circumstances, completely inappropriate. Pushing abruptly away, she forced her mind back to the dreaded chore that awaited her. "I have to tell Carolyn that there won't be a present from her father. It's going to break her little heart."

As she took a step toward the living room, Roberto touched her arm, stopping her. "Don't tell her yet."

"I have to," she said miserably, then turned away and went out the front door, to where Carolyn was curled in her grandmother's lap.

The child looked up expectantly.

Erica licked her lips and tried to stretch them into an encouraging smile. From her father's dour expression, she assumed that she'd fallen short of the goal. She focused instead on her mother. "What's this, story time?"

Jacqueline's smile wasn't particularly convincing, either. "What a fine idea. Would you like Gramma to read you a story, dear?"

Carolyn shook her head and spoke to her mother. "Can I call Daddy?"

Erica felt sick. "I just did, sweetie."

She brightened. "I'll bet he's real mad that my present is late."

God, this was difficult. Squeezing her hands together, Erica fought to control the telltale quiver in her voice. "As a matter of fact, he isn't angry because—"

Roberto suddenly appeared to complete the sentence. "Because your present isn't late at all."

The child's eyes rounded. "It isn't?"

"Nope. It seems that while everyone was mulling around out here, someone delivered it to the back yard."

"Really?" With a gasp of utter delight, Carolyn leapt off her grandmother's lap. "Where is it? Can I see?"

As she dashed within reach, Erica tried to grab the excited child. She missed and Carolyn fairly flew around the corner of the house. Erica was completely baffled by the odd turn of events and frustrated to the point of tears. Putting off the inevitable wasn't going to help Carolyn; it could, in fact, cause her even more grief in the long run. She snagged his arm, whispering harshly, "What on earth are you trying to do?"

"Come join the party and you'll see." With a secretive wink, he sauntered toward the back yard, gesturing for the stunned adults to follow. Since their other options were even less enticing, they all complied with the peculiar request.

At first, Erica didn't recognize the object that was surrounded by the entire gaggle of partygoers. Then she saw the flash of lavender, the gleam of chrome, as Roberto lifted the radiant birthday girl onto her new bicycle. Carolyn was grinning so broadly that Erica feared the child might actually burst from pure joy. "Mommy, Mommy," she squealed, waving. "Look what Daddy gave me!"

"Well, what do you know?" Kenneth murmured, stroking his chin.

Erica couldn't have replied if she'd wanted to. Her throat had closed up and her chest ached as if squeezed by a giant hand. She simply stood there, frozen, touched to the core by the selflessness of the one man who truly did care more for a little girl's happiness than anything else in the world.

Erica had known for weeks that Roberto Arroya was a very special man. But she hadn't realized that she was deeply in love with him. Until now.

Chapter Nine

The girls were angelic in slumber, each sprawled across matching beds littered by remnants of prebedtime play. Cathy was curled into a ball with her knees tucked under her chin. Beside her, Buddy stretched comfortably, eyes closed, paws askew. Erica adjusted Cathy's covers without disturbing either of the bed's occupants, then removed Barbie doll clothes, books, and shiny new shoes from Carolyn's bed before snugging up her older daughter's blanket. Even asleep, the birthday girl was still smiling.

Earlier that evening, Carolyn had told anyone who'd listen that this had been the very best birthday she'd ever had in her whole life. All six years of it.

Had it not been for Roberto's selfless generosity, the day could very well have turned into one of heartache and emotional devastation. Erica was almost as furious at Carter for having given so little thought to Carolyn's feelings as she was grateful to Roberto for having given so much. His gesture had been so pure and noble, so truly gallant that Erica had been moved to tears.

And she hadn't been the only one affected. Her mother's eyes had been moist most of the afternoon and even her father, who'd been quite clear about having preferred a gall bladder attack to sharing his granddaughter's birthday with Roberto Arroya, wound up behaving in an uncharacteristically charitable manner.

Actually, the only unimpressed adult at the party had been Roberto himself. Stammered attempts to offer appreciation had been dismissed with expressions of surprise, bewilderment and finally, complete chagrin. He honestly hadn't understood what the hoopla was all about. From his perspective, he'd simply seen a problem and solved it. Period. No big deal.

To Erica, it was one heck of a big deal.

Her thoughts were interrupted by the front door's squeaking hinge, which alerted her that Roberto was finished loading the borrowed folding tables into her father's car. She left the girls' bedroom door ajar, went down the hall and found Roberto standing in the living room, scrutinizing the floor.

He looked up as she entered. "Where's Buddy?"

"Asleep on Cathy's bed. Did you know that he snores?"

"Don't tell him. He swears that he doesn't." Smiling, Roberto rubbed the back of his neck and glanced toward the hallway. "I'd better get him before he wakes up the kids."

"An earthquake wouldn't wake up them up now. I can't remember the last time they were so exhausted."

"You're probably tired, too. We should be going and let you get some rest." Even if he made a move to leave, which so far he hadn't, Erica presumed that he wouldn't go anywhere without his beloved little mutt and she was strategically blocking access to the hallway.

She simply didn't want him to go. Not yet. There were things to be said, perhaps even confessions to be made. The mere concept of revealing aloud feelings that she'd barely admitted to herself was terrifying; but so was the thought of letting him leave without understanding how deeply she cared for him.

However, such things had to be done slowly, as time and courage permitted. And the room suddenly seemed ungodly hot.

She mopped her forehead with the back of her hand, nodding toward the kitchen. "Would you like some iced tea?"

"No, thanks."

"Wine?"

"I don't think so."

"A glass of milk?"

"And cookies, too?"

"Sorry," she murmured, embarrassed by his tolerant grin. "The mommy in me comes out at the most inappropriate times."

"Don't be sorry. I think it's great." Reaching out, he stroked her cheek with his knuckles, his eyes darkening with undisguised longing.

The air thickened, crackling with electric intensity. Erica's pulse raced. Her chest tightened and throbbed with vague anticipation. Something was happening between them, something wonderful.

At least, it was wonderful to Erica. Roberto seemed curiously distressed. His breathing appeared labored; he repeatedly moistened his lips; a small shudder rippled through his body, a minuscule movement that was monumental to Erica, because she felt his emotional withdrawal as tangibly as one feels a fist in the stomach.

As he withdrew his hand, she caught it, turned it and brushed her lips across his warm palm, catching a subtle scent of soapy pine that was oddly arousing. Closing her eyes, she pressed his hand to her cheek. It took a moment before she dared test her voice. "I'll never forget what you did for Carolyn today. I know how badly you wanted to give that bicycle to her." A slight tremor stiffened his wrist. Reluctantly, she allowed him to retrieve his hand. As he tucked it protectively beneath folded arms, his nurturing warmth seeped away.

"I wanted her to have the bike," he said. "I told you before that it didn't matter whose name was on the card."

"You really mean that, don't you?"

"I usually mean what I say. Why would you think otherwise?"

"Most people say what's expected or what will give them an advantage, regardless of how they feel. But truth is very important to you, isn't it?"

"Not necessarily. Justice is what really counts."

Initially, Erica thought that a strange comment. All her life, she'd been taught that truth and justice fitted together as neatly as did peanut butter and jelly. But if that was correct, Carolyn would have to be told that her father had never loved her and didn't give a damn about anyone but himself. To reveal such a cruel truth would break the child's heart; and there was certainly no justice in that.

"Did you let Carter know what's going on?" Roberto asked suddenly.

"Yes." Much as it had pained her to do so, Erica hadn't wanted the foolish fellow to let the cat out of the bag when his daughter telephoned with profuse appreciation for her beautiful new bike. "I left a message that if he didn't play along, I'd not only sue for back child support, I'd personally spearhead a contempt of court prosecution for his failure to pay in the first place."

Roberto considered that for a moment. "Do you think he'll cooperate?"

"It's in his best interest to cooperate and since Carter always does what's best for Carter, I don't think we have anything to worry about."

Apparently disgust for her ex-husband was reflected in her expression, because Roberto's eyes clouded with concern. "Are you going to be all right?" he murmured, brushing a wayward strand of hair from her brow.

Intuitively she realized that he was also referring to last night's tragedy, and the loss of a woman that Erica had considered to be a friend. "I still can't believe that Sara is really gone. It's so senseless, so very sad. I keep hoping that she'll walk in the door Monday morning and we'll find out that it was all a big mistake."

Roberto took a step forward, enfolding her in a comforting embrace. "That's not going to happen."

"I know," she whispered against his chest. "I know."

A buttery softness flowed through her veins, a feeling of well-being that was more sensual than anything she'd ever experienced. She belonged here, wrapped in Roberto's arms, listening to the rhythmic pulse of his heart and absorbing his soothing strength. It was so simple, really. She loved him. Deeply. Completely. Without reservation.

As his fingers massaged her lower back, he rubbed his face against her hair. "You smell good," he murmured. "Like night flowers."

Since the comment wasn't accompanied by a more intimate touch, a small voice in the back of her mind suggested she might consider switching shampoos. An erotic scent like Love Musk or Aphrodisia would be more appropriate to seduction than a scent used in air freshener.

Her eyelids flew up like sprung shades. *Seduction?* Is that what was happening here? And if so, who was doing the seducing?

The answer became clear when Roberto's muscles tightened as if preparing to release her. Her arms slipped around him and before she could contemplate the consequence of such boldness, she was hanging on as if he were the only life raft in a storm-tossed sea.

After a hesitant moment, his arms settled around her now-rigid body. She was certain that if she looked up, she'd see shock on his face; perhaps even disapproval. So she didn't look up. Instead, she buried her face against his cotton polo shirt and squeezed him so hard it was a wonder he didn't pass out. "Please don't leave," she whispered, hating the broken desperation in her voice. "I...don't want to be alone."

For a moment, neither of them moved. Erica was petrified that Roberto would simply step away and run screaming out the door. But he didn't. As his lips brushed against her hair, one hand slid up to the back of her neck, then around to cup her throat and tilt her head back. She felt his warmth, the heat of his body radiating into every fiber of her being; and she saw her own love reflected in his eyes. It took her breath away.

He kissed her then, so softly and sweetly that she nearly cried out from sheer joy. Their lips met again and again, moving, tasting, parting for a more intimate touch. Each flick of his tongue sent a flame down her spine. She returned the favor with short, tentative probes that became more reckless, more brazen, fusing them in a fiery mergence of body and soul.

It was Roberto who finally broke away, panting. He mumbled something in Spanish that Erica loosely interpreted as a request for divine guidance, then untangled her fingers from his shirt and held her at arm's length. "You know I want you, Erica. It would be foolish to pretend otherwise. But you're vulnerable now and I won't take advantage of that."

"Vulnerable?" She repeated the word weakly. "I don't understand."

He gathered his thoughts for a moment. "You've been hurt by Sara's betrayal and saddened by her death. You're also angry with your ex-husband, which I certainly understand."

"What does any of that have to do with . . . with, ah—"
Her struggle for words ended with the obscure. "With what
is happening between us?"

"It doesn't have anything to do with it. Or at least, it
shouldn't. But you've been under a tremendous amount of
stress and I don't want you to—" After biting off the final
word, he hesitated, having difficulty choosing the words to
express his feelings. Finally, he blurted, "I don't want you
to feel a misplaced sense of gratitude here."

It took a moment for her to catch his meaning. When she
did, her eyes widened in disbelief. "You think that I'm offering myself in payment for what you did for Carolyn?"

He flinched visibly. "I don't think I'd put it quite that
way—" A snort of tickled laughter cut him off. He stared
at her, stunned. "Did I miss a punch line or something?"

"No. . .sorry." She muffled a giggle with her hands, then
swallowed hard, caught her lips between her teeth and
fought off another convulsive surge. Upon regaining at least
partial control, she tried again. "I, ah, was just wondering
how receptive you'd be if I stuck a bow on my head. I mean,
since you apparently believe that I'm serving myself up as a
gift, I might as well look the part, don't you think?"

He regarded her warily. "Have I insulted you?"

Sobered by the question, Erica shook her head. Suddenly, nothing seemed very funny. Nothing at all. She massaged her eyelids and heaved a weary sigh. "Apparently I've
insulted myself by assuming facts not in evidence. That is
the correct terminology, isn't it, counselor?"

The corners of his eyes crinkled adorably. "It would be,
except that even a cursory scan reveals that the facts are indeed in evidence."

When a sneaked glance provided confirmation of his
arousal, Erica's heart gave a hopeful leap. "Should I start
looking for that bow?"

Releasing his grasp on her shoulders, he framed her face with his hands. "This is a big step," he murmured. "Are you certain that you're ready for it?"

"I've been ready since the day you jogged into the park looking sexier in sloppy sweats than Daniel Day Lewis in buckskins."

"Is that good?"

"If you'd seen *The Last of The Mohicans,* you wouldn't have to ask."

"I did see it. If you're talking about the tall one with hair, he didn't do a thing for me." After scooping her into his arms as easily as he'd have lifted one of the children, Roberto carried Erica to the edge of the hallway, then paused. "What about the girls?"

"They're asleep."

"They might wake up."

"There's a lock on my bedroom door." She wrapped her arms around his neck to discourage any traitorous thought he might have about putting her down, and purred, "The previous tenants must have had kids, too."

Apparently satisfied, he carried her down the hall, backed into her room and let her legs slide to the floor. It was Erica who reached out and quietly closed the door. Never having bothered with the lock before, she had to fiddle with it for a moment before it clicked into place. She managed a nervous smile, grateful that there was little more than a shaft of moonlight to illuminate the room. The enormity of the commitment they were preparing to make was enough to weaken her knees.

Fortunately, Roberto still had an arm around her waist. He tightened his grasp, pinning her against him. She clung to him, her heart thumping madly. Or maybe it was his heart. She couldn't tell.

He tipped her chin up and gazed deeply into her eyes. Moonlight reflected from his own dark pupils with an almost ghostly glow that was oddly erotic. Her lips parted to receive a kiss that was even more provocative than before, and more deeply arousing.

By the time he slipped his hands beneath her casual knit top, Erica was literally trembling with passion. Every inch of her skin was on fire and blood pulsed through her veins like rivers of burning lava. She lifted her arms, allowing him to pull the garment over her head, then fumbled with the hem of his knit shirt until he took pity and removed it himself.

The sight of his bare chest made her gasp in awe and amazement. He wasn't built at all like Carter, whose flat chest mushroomed down into a floppy flap at the belt line. Roberto was sculpted, formed, molded like art and smooth as polished granite. She touched him greedily, her fingers memorizing every curve and ripple of his muscular torso.

She was so busily engrossed in her own exploration that she didn't notice him removing her bra until his thumb brushed her nipple and sent a shock from her breast straight down to her quivering belly. With a small gasp, she looked up and was instantly lost in the intensity of his gaze. Her breath slid out all at once.

"Do you like that?" he asked softly.

Since her lungs were completely deflated, the best she could manage was a jerky nod.

"How about this?" Using a gentle, circular motion, he massaged both of her soft breasts with his flattened palms.

The effect was startling enough to elicit a sharp cry following by a long, low moan that Erica didn't even recognize as coming from her. She felt boneless, out of control. As her head lolled backward, she grasped at his slick shoulders but they slid out of reach. Only when her seeking arms wrapped around his head, hugging him to her bosom, did she realize that he was kneeling.

Embracing her hips, he pulled her close and nestled against her breasts, kissing and tasting each delicate tip until Erica was certain that she would die from sheer joy. She felt a tug at her waist a moment before her slacks glided down to pool around her ankles. After stepping out of the bunched fabric, she pushed it away with her foot.

From the corner of her eye, she saw the remainder of Roberto's clothing heaped on the floor and realized that after having dispensed with his shirt, he'd managed to disrobe discreetly enough that she'd been blissfully unaware of the activity.

Blissful was the operative word, because Erica was completely entranced by what was happening inside her own skin. Roberto was making love to her body, every inch of it, from her aching breasts to the velvety mound below her navel and the exquisitely sensitive flesh of her inner thighs.

And then, when her body had been cherished to the very brink of completion, he took her to bed and made love to her soul.

It would be dawn in an hour. Erica would wake Roberto then so he'd have time to dress and be at the breakfast table when the girls got up. They wouldn't be surprised to find him there. They'd already been told that Roberto would be spending Sunday with them because Mommy had an early appointment at the shop.

Erica shifted in the bed and continued to stroke the sleeping head nested between her breasts. She loved the feel of his hair, the springy texture pushing against her palms. The thick strands swirled around her fingers with a determined softness that was appropriate to the man himself.

She traced a funny twist of hair that, despite his constant attempts to tame it, fought off the spray and consistently returned to its natural state, a haphazard whirl across one side of his forehead. That, too, was a reflection of the man. Roberto forced an image for himself that contradicted his true nature. To the world, he was the steely, unforgiving and vengeful prosecutor who could destroy lives with the snap of a finger; to Erica, he was softhearted and sensitive, a tender man who couldn't bear the sight of a child's tears. Although Roberto was eminently comfortable with the persona of the polished professional, Erica believed he was happier wearing sloppy sweats and chatting with his dog. And that was the part of him she loved best.

Last night, she'd gone to him as an emotional virgin. Now she was reborn. Sighing, she laid her cheek against his head and wished dawn would never come.

"This is Poison Control, what is your emergency?"

"Bow-Wowies," Roberto blurted. "Can they hurt a three-year-old?"

There was a brief silence. "A three-year-old what?"

"Girl. A three-year-old girl."

"And exactly what did the child ingest?"

"I told you. Bow-Wowies. She ate four of them." Clamping the telephone between his chin and shoulder, Roberto shifted Cathy to his right arm, grabbed the bright yellow package and read directly from the label. "They're 'chewy sausage style snacks for dogs'... beef flavor, containing fifteen per cent crude protein and a list of ingredients it would take a month to recite." He dropped the package, spun around and sagged against the counter. "Should I make her throw up or something?"

"Does the child seem ill?"

"Not yet," Roberto muttered, inspecting Cathy's grinning face for the umpteenth time. At that point, Cathy issued a series of loud giggles that could apparently be heard on the other end of the line.

"I don't think you have anything to worry about," came the amused reply. "Canine dietary supplements are nontoxic to humans, even very small humans. Besides, my dog loves Bow-Wowies."

"Yeah, so does mine."

The back door opened as Carolyn and Buddy came in from the back yard.

"Wanna get down," Cathy announced impatiently.

"I'm sure everything will be just fine," said the voice on the phone. "But if the child should exhibit any symptoms—"

"Symptoms?"

"Listlessness, nausea—"

Trying to juggle both the squirming child and the receiver, Roberto turned around and nearly strangled himself with the telephone cord.

"—fever, anything that concerns—"

The receiver slipped off his shoulder and bounced along the floor. Wheezing, he untwisted the coiled cord that was wrapped around his throat and managed to retrieve the phone. "Hello? So what do I do if she exhibits, ah, symptoms?"

"Contact the child's physician."

"Her physician?" he repeated, beginning to panic again. "I don't even know who that is."

Cathy grabbed his face with both hands and jerked his head around. "I wanna get *down!*"

"Mr. 'Roya," Carolyn said, tugging on the hem of his knit shirt. "I'm bleeding."

"You're *what?*" The receiver hit the floor again as Roberto frantically reached for Carolyn. "Where? Show me..." He moaned as the girl held up a scraped elbow. "Oh, Lord. Geez... does it hurt, honey?"

She nodded solemnly.

"Down!" Cathy screeched.

Roberto let out a yelp, covering his ear as the irked three-year-old squiggled out of his grasp.

With a devilish grin, Cathy snagged the Bow-Wowie bag from the counter and would have bolted out the door if Roberto hadn't scooped the telephone off the floor and lassoed the scampering child with the cord. He plucked the package of dog treats from her hand, clamping it between his teeth while he held a tea towel under the kitchen faucet.

A few minutes later, Erica returned to find her youngest daughter harnessed to the wall phone by an improvised, spiral cord leash while Roberto, who for some inexplicable reason had a bag of Bow-Wowies clamped in his teeth, was frantically dabbing Carolyn's elbow with a wet towel.

She stood there, stunned.

Cathy spotted her first. "Hi, Mommy! I'm a doggie."

Roberto's head snapped up, his dark eyes wide with horror. "Oor Ack," he mumbled, then crossed his eyes to focus down at the bag hanging out of his mouth. He spit it out and looked up with a pathetically thin smile. "You're back. Uh . . . how'd the interview go?"

Erica laid her purse on the table. "Very well, thank you. Marge Cowen seems like a lovely woman."

"Good. That's . . . ah . . . good."

"I'm bleeding," Carolyn said cheerfully.

Roberto winced, straightened and dropped the towel into the sink, avoiding Erica's gaze. "She fell off her bike."

"Oh-h-h." Erica bent to inspect the reddened patch on her daughter's elbow. "That doesn't look too bad. Why don't you run and get the bandages from the bathroom."

"Okay."

As Carolyn scurried away, Erica focused attention on her youngest child, who was still pinioned to the telephone and at the moment, was belting out the lusty improvisation of a barking dog. "And what have we here?"

Roberto swallowed a groan and bent to unwrap the cord from the little girl's waist. "Cathy decided that she wanted Buddy to be her brother," he explained, hanging up the telephone. "She started crawling around, arfing and barking all over the place. It seemed harmless enough, so I went along. I, ah, even put her cookies on the floor."

"Excuse me?"

"Oh, they were on a plate," he added quickly. "And so were Buddy's dog treats. It didn't occur to me that she'd…ah, well…eat the Bow-Wowies and give her cookies to the dog."

"Oh, dear." Erica bit her lip, trying desperately not to laugh.

Apparently Roberto misread her expression. "It's all right," he assured her. "The woman at Poison Control said—"

"What?" Erica couldn't believe her ears. "You actually called Poison Control?"

"Well, sure, I mean, I don't know what's in those things."

"They're probably healthier than the cookies," Erica said, then lost it completely and nearly doubled up, laughing. The image of what the poor man must have gone through shouldn't have been funny, but it was. She couldn't help herself. By the time she straightened and wiped her eyes, Roberto was standing there with his arms folded, sulking. "I'm sorry." She sniffed, swallowed a giggle, and cleared her throat. "Maybe you'd better just start from the beginning and tell me everything."

Erica had to coax him for a few more minutes but eventually, he broke down and relayed the morning's events, every traumatic one of them. When he'd finished, she sympathetically patted his hand. "I'm sorry you had such a bad day."

"Are you kidding? This has been just about the best day of my life." Roberto pulled her into his arms and gave her a kiss that curled her toes.

Sighing, she reached up to wipe a lipstick smudge from his mouth. "The day isn't over yet," she whispered. "I have a hunch that it's going to get even better."

The next morning, Roberto received the best news he'd had in weeks. Maryland police had picked up a three-time loser who'd confessed to having killed Caricchio's competitor and dumping the body outside of Victorville. The guy confirmed just about every facet of George Mercier's story, so when Edith Layton came into his office, Roberto was still gloating. "We've got him," he told her, unnecessarily. Everyone in the office had heard the news, but Roberto loved saying the words out loud. "After all these months, hard evidence on Caricchio's complicity in murder."

Edith's smile was, he thought, a bit weak considering the monumental occasion. "Yes, we've got him, and that's not all we've got." As Edith closed the office door, Roberto noticed a black plastic case in her hand.

"Is that a surveillance tape?"

"Yes."

Instead of pulling up a chair, Edith crossed the room and popped the tape into a VCR on the credenza, although Roberto couldn't for the life of him figure out why. Over the past weeks, surveillance teams hadn't taken their lenses off Caricchio but had little to show for it. They'd gotten footage of suspicious activity, only to have what appeared to be a payoff blocked from view by a passing bus. Roberto had been disappointed, but not surprised. Ordering surveillance had been a desperate measure. Thank God, it was no longer necessary.

Leaning forward, Roberto propped his elbows on his desk, bothered by Edith's dour expression. "We've got enough evidence to sink a major mobster. This is a good day and around here, we try to smile on good days."

Avoiding his gaze, Edith scooped up the remote control and a wooden pointer. "After you see this, you may not feel much like smiling."

A nervous tingle lifted the hairs on his nape. "Why, did we pick something up on surveillance?"

"You could say that." She adjusted her glasses and peered over the rims. "But I don't think you're going to like it."

Roberto's heart sank, assuming that something on the tape would throw a monkey wrench into what he'd considered to be an airtight case against Frank Caricchio. Frustrated, he gestured for Edith to start the tape. She did.

A grainy, black-and-white film flickered across the television screen. "This took place outside the library. Caricchio is inside the Lincoln Continental, right here." Edith tapped the screen with the pointer, indicating where the car was parked. "Now in a moment, you'll see a man come in from the left ... there, see him?"

Roberto leaned forward, scrutinizing the anonymous figure. "His back is to the camera."

"He'll turn around in a few minutes. Look ... the car window is going down and there's Caricchio, leaning out, talking to the man. Keep your eye on his hand ... there!" Edith hit the pause button, stopping the film, and aimed the pointer at a white splotch on the screen. "That's an envelope of cash."

A thrill of anticipation skittered down Roberto's spine. Still, he was cautious. "It's an envelope, all right. But how do you know what's in it?"

"Because we've got film of Caricchio counting out cash and putting it inside." As Edith hit the play button, the anonymous man took the envelope and appeared to tuck it in his breast pocket. "Bank employees cooperated, so the bills are marked," she said. "We've been monitoring Caricchio's account activity for months, so we can follow the paper trail right into this guy's bank account."

Roberto could hardly believe his eyes. "This is great. We can add bribery and corruption charges, too."

Edith hit the pause button again. "I suppose so."

"You don't seem particularly enthused about that."

"Thing is, this guy—" She tapped the image of the anonymous man's back. "Oh, hell. I might as well let you see for yourself." She pushed the play button.

As the film continued, the man stepped away from the car. Then, with Frank Caricchio's blood money bulging from his coat pocket, Kenneth Mallory turned around and stared straight at the camera.

Chapter Ten

The tape had ended. Roberto stared in stunned disbelief, his mind as empty as the black screen. "Who knows about this?" The question was posed by a rasping voice he barely recognized as his own.

"The field crew, a few technicians." Edith laid down the pointer and ejected the tape. "I doubt any of them recognized Mallory and even if they did, bribery of a local official isn't a federal matter. Besides, this video came in about the same time Caricchio's shooter was located, so no one was paying much attention to surveillance results."

Roberto rested his head on his hands. As he tried to reignite a shock-numbed brain, the image of the tape repeatedly flickered through his memory. He lifted his head to peer above his fingers. "Everything on that tape is purely circumstantial. So what if we have additional film of Caricchio stuffing cash into a hundred envelopes? There's no proof that there was money in the one he gave Mallory."

Edith nodded without comment.

Roberto continued to embellish the feeble rationalization. "Without corroborating evidence, the tape can't even be used as probable cause for a warrant to inspect Mallory's bank records." This time, Edith remained motionless. Roberto knew he was stretching but couldn't help himself. "And even if the damned bank accounts showed corresponding activity, that's still not enough to indict. It's all too circumstantial. There'd have to be witnesses, credible witnesses, not just the word of a bunch of murdering racketeers...."

Even Roberto couldn't believe the idiotic drivel coming out of his mouth. The murder charge notwithstanding, Frank Caricchio was a land developer of questionable repute for whom county contracts were worth a tidy fortune. Kenneth Mallory was the planning commissioner, a public official with the power to swing crucial votes on zoning, lucrative permit waivers and millions in redevelopment funds. There was no legitimate reason for these two men to exchange Christmas cards, let alone a fat envelope appearing to contain large amounts of cash. The impropriety revealed by the tape was more than enough to launch a full-scale investigation by the district attorney's office. Roberto knew it; Edith knew it.

But Roberto had been introduced to other facets of Kenneth Mallory—the loving husband, devoted father and doting grampa of two precious girls. If this tape was released, Mallory would be destroyed. Maybe he deserved what he got, but his family didn't.

God, this would kill Erica.

With a violent curse, he angrily swiped a fist across his desk, sweeping away everything in its path. A stapler bounced off the wall, landing on the floor beside scattered files and an upturned pencil holder. Unable to face his colleague, Roberto swiveled his chair, turning his back to her. Outside, he saw gray clouds forming to the west. A storm was coming. A big one.

"This isn't a federal matter," Roberto said softly. "It doesn't concern us."

Behind him, silence stretched like a shroud. After several long minutes, Roberto heard his office door open, then close with a soft click. It took another moment before he looked over his shoulder. The room was empty. And the incriminating tape was lying in the middle of his desk.

Erica rinsed a soapy dish under the faucet and slid a glance at Roberto, who was absently staring into space, polishing the same plate he'd picked up five minutes earlier. "I don't think that one is going to get much drier. Maybe you could lavish a little attention on some of its relatives?" She gestured toward a rack heaped with drippy dinnerware.

He blinked, glanced down at the rack in question, then set the dry plate aside and picked up a wet one without comment.

Erica laid her sponge on the sink. "Are you okay?"

"Hmm? Oh, sure."

"You've been a bit distracted tonight. Bad day at the office?"

"The usual," he mumbled without looking up.

Quickening the pace, he focused attention on the wet dishes, although it seemed to Erica that the effort was directed more toward avoiding conversation than completing the chore. In fact, he'd barely spoken to her all evening and had looked at her even less.

At first she'd been concerned that he might be ill; later, she'd wished that he had been. Physical sickness was, for the most part, transitory. It could be treated. But there was no cure for regret.

That was at the heart of Erica's anxiety. She was petrified that Roberto was having second thoughts about the intimacy they'd shared. For her, their lovemaking had been the most incredibly beautiful experience of her life; that it might have meant less for him was a crushing concept. Even more shattering was the creeping dread that he might actually consider making love to her as having been a mistake.

The mere idea was so devastating that Erica dismissed it instantly. She grabbed the damp sponge and set about washing down the counters with a vengeance that brought Roberto out of his comatose state.

He picked up a salt shaker upended by her vehement scrubbing and, after regarding it thoughtfully, he carefully positioned the container beside its pepper-filled twin. "It's getting late," he said quietly. "I have some briefs to review for court tomorrow."

Every trace of moisture evaporated from Erica's mouth. "I thought you and Carolyn were planning on a game of checkers."

"I'll talk to her. She'll understand."

Perhaps she would, but Erica didn't understand. She didn't understand at all, and it was eating her up inside. "I'd hoped that you...I mean, I'd thought you might stay awhile and... and..." She turned away to hide her misery. She'd hoped, of course, that they'd make love again. That he'd *want* to make love again. And again, and again—

"I'm sorry." As he laid the dish towel on the counter, his hand brushed her arm. "Another time, perhaps."

She spun around, horrified. *Perhaps?* As in, maybe never?

To her chagrin, Roberto simply brushed a chaste kiss across her forehead, and with a murmured good-night, he left the kitchen.

As Erica stood there, immobilized by fear and bewilderment, she heard Roberto speaking to the girls. Then the front door hinge creaked. She knew that he was gone.

Buddy padded across the dimly lit room to sit at Roberto's feet and cast an inquisitive glance at the fireplace. Since the sweltering September day had turned into a muggy, uncomfortably warm night, the animal seemed perplexed by the roaring fire his master had stoked. Still, Buddy was nothing if not loyal and despite the intense heat, he curled up beside Roberto's chair and lay there, panting.

Roberto clutched the surveillance tape and stared into the mesmerizing flames, barely aware of the dog's presence. His mind was in turmoil, his gut twisted into a throbbing knot. All he had to do was toss the video cartridge into the fire and evidence of Kenneth Mallory's dirty little secret would go up in smoke.

Other evidence might surface, of course—people without respect for the law usually made more than one mistake—but it would be up to someone else to find that evidence. Then someone else could make the hard decisions, the devastating revelations that would break Erica's heart. But it wouldn't be Roberto. He simply couldn't do it, couldn't be the one to tell Erica that the man she adored above all others was nothing but more than just another sleazy politician on the take.

Damn Kenneth Mallory. Damn him to hell. He'd betrayed his family by using power to further his own ambition. Roberto couldn't forgive him for that; he wondered if Erica could.

The fire crackled with invitation. One small toss and his torment would be over. Mallory would be safe, for the moment. Erica would have at least a temporary reprieve. All Roberto had to do was toss the damned tape into the fire.

And watch his own career go up in flames.

Because it would. Ignoring a potentially illegal act was not only a gross violation of the unyielding morality on which Roberto had built his life, it was an unpardonable breach of professional ethics and a desecration of his duty as an officer of the court.

Eventually, he'd have to answer for what he'd done, because his own conscience would require it. Then Edith Layton would be brought into the fray. Roberto wouldn't be able to cover for her or conceal the fact that out of loyalty and friendship, she, too, had conspired to withhold crucial evidence.

In the end, Roberto knew what he had to do. There was no choice, really. No choice at all.

"Here you go, Mama. Spinach salad, sour dough rolls and iced tea. Lunch fit for a queen, if I do say so myself." Erica set the tray on a patio table beside her parents' pool, then pushed one of the chairs aside to make room for her mother's wheelchair.

As Erica wheeled Jacqueline into position, the woman reached over her shoulder to pat her daughter's hand. "It looks lovely, dear. But you really shouldn't give up your Saturday just to look after me. Your father will be back any minute now."

"We've been through this before, Mama. I'm not looking after you," Erica said, arranging the luncheon plates on the table. "I'm visiting my mother, which is a treat I've been denied for far too long. By the way, where is Daddy?"

"I'm not sure. He left after receiving a call from Oscar. Probably an important meeting on the eighteenth green," she added with a wink.

Erica laughed, knowing that Oscar Watson, who'd been her parents' attorney ever since she could remember, was also one of her father's favorite golfing buddies. "Well, Daddy's entitled to a little R and R and so are we. So let's eat. I'm starved."

"Well, we can't have you starving now, can we?" Jacqueline reached for her napkin using her left hand, the only hand she'd been able to use since the stroke. After spreading the linen cloth neatly in her lap, she slid Erica a secretive smile. "Would you like a roll, dear?"

"Yes, thank you." Erica glanced up and, noting the plate of dinner rolls had been set to her mother's right, automatically reached across the table to retrieve one.

Jacqueline stopped her. "Allow me."

Erica was a bit confused by the request, but honored it, assuming that for whatever reason, her mother wanted to reestablish the strict table etiquette upon which she had insisted before her illness. Erica did note, however, that instead of simply reaching for the requested item with her left hand, Jacqueline was staring down at her right arm as though willing it to fly.

Then, in front of Erica's shocked eyes, the paralyzed arm started to quiver and after a moment, moved slowly upward. "Mama?"

Jacqueline, completely focused on the effort, didn't respond. Tiny beads of perspiration dotted her brow as her trembling hand cleared the table and moved inch by painful inch toward its destination. Then, with her entire arm shaking violently, her fingers went into a spasm and seized a fat, crusty roll.

With a victorious smile, Jacqueline offered the hard-earned prize to her stunned daughter. "Would you like the butter, too?"

"Oh, Mama." Erica took the roll, blinking back tears as she laid it on her plate. "I had no idea..." As the words drifted away, she simply sat there, overwhelmed.

"I wanted it to be a surprise. My therapist is very pleased." Judging by the proud gleam in her eyes, Jacqueline was pretty darn pleased herself. "He tells me that I might even be using a walker by Christmas."

Erica could barely believe it. A few months earlier, Jacqueline had given every indication of being a woman who'd given up on herself. To have made so much progress so quickly was beyond anything Erica could have even hoped for. A rush of emotion choked her, making it difficult to speak. "That's... so... wonderful."

"Yes," Jacqueline replied, grinning. "It is, isn't it?"

Laughing and crying at the same time, Erica leaned over to embrace her mother. "I'm so proud of you. Remind me to send flowers to your therapist. He's an absolute wonder."

"At those prices, he should be," Jacqueline replied, dabbing her own moist eyes. "I didn't think therapy would be worth the expense, but your father insisted."

"Thank goodness he did. At this rate, you're going to be back on the tennis court in no time."

The older woman winced. "Oh, dear. I've always hated tennis."

"Then why did you play?"

"Because your father enjoyed it." Sighing, she used her left hand to lift her salad fork. "I was hoping the stroke would give me an excuse to sit and watch."

"Just tell him you don't like it. He'll understand."

"I suppose, but I do so hate to disappoint him." Jacqueline poked at a leaf withered by warm vinaigrette and slid her daughter a sly glance. "Speaking of disappointments, I was hoping you'd invite Mr. Arroya to join us for lunch today."

Erica feigned a sudden interest in moving a cherry tomato from one side of her plate to the other. "He had other plans."

"Oh?" Jacqueline smiled pleasantly, awaiting details. When none were forthcoming, her smile faded. "Is something wrong, Erica?"

"Of course not." She stabbed at her plate and spoke through clenched teeth. "What could possibly be wrong?"

"Well, I don't know, dear, nor do I understand what that tomato has ever done to deserve such punishment."

Erica stared down at the mushy red puddle and promptly burst into tears.

"Mommy!" Carolyn hollered from the house. "I'm trying to watch Power Rangers but Cathy keeps turning to Barney."

While Erica wiped her eyes with a napkin, Jacqueline slid an arm around her sobbing daughter and spoke over her shoulder. "There's a television in Gramma's room," she told Carolyn. "You may watch your program in there."

Carolyn hovered in the doorway. "Is Mommy crying?"

"No, dear," Jacqueline lied. "She just has something in her eye."

Appeased by the explanation, Carolyn disappeared back into the house and Jacqueline returned her attention to Erica. "There, there, dear. It can't be as bad as all that."

"No. It's worse." Sniffing, Erica stared at the wet napkin which was now smudged with mascara. She felt weak and foolish and frighteningly out of control. "I've done something terribly wrong, Mama, and I'm not even sure what it was."

"Why? What has happened?"

"Nothing has happened. Absolutely nothing and that's the problem." Erica took a deep breath, held it, then exhaled slowly.

When she'd gained some modicum of control, she quietly confessed that she and Roberto had been intimate. Jacqueline blinked but made no comment. Instead, she gave her daughter's hand an encouraging squeeze, providing Erica with enough courage to continue. "Over the weekend, everything was wonderful. Roberto was so affectionate and loving, he couldn't seem to go more than ten minutes without giving me a hug, a kiss, or teasing me with, ah, well..." She coughed, felt her cheeks heat and lowered her voice. "An erotic suggestion."

The older woman gave a sage nod. "How has his behavior changed since then?"

"It's so strange," Erica murmured, not sure where to begin. "Roberto still calls every morning and sounds like he really cares about me. In the evenings, he comes over with a rented video or a bag of takeout under his arm and plays with the kids, just like he always has. But when he looks at me, there's...I don't know...a sadness in his eyes that scares me to death. And as soon as the kids go to bed, he leaves."

"Without, ah, doing . . . well, you know."

"Yes." Erica stared at her lap and wished she could die on the spot. "It's as if he's trying to pretend that nothing ever happened. But I can't do that, Mama, and I don't understand how he can. Or why he would even want to."

"Oh, my," Jacqueline murmured. "That is peculiar. Have you spoken to him about your concern?"

"Lord, no."

"Why not? I mean, there could be a perfectly reasonable explanation that might not have anything to do with your, ah, personal relationship."

God knew how desperately Erica wanted to believe that. But the memory of how he'd watched her with a poignant, almost wistful expression, was convincing evidence that Erica herself was somehow the cause of his melancholy mood.

Erica pushed her untouched salad away and laid the smudged napkin on the table. "I think he's sorry it happened, Mama."

"Nonsense," Jacqueline insisted with a dismissive flick of her hand. "I saw the way Mr. Arroya was looking at you over the birthday cake. If that wasn't love in his eyes—"

"Love?"

"Yes, love. The heart-pounding, breath-catching, moonlight-and-madness, now-and-forever, wedding bells kind of love. Now don't tell me you haven't noticed because I know you, Erica. You would never be intimate with any man unless you were deeply in love with him, and he with you." Jacqueline smoothed her daughter's hair, as she'd done when Erica was a child. "You know that I'm right, don't you?"

"You're half-right, Mama. I do love him, more than I would have ever dreamed possible."

"And he loves you, too, dear."

"I thought he did, but..." She turned away, chewing her lip.

If Erica was riddled by doubt, her mother had no such problem. "There are no 'buts'," she said firmly. "The man is quite definitely in love with you."

True or not, the words were music to Erica's ears. She loved hearing them, even if a tiny voice of reason continued to blunt optimism by reminding her that Roberto was not at all behaving like a man in love. "Then how do you explain his behavior, Mama? Roberto has become so distant, it's almost as if he'd pulled a plug and emotionally detached himself."

Considering that, the woman absently scratched the motorized control box on the arm of her wheelchair. "Only he can explain what he's feeling," she said finally. "You must speak to him at once. Clear the air, get things out in the open. Silence is the enemy, Erica, and communication is the only weapon available to us. Use it."

The suggestion sounded simple enough. Just ask him. But what if the answer was one Erica couldn't live with?

So what? replied a peevish voice in her mind. *Is it better to go on pretending, living a lie?*

Well, of course not. Still, there was an emotionally frail part of her that really didn't want to know—

The sliding glass door opened as Carolyn emerged from the house. "Mommy, Mommy!" she hollered. "Grampa's on TV!"

Twisting in the chair, Erica peered over her shoulder. "Now, Carolyn, you know better than that."

"Really, Mommy! It's Grampa. Come look."

She gave her mother a long-suffering look, to which Jacqueline replied with a shrug. "Perhaps they're televising a golf tournament and Carolyn caught a glimpse of Kenneth among the spectators."

Erica allowed that given her father's love of the sport, the scenario was possible, albeit unlikely. "I doubt Carolyn would choose golf over Power Rangers."

"Mommy *hurry!*"

"I'm coming, sweetie." Rolling her eyes, Erica stood and patted her mother's shoulder. "You stay here, Mama. I'm sure it's a false alarm."

Apparently, Jacqueline thought so, too, since she'd made no attempt to wheel away from the table and had returned to enjoying her lunch.

"Mom-m-my!"

With a pained sigh, Erica followed her frantic daughter into the family room. Cathy, who was sitting on the floor two feet from the large-screen console, pointed at the TV with a shriek of excitement. "Grampa!" she squealed.

Erica's gaze followed the wriggling little finger, but all she saw was a vaguely familiar man leaving a podium studded by microphones and decorated with a replica of the county crest.

Suddenly a reporter appeared on the screen. "There you have it," she said. "District Attorney Calvin McMahon confirming the grand jury investigation of bribery charges against one of the county's most powerful political figures. McMahon also made the surprise announcement that indictments are expected early next week. A few moments ago, Channel Seven got exclusive footage of Commissioner Mallory leaving the courthouse."

Erica jolted to attention at the mention of her father's name. Her first thought was one of numb surprise that Carolyn had been right. Grampa really was on TV, although Erica still hadn't figured out the reason. Even as the video flickered across the screen, her benumbed mind wondered why film of her father and his attorney hustling down the courthouse steps into a waiting car was considered newsworthy.

That's when the telephone started to ring.

Erica ignored it because the reporter was back on the screen with an expression so somber one would think she was reporting the advent of another world war. "Commissioner Mallory had no comment about the impending indictments. This has been a Special Report, live from downtown Los Angeles. We now return to regular programming, but stay tuned to Channel Seven for further developments on this breaking story.''

Carolyn let out a triumphant whoop. "See, Mommy, I told you!"

"Hmm? Oh, yes, you did.'' Bewildered, Erica absently reached for the phone just as the answering machine in the living room picked up. As she decided to retrieve the message later, Erica's attention returned to the television, which was now showing some kind of cartoon. Apparently the special report was over, although she was still confused as to exactly what was going on.

She massaged her head, wondering what on earth was happening and why her father had looked so grim.

"Where was Grampa going?" Cathy asked.

"I don't know," Erica murmured. Since she needed a few minutes of peace to try and figure things out, she sent the girls into the kitchen for some juice. When they were happily occupied, Erica decided to call her father at Oscar Watson's office. As soon as her hand touched the receiver, the phone rang again.

This time she answered and was greeted by a reporter for a local news station, who immediately went for the jugular. "According to the district attorney, bribery and corruption charges against Commissioner Mallory will be filed next week. Do you have any comment?"

The room started to sway. Bribery? Corruption? Against her father? She couldn't believe it. There had to be some mistake. Kenneth Mallory was the most decent, most honorable man she'd ever known. It couldn't be true. The D.A., the grand jury, the reporters . . . they must be talking about one of the other six planning commissioners. That had to be it, of course. Since her father was head of the commission, he'd obviously been called to testify against the real culprit.

A buzzing in her ear jarred her from her shocked stupor. She stared at the phone and, realizing that the reporter was still on the line, slammed the receiver back into its cradle. Within three seconds, the phone was ringing again. She backed away as if it were a snake.

It was all a mistake. It had to be.

It had to be....

"How the hell did this happen?" Roberto shouted into the phone.

"It's a slow news day and the D.A.'s running for reelection," came the weary reply. "Look, Rob, I've checked with our county sources and they all say the same thing. McMahon's behind in the polls and a juicy political scandal was just what he needed to gain points with the hard-liners."

"But the grand jury only started taking evidence yesterday. How in God's name could they be ready to indict?"

Edith's pained sigh filtered through the line. "From what I hear, they were ready to indict five minutes after viewing the tape. Since Mallory wasn't shrewd enough to launder the funds through foreign accounts, the jury considered his bank records as a signed confession."

Cursing under his breath, Roberto paced the living room, feeling as if he were about to explode. All he could think about was Erica. If she'd seen that press conference— The thought was too horrible to contemplate. He gripped the receiver and fought to control his fury. "Grand jury proceedings are supposed to be secret, dammit!"

"So are the directions for making a nuclear bomb, but you can order them by mail," Edith said, then lowered her voice. "Whispers at the water cooler say that McMahon himself leaked the transcripts. Naturally, no one who values his job will officially confirm it but those in the know have little doubt about the source. Apparently the district attorney and the planning commissioner haven't exactly been partisan soulmates."

As far as Roberto was concerned, that made absolutely no sense. "So for nothing more substantial than a chance to embarrass a political foe, McMahon would violate the ethics of his position and risk disbarment?"

"What risk? We're talking about the district attorney here. Who with a brain has the round chutzpahs to rat him out? Besides you, of course." Edith's tone abruptly changed from impatient to apprehensive. "Have you gotten hold of Erica yet?"

He dropped into the nearest chair. "I've called her house three times. There's no answer."

"Maybe she's with her parents."

A chill of trepidation slid down his spine. "I'll try her there."

Indicating that she'd talk to him later, Edith hung up. No sooner had Roberto pressed the hook switch when the phone rang. It was Erica, erasing his last hope that she might not have heard the news.

She was nearly hysterical, but Roberto didn't have to understand each word to know what she was saying. "Mistake...horrible mistake...my father...would never—"

"Shh," he whispered, trying to calm her. "I know how difficult this must be for you."

"Can you call someone...tell them it's not my father who...did those awful things?"

"Erica, honey, listen to me."

Listening was the last thing Erica was willing to do. Words rushed out in a distressed torrent. "But it's a lie. Everything that man on television said is a lie. It's all a terrible mistake—"

"No, Erica, it isn't a mistake." The silence on the line was almost as heartbreaking as her frenzied plea had been. Roberto's hands were shaking. He took a deep breath and spoke slowly, enunciating carefully so that even in her frantic state, she'd be certain to understand. "The man you saw on television is the district attorney. He has a tape of your father taking an envelope from a known criminal. That envelope allegedly contained a large amount of cash.''

A tiny gasp crackled in the handset. After a moment, she whispered, ''That's a lie.''

''I wish it was a lie, Erica, but it's not.''

There was another infinite silence. ''You . . . knew about this?''

''I knew about the tape but not about the press conference or the indictment. I swear to God, Erica, I had no idea this would go public so soon.'' Scouring his aching forehead with his fingertips, Roberto swallowed hard. ''Where are you? I'll come over and we'll talk—''

She interrupted, repeating herself in a dull monotone. ''You knew about the tape.''

''I, ah . . . yes.''

''How?''

''I saw it.''

''You . . . what?''

''Erica, listen to me. It was an accident. My people were surveilling someone else and suddenly there was your father, big as life. Believe me, he was the last person on earth I expected to see—''

''*You* made that tape?''

''Not personally, but my office was responsible for the initial surveillance activity.''

She made a sound somewhere between a soft mew and a choked gurgle. She spoke again, her voice cold and raw. ''Perhaps you could enlighten me as to how this 'alleged' tape found its way from your office to the district attorney?''

Roberto closed his eyes. Damn, his hands were shaking again. ''I gave it to him. Erica, listen—''

The dial tone buzzed in his ear. She'd hung up on him.

Roberto didn't know how long he sat there, staring at the receiver. By the time he cradled it, he knew without doubt that everything he'd feared most had happened. Erica had been devastated.

She'd never forgive him, of course, but at least his precious ethics were still in tact. Yep, that was what really counted, all right. Now he could sleep like a baby, secure in the self-righteous knowledge that regardless of how many lives he'd destroyed, justice had been served.

"Hey, Bobby."

Blinking, Roberto scanned the empty room.

"Over here, man."

As he turned toward the sound, he saw a translucent image shimmering by the hallway. He rubbed his eyes and looked again. The illusion was still there.

"Yeah, it's me, Bobby. I haven't changed so much, have I?"

"No, Tommy. You haven't changed at all." Rationally, Roberto knew he was talking to a figment of his own mind. For some reason, that didn't upset him.

The familiar grin appeared as the image cocked its head, studying him. After a moment, the figure faded away and from the darkness of Roberto's mind came the final words: "What happened to you, Bobby? How come you went over to their side?"

Squeezing his eyes closed, Roberto simply shook his head. The path that he'd once traveled with such ease had turned into a muddy rut of confusion and contradiction. He didn't know when it had happened—or how, or why. He only knew that he'd lost his way and feared he might never find it again.

Chapter Eleven

She felt as if she were going to pass out.

This had to be a dream, a horrible nightmare from which she'd awaken at any moment. It had to be; the man she loved wouldn't have, couldn't have betrayed her. That was someone else on the phone, someone pretending to be Roberto, someone trying to drive her mad with cruel lies.

The room was spinning.

Erica stumbled to her father's favorite lounge chair and sat with her head resting on her knees. Her stomach soured; a wretched taste flooded her mouth. She prayed to wake up, begged God to let her wake up.

"Erica!"

Her head snapped up. "Daddy," she whispered, pushing herself out of the chair, struggling to focus through a sudden rush of tears. She reached out and would have run to him except her legs wouldn't move.

He dropped his briefcase on the floor and crossed the room to embrace her and stroke her hair, whispering fatherly assurance and endearing sobriquets of her child-hood. But those words, once the most powerful in Erica's small universe, had lost their mystical power to heal. She was still in pain, terrible pain, an agony of spirit that her father couldn't mend anymore. That was most frightening of all.

With a shaky step backward, she held him away with stiff arms and a heavy heart. Gazing into his worn face, she saw the weariness in his eyes; and the fear. A thin, quavering voice—her own—broke the silence. "Why are they doing this to you, Daddy?"

Kenneth Mallory's gaze skittered away, out the sliding glass door to the patio where his wife still lingered over lunch. "Does your mother know?"

Erica shook her head, acutely aware that he hadn't re-sponded to her question. "Daddy—"

"Grampa!" Carolyn dashed in from the kitchen and bounced around her grandfather's feet like a spirited puppy. "I saw you on TV!"

Squatting to the child's level, Kenneth gave his grand-daughter a fervent, almost desperate hug. His smile was flat and, Erica thought, painfully forced. "Would you do Grampa a big favor and take your sister upstairs for a while?"

"How come?"

"Your mommy and I have some things to talk about." He brushed a kiss on the child's forehead before standing. "Run along, honey-bunny."

Carolyn's disappointed frown melted into a pout of res-ignation. She heaved an exaggerated sigh, muttered, "Okay," and trudged away. In a few minutes, little foot-steps clamored up the stairs.

Erica clasped her trembling hands. "I want to know what's going on, Daddy. Please, tell me the truth."

Kenneth raked his hair, glanced out at the patio again, then jammed one hand in his slacks pocket and used the other to wipe his moist forehead. "It's politics, Erica. Nothing for you to worry about. I'll handle it."

She ardently wanted to believe that, but she didn't. There was terror in her father's eyes, terror of the truth. Her heart fluttered in a final, silent scream before her entire chest went cold inside. "What was in the envelope?"

He paled visibly. "I don't know what you mean."

"The envelope that mobster gave you. There's film of you putting it in your pocket. What was in it, Daddy, a fax of the Sunday comics?"

An invisible weight came down on Kenneth's shoulders. He shrank before her eyes, stooping under the staggering mass of guilt.

"It's true, isn't it?" she whispered, unable to focus through a renewed rush of tears. "Everything they've said about you, everything they're going to say... it's all true."

Kenneth reached out, eyes filled with misery. She stepped back, shielding herself with upraised palms. His fingers flexed once, then his hand dropped to his side. "Yes, it's true."

The answer struck with the force of a blow. Turning away, she clutched her stomach, whispering "Why?" over and over again.

"Sit down, Erica. Please."

Since her legs couldn't support her, she did. After a moment's hesitation, Kenneth sat on the sofa, across from her. Staring at the polished hardwood floor, he slouched forward, propping his forearms on his knees, and spoke without looking up. "You asked why, Erica, and it's a fair question. I'm not certain the answer will satisfy you, but all I can do now is tell the truth and hope you can accept it."

He waited a moment, as if expecting her to comment. When she didn't, he went on. "The problems started five years ago, after my heart attack. Bypass surgery is immorally expensive, Erica. Afterward, I wasn't able to work for nearly a year and by the time we'd paid off the uninsured portion of medical bills, our savings had been severely depleted." He straightened, proudly lifting his chin with the force and confidence Erica remembered. "Still, we managed. I went back to work, part-time at first, but it was enough to keep the creditors at bay."

Kenneth met his daughter's eyes, apparently didn't like what he saw and returned his gaze to the floor. "Yes, there were many creditors. One doesn't maintain a comfortable life these days without incurring debt. Eventually, however, I discovered to my delight that there was a little money left over each month. I thought the crisis was over. Then your mother..." His voice trailed away. He shook his head, unable to complete the statement.

Erica finished for him. "Then Mama got sick."

Sighing, he gazed up with dull eyes. "Insurance covered even less this time because the benefits had been reduced after my surgery. By liquidating most of our remaining assets, I was able to pay the initial medical costs but there was no money left over for therapy or nursing care, which were vital to your mother's recovery."

For some reason, Erica couldn't completely comprehend what she was being told. Her father had always been a successful man, surrounded by material expressions of wealth that the family had taken for granted. As far as she could see, nothing had changed. The house was still here, furnished with exquisite antiques that were worth a tidy sum in their own right; and the cars, luxury models so favored by those of privilege, were still parked in a garage larger than some homes. So she had difficulty grasping the excuse of financial need. "I don't understand," she said slowly. "Equity in the house must have increased at least three-fold since you bought it."

Kenneth's head snapped up. He stared at her as if she'd committed heresy. "This is your mother's home. After all she has endured, do you think I would take that away from her?"

"It's just a house. If things were so bad, I can't believe Mama hasn't already suggested selling it—"

"Enough!" Kenneth bolted to his feet, clasping his head between his hands as if expecting his skull to explode. "Don't speak of this again."

That's when the depth of her father's deception sank in. "Oh, Lord. Mama doesn't know about any of this, does she? You never told her that you were having financial problems."

His hands slid from his temples to cover his face. A shudder vibrated the strong shoulders to which Erica had so often clung for solace. But those shoulders weren't strong anymore; they were sunken, sloped, collapsing into themselves. Kenneth lowered his hands slowly, gathering himself into the practiced, proud demeanor that no longer seemed to fit. "I don't want your mother to worry. Please don't tell her."

Erica was numb inside. "I won't tell her, Daddy. You will."

"I . . . can't."

"You don't have any choice. Reporters have been calling all morning. By sunset, they'll be clustered around the gate like starving vultures. You can't hide the truth anymore, not from Mama and not from yourself."

He closed his eyes, whispering, "I know."

A silence stretched between them, an invisible rift in their universe widening the breach between father and daughter until Erica could barely recognize the man who had once been her entire world.

Then a thought struck her, a realization slamming into her brain with such force that she gasped aloud. "The loan . . . the money to open my shop . . . Oh, Daddy. Please tell me it didn't come from those gangsters."

Kenneth seemed surprised that she'd even asked. "It was necessary, Erica. Your mother needed you here."

"Oh, no. Oh, God." She sagged back against the soft cushions of the lounge chair, her head reeling. Blood money. Her shop had been opened with blood money. "I can't believe this is happening."

"Erica . . . my sweet, sweet child . . ." Distraught, Kenneth crossed the room and knelt at his daughter's side. "Please understand, I had no choice. If anything happened to me, your mother would have been left penniless, unable even to care for herself. I couldn't let that happen, don't you see? I wanted you close enough to care for her, to keep her from being alone."

"So you took bribes?"

"That's harsh, Erica."

"So is selling your vote to the highest bidder."

He winced. "I took money, yes. I've admitted that, but I never cast a vote I didn't believe in. I never sold my integrity."

She looked into his eyes without wavering. "Didn't you?"

Kenneth stiffened as if he'd been slapped. Erica felt neither pain nor remorse for having hurt him; she felt nothing at all and wondered if she was dead inside, or merely shattered. All of Erica's life, Kenneth Mallory had been her rock and her role model. Discovering that the father she'd worshipped as a god was nothing more than a mere mortal—and a deeply flawed one at that—was more than she could bear.

Over the years Erica had survived her share of heartache and disillusionment; for her children's sake, she'd find the strength to survive again. But she'd never be the same. Something had cracked inside, and her innocence had drained away. Almost everyone she'd ever cared about, from her ex-husband to Sara Rettig, now her father and Roberto, had in one way or another betrayed her trust.

It was the bleakest moment of her life.

The third time Roberto rang, he pressed his thumb on the bell and left it there. After a full minute of tooth-rattling ding-dongs, Erica yanked open the door with such force he feared she'd rip it off the hinges.

"Go away."

The chill in her eyes made his blood ice. "We need to talk."

"Please don't ring the bell again. You'll wake the girls."

He wedged a foot in the door to keep her from closing it. "If you don't let me in, I'll wake the whole damned neighborhood."

She scrutinized him for a moment, then, apparently deciding that he was capable of following through on the threat, abruptly released the door, spun around and walked back into the living room. When Roberto entered, she was standing with her back to him, arms folded, shoulders rigid.

Before Erica had turned away, he'd noticed her reddened eyes and pale complexion, devoid of makeup and saw that her silky, scented hair was alluringly disheveled. A floppy knit tunic hung to her thighs, covering most of the worn blue jeans that he knew were clinging to her lush hips as comfortably as a lover's hand. She was barefoot, her shoes piled under the coffee table along with some bright plastic beads and a few parts from the girls' Candy Land game.

Despite her rumpled appearance, Roberto considered her the most beautiful woman on earth. Around him, the room was filled with the enticing sights and smells of family life; colorful children's books strewn across the floor; warm kitchen scents—hamburgers, he thought, and the summery fragrance of fresh steamed vegetables; the lingering bouquet of Little Mermaid bubble bath faintly detectable in the humid air. And honeysuckle, Erica's scent; sweet essence of tousled sheets and slickened skin and unforgettable passion.

He was mesmerized, drugged by wistful memories and hopeless hope, until the spell was broken by a voice, Erica's voice, cold as regret and stiff as her spine. "What do you want?"

"To tell you the truth, I'm not quite sure."

She turned her head just enough to toss a frigid glance over her shoulder. "The truth? That word from your lips... lightning should strike."

"I can see that you're angry—"

"Angry?" She spun to face him, planting her fists on her hips. "I'm not just angry, Mr. Arroya, I am livid. Even if sneaking around like some voyeuristic pervert is part of your so-called job—"

"Now wait a minute, I wasn't sneaking anywhere—"

"How dare you use me and my children as pawns in your dirty little scheme?" Erica shook her finger at him as he stood there, mute with shock. "If you don't give a tinker's damn about me, which is fairly obvious at this point, what about the girls? They're children, for heaven sake! How could you deceive them like that?"

Midway through her furious spiel, Roberto regained his voice. "I haven't deceived anyone."

"No? So last week, while you were reading stories to the girls and playing checkers with them, you didn't know that their grandfather was being investigated?"

His indignation dissipated. "I've already admitted that I did."

"But you didn't think it worth mentioning, right?"

"I couldn't, Erica, you know that."

"I know it now, but at the time, fool that I am, I actually thought you cared for us... cared for me."

"I did... I mean, I do. Erica, listen to me—" As he stepped forward, she backed away, her eyes filled with tears.

She angrily wiped her eyes, her voice quivering with emotion. "God, you must have thought me such a dimwit. I believed everything you said, and all the time you were just using me to get to my father."

The accusation sliced him to the core. "You can't believe that."

"Why did you pretend to have feelings for me? Why couldn't you be honest and tell me what you really wanted? I would have told you to go to hell, but at least I wouldn't have ended up feeling like a tramp—"

"Stop it!" Roberto grasped her shoulders and, not knowing whether to shake her or embrace her, did both. She melted against him, sobbing, and buried her face in the curve of his throat. He held her, stroking her hair, kissing her wet cheek, and damned near broke into tears himself.

It took a few moments before his throat spasm eased enough for him to speak. "Don't ever say that again. Don't even think it. What we shared was something so pure and special, just thinking about it makes me ache inside. I meant everything I said when we were together. Everything."

He allowed her to step back far enough to wipe her face, but not so far that he couldn't touch her. She hiccupped, bit her lip, and, curling her fists under her chin as Cathy so often did, she focused her gaze on the center of his chest.

When he realized she wasn't going to respond, he took a deep breath and continued. "That morning when we first met in the park, you were so beautiful you took my breath away. I didn't know who your father was and I damn well didn't care. All I knew was that I was completely entranced by your intelligence, your wit, that funny half-giggle thing you do when you're embarrassed and yes, the fact that you have a body to die for didn't escape my notice, either." He smiled at the top of her head, but her gaze remained fixed somewhere around his solar plexus; he presumed that she was not amused. Sighing, he slid his palms along her upper arms. "What I'm trying to say is that up until last Monday, your father had absolutely nothing to do with our relationship."

She went rigid in his arms, then lifted her face to peek out from beneath glistening lashes. "Did you say Monday?"

"Yes."

Her eyes darkened, intensified. "Then over the weekend, when we . . . that is, while we were . . ." Unable to articulate the words, her gaze skittered away.

"When we were making love?"

She nodded without looking at him. He slid a thumb under her chin, urging her head back and gazing deeply into
her eyes so there would be no misunderstanding about what
he was going to tell her. "Making love with you was the
most beautiful experience of my life. I wish I could find the
words to tell you what I was feeling, what was going on inside of me. I can't. It's too complicated. I'm not even sure I
understand it myself. But there is no doubt as to how much
I care for you. Erica, I . . ."

The word *love* danced on the tip of his tongue. Roberto
had never used that word before, at least not in this particular context. But then again, he'd never been in love before. And if he'd hadn't been in love, how could he possibly
be certain that he was in love now? In truth, he couldn't. He
felt something strange, something deep, something inordi-
nately powerful. It might be love. It must be love.

Yet when he tried to utter the word, it backed into his
throat and he swallowed it. What finally came out was the
bland utterance, "I have feelings for you."

If there had been a trace of expectation in her eyes, it died
then. "I see."

"No, you don't see," he said miserably, knowing that she
couldn't possibly understand what he was unwilling or unable to express freely. "I'm trying to say that what is happening to your father, unfortunate as it might be, has
nothing to do with us. You're not responsible for his mis-
deeds and I certainly don't blame you for anything that he
has done."

Her eyes widened only a moment before narrowing into
furious slits. "Is this where I'm supposed to fall into your
arms, blubbering with gratitude that you don't *blame* me for

crimes my father is *alleged* to have committed? Well, be still my heart. Aren't I the lucky one?''

''I only meant—''

''I know exactly what you meant.'' She shook off his hands, backing away and warning him off with her eyes. ''You've made your opinions excruciatingly clear over the past weeks and if memory serves, my father has just stepped over that invisible line you've so pompously drawn to separate bad people from good people, right?''

Roberto, having cleverly ascertained that he'd managed to offend her, now chose his words with more care. ''If— and I stress the word *if*—your father is guilty of the charges, then he has abused a position of public trust for personal gain. In the eyes of the law, that is a criminal act.''

''Therefore, my father is a criminal?''

''If he's convicted, yes.''

''Regardless of circumstance?''

''There is no circumstance that justifies breaking the law.''

Erica stared at him with an expression he couldn't quite define and most certainly didn't like. ''That, counselor, is a reeking heap of bunk.''

''Excuse me?''

''Let's assume for the sake of argument that Daddy did everything he's accused of. What was his motive? Why would a supposedly wealthy man risk everything—career, family, a lifetime of achievement—for a few paltry dollars?''

It was a question Roberto had been asking himself for almost a week. Since he hadn't been able to come up with a reasonable answer, he responded to Erica's query with an ambiguous shrug.

''Well then, what if those paltry dollars represented more than mere money?'' Her voice dropped to a nearly inaudible whisper. ''What if they represented life or death for someone he loved? Would you consider that an extenuating circumstance, counselor, or just another lousy excuse?''

The pain in her eyes sliced him to the core. He felt cold, sick inside. He wanted to reach out, take her hand and hold it forever, but knew she'd pull away. So he clasped them behind his back to avoid the temptation. ''Is this extenuating circumstance something you'd like to discuss?''

''That depends.'' She stared straight at him. ''Off the record?''

''Yes.'' When she hesitated as if weighing potential harm against the measure of his veracity, Roberto realized how deeply he'd hurt her. ''You don't trust me, do you?''

''Should I? Never mind. It doesn't matter.'' With a defiant toss of her head, her hair rippled around her shoulders, catching the light. ''Even if you have a tape recorder in your pocket, everything I'm about to say is purely hypothetical. Do you understand that, counselor?''

''Erica, I—''

''Do you understand?''

He sighed. ''Yes.''

''Good.'' She turned away, rubbing her upper arms and staring into space. Then she started to speak, slowly, softly, in a shaking voice that occasionally failed her completely. She described a robust, confident man who'd been decimated by sudden illness and subsequent realization of his own mortality. Erica relayed—hypothetically, of course— how an overly proud man, weakened by an arduous recovery and stressed by financial hardship, might have concealed his financial burden from his family out of protectiveness and misguided concern.

As she spoke, each revelation chipped at Roberto's resolve. Erica described a man obsessed with love for his family, a man who would do anything, pay any price to assure that his stricken wife would always be cared for. The cost had been high: his career; his reputation; his freedom. Yet Kenneth Mallory had paid willingly, out of love.

A smothering silence fell over the room. Roberto realized that Erica had stopped speaking. He cleared his throat. "Is that what your father told you?"

She shivered, turning slowly to face him. "Would it matter if it was?"

"I don't know." The response was an honest one, yet obviously not what she'd hoped to hear. "It might explain his actions, but it can't excuse them. If your father abused the power of his position, he'll have to live with the consequences."

Other than a minute muscle twitch below her jaw, she remained motionless. "As will you."

The obscure statement baffled him. "I don't know what you mean."

"You once told me that you'd become a lawyer to see justice done. At the time, I believed that. Now I don't." She walked to the front door and opened it. "Go home, Roberto. Go home and look in a mirror."

He followed her to the doorway but made no move to leave. "Just what is it that you think I'll see?"

"The thing you purport to despise most in this world," she whispered. "A man who wields power without conscience."

A mule kick to the belly couldn't have shocked him more. The breath erupted from his lungs in a single surge, leaving him empty, flat inside. He stumbled backward, still struggling to breathe as light from the living room compressed to a sliver, then dissipated into darkness with the click of the closing door.

Roberto vaguely realized that he was on the porch, a locale which meant nothing in comparison to the enormity of what had just happened. Erica had sent him away. Forever. He'd expected that to happen. He just hadn't realized how much it would hurt.

* * *

Erica turned off the lamp, plunging the room into darkness, and fought a valiant battle with herself. In the end, pride won. She didn't rip the door open and beg Roberto to return. She didn't even peek through the blinds for a final, yearning look as he strode down her walk for what would certainly be the last time.

Instead, she felt her way through the shadowed hall into her own bedroom and collapsed on the bed. She sat there, hunched like a cornered mouse, twisting her hands, biting her lip, wishing to God that Roberto had thrown that damning tape into the Pacific Ocean. If he'd only destroyed the thing, none of this would have happened.

With a sigh that sounded more like a sob, Erica rubbed her stinging eyes and shook off the foolish notion. Someone—she couldn't remember who—had once told her that wishes were free; now she realized that even with wishes, one got what one paid for. All the wishing in the world wouldn't loosen Roberto Arroya's uncompromising code of ethics; and deep down, Erica didn't want to loosen them. Roberto wasn't a man capable of lying or cheating or bending moral rules, as was her ex-husband; that honor and unquestioned integrity was an essential part of the man Roberto was, the man she had come to love.

But Erica loved her father, too, and now faced the agonizing decision of choosing between the two most important men in her life. In the end, there was no choice. Her father needed her. Roberto didn't.

With her heart breaking, Erica flipped on the overhead light, then dragged a suitcase out of the closet and started to pack.

Chapter Twelve

Carolyn slouched on the family room sofa, brows furrowed, expression grim. "I don' wanna ride my bike. I wanna go home and play with Buddy."

Since that was all Erica had heard for the past two days, it was becoming more and more difficult to issue the same tolerant response. "You know that's not possible right now, sweetie. While we're staying with Gramma and Grampa, Buddy lives too far away to come play with you."

"Mr. 'Roya could bring him."

As always, the sound of Roberto's name made her heart ache. She glanced out the patio window, partly because she found the view calming and partly so her daughter wouldn't read the truth in her eyes. "Mr. Arroya is busy, Carolyn. He doesn't have time to come visit."

"Doesn't he like us anymore?"

"I'm sure he likes you very much," Erica said, hoping that Carolyn, who missed Roberto almost as much as she did, wouldn't start crying again. To forestall the inevitable, she gave her daughter a comforting hug and tried to redirect her attention. "How about a game of checkers?"

Pulling away, Carolyn shook her head. Two more fat tears slid down the child's unhappy face. "Maybe Mr. 'Roya doesn't know where we are."

"I'm sure he does," Erica mumbled, although she wasn't sure at all. In fact, she doubted that Roberto was even aware that she and the children had left the neighborhood. After the bitter argument Saturday night, he'd certainly not want to see or speak to her again. In a sense, that had been the plan. Blaming him for her father's problems had been unfair, of course; but Erica couldn't get past the fact that he'd deliberately deceived her.

Most devastating, however, had been the discovery that Roberto's sensitivity and compassion were, in fact, rationed, doled sparingly to the deserving few who conformed to his strict moral standards. Those deemed unworthy were simply cast aside and left to drift in their own misfortune. Like Sara, for example.

There was, Erica had decided, too much anger in Roberto's heart to leave room for forgiveness. He couldn't understand that good people occasionally stumbled; sometimes they even fell down. That didn't make them bad or evil. It made them human.

As much as she loved Roberto, Erica couldn't take the chance that if she or, God forbid, one of the children ever made such a mistake, they, too, would be categorized and ostracized as unworthy of love.

"Can I call him?"

Blinking, Erica turned to Carolyn, who was looking up expectantly. "Call who, sweetie?"

"Mr. 'Roya. Maybe he can come see us tonight and we can watch the Snow White movie Gramma gave me for my birthday." Apparently Carolyn read the word "no" on her mother's face because she instantly went into begging mode, clutching her hands together and repeating, "Please, Mommy," until Erica's head felt as if it would explode.

Finally she shushed her pleading child, massaged her own throbbing forehead and struggled to explain what she didn't completely understand herself. "This isn't a good time for that, Carolyn. Gramma and Grampa have some, ah, things to deal with and I doubt they're in the mood for company."

Carolyn wasn't ready to give up. "Maybe we can go over to his house. Mr. 'Roya likes us to come over. He said me and Cathy make his house all noisy, but he said it was a good kind of noise."

"I've already told you that Mr. Arroya is extremely busy with his own work—"

"He's never too busy for us," Carolyn announced confidently.

"Now how do you know that?"

"'Cause he told me so."

"Yes, well, things change." Erica's heart sank as a fresh flood of tears splashed down Carolyn's face. She frantically searched her mind for something that might redirect her daughter's attention and was relieved when the answer popped into her head. "I know! You can call your daddy and leave a message telling him all about the wonderful mural your class is painting. Would you like to do that?"

"Uh-uh."

Since Carolyn had never passed up an opportunity to call her father, the unexpected refusal was a bit of a jolt. "Why not? I thought you liked to call your daddy."

Her lower lip quivered. "Wanna call Mr. 'Roya."

Erica sighed. "I'm sorry, Carolyn. I've already explained why that's not possible."

Sniffing, Carolyn scrutinized her mother's face, concluded that further entreaty was pointless and burst into tears. She scooted down from the sofa, dashed past her grandmother, who'd just wheeled into the doorway, and charged upstairs, wailing at the top of her lungs.

Jacqueline twisted in her chair, casting an awkward glance over her shoulder. "Gracious, why is that poor child so upset?"

"Thwarted youth," Erica mumbled, hoping to avoid a detailed discussion.

Her mother, however, was much too astute to be side-tracked by obscure murmurings. "Roberto again?"

Since Erica assumed the answer must be written all over her face, she didn't bother to dispute it. "Yes."

With a soft cluck of disapproval, Jacqueline pressed the control button and rolled into the room. "Carolyn doesn't understand what has happened between you and Roberto, and quite frankly, dear, neither do I. The point is that whatever problem you two have, you mustn't allow it to affect the children."

"You're acting as if Roberto and I are married, Mama. We aren't."

"I know that, Erica, but by your own admission, the two of you have been very close friends. The girls sensed that closeness, just as they now sense tension and alienation. They're frightened." Jacqueline parked beside the sofa, close enough to reach her daughter's hand. "I saw how Carolyn and Roberto interacted at the birthday party. They adore each other. I can't believe there's anything on earth that man wouldn't do for that little girl. Call him, Erica, for the children's sake."

"It's for their sake that I won't call him." Erica squeezed her mother's hand. "Try to understand, Mama. The girls have already been disappointed and emotionally abandoned by one man whom they loved deeply. I won't let that happen to them again."

"You won't let it happen to them, Erica . . . or to you?"

Her mother's kind smile couldn't ease the sting of that question, or the icy fear it invoked. Erica *was* afraid of being hurt again, but she was also afraid for her children. Roberto was a man of enormous principle, of moral values which left no room for human error; yet he'd failed to recognize that forgiveness is the most crucial component of love.

To Erica, that was a fatal flaw. An unforgiving environment splinters the spirit, shatters the soul. That was not what she wanted for her children. Or for herself.

But she couldn't consider that now, while the rest of her family was in crisis. "Can I get you something to eat, Mama? You didn't have much lunch."

"No, thank you, dear. I'll wait until your father gets home."

Following her mother's worried glance at the domed anniversary clock on the mantle, Erica noted that it was nearly dinnertime. Her father, who'd left for an early morning meeting with his attorney, should have been home hours ago. "Perhaps the district attorney finally agreed to meet with him," Erica speculated aloud. "That would certainly be a good sign."

"Yes," Jacqueline murmured, preoccupied by the ticking clock. "Although I'd have thought Kenneth would have called by now."

"He'll be home any minute."

"I hope so. This nasty business has taken so much out of him. He barely slept a wink last night and was so tired this morning, he could hardly get out of bed." As was her habit when distressed, Jacqueline absently twisted the diamond wedding band which had been a gift from her husband on their twenty-fifth anniversary.

Erica watched silently, marveling at her mother's unwavering strength. When Kenneth had finally told his wife of the impending indictments, Jacqueline had listened without comment, her expression impossibly calm. Afterward, all she'd said was, "Whatever you've done, dear, I'm sure you had your reasons."

That was it. No questions. No recriminations. No tears.

As far as Erica knew, her mother was still in the dark about their current financial crisis, a situation that Erica charitably considered as unfortunate, if not intolerable. Jacqueline was an articulate, intelligent woman. She had a right to know that the family's economic security had been badly eroded. Had it not been for the untimely promise her father elicited during a particularly vulnerable moment, Erica would have remedied the situation by telling her mother the unvarnished truth.

What she knew of it, anyway. Erica couldn't suppress a growing suspicion that there had been more to the story than her father had been willing to share. There'd been a quaver of avoidance in his voice, along with an odd aversion to meeting her gaze that had disturbed her. She was certain that he'd been holding something back, although she couldn't fathom anything more devastating than the facts he'd already revealed.

Thoughts of even more terrifying possibilities were interrupted by the hum of her mother's chair. Erica glanced up as Jacqueline cruised toward the kitchen. "What do you need, Mama?"

"I thought a glass of sherry might do us both good." She swung in front of the wet bar, easily lifting the bottle from the polished burl counter. "Oh, dear," she murmured, eyeing the neat row of inverted wineglasses suspended out of reach on the underside of the liquor cabinet.

Erica crossed the room, reaching over her mother's head to retrieve two crystal goblets and set them on the counter, so her mother could pour a short shot in each. Recorking and returning the bottle to its original location, Jacqueline offered her daughter one glass and took the other for herself, slipping the stem between her fingers to balance the bowl portion in her palm.

After taking a delicate sip, Jacqueline rested the flared crystal base on her knee and turned her attention to Erica, who was rolling her head in a futile attempt to unknot her neck muscles. "You look tired, dear. Are things at the shop very busy?"

"Thankfully, yes. I've had to hire a second counter person. Marge is training her." By casually tossing out the information, Erica hoped her mother wouldn't suspect the need for an additional employee was due more to Erica's increased absence than by an inordinate influx of customers.

Jacqueline, however, was not easily fooled, and her perceptive gaze made Erica squirm. The question had already formed in her mother's eyes when her attention was diverted by the ringing telephone. She immediately set her glass on the bar and grabbed the control switch. The wheelchair buzzed back a few feet, did a ninety-degree turn and hummed into the family room.

"Maybe you should let the machine answer, Mama. It might be another reporter—"

Jacqueline anxiously snatched up the receiver. "Hello? Oh, hello, Oscar. Did the meeting go well?"

Once Erica realized the call wasn't another news media assault, she found a towel behind the bar and wiped up a puddle of sherry sloshed from her mother's glass. At this hour, a call from her father's lawyer probably indicated even more of a delay. Since the children wouldn't be able to wait much longer for dinner, Erica decided she'd better whip something up for them.

As she contemplated a meal that would be easy to reheat when her father got home, she became aware that the room had become uncomfortably quiet. She turned and saw her mother sitting there, ashen, staring down at the telephone receiver lying in her lap. Erica dropped the towel on the bar. "Mama? What is it?"

Jacqueline looked up, her eyes wide with bewilderment and pain. She said nothing; she didn't have to. Erica knew instantly that something terrible had happened to her father.

Emerging from his car, Roberto glanced across the street at a cinder block fence so littered by graffiti that it was impossible to ascertain its original hue. The narrow alley where he'd parked was a ribbon of garbage, strewn with crushed cellophane, dented beverage cans and crumpled food wrappers. It was uncomfortably similar to the neighborhood where Roberto had grown up, so he couldn't for the life of him figure out why Larkin McKay had picked such a woebegone place for his youth services program.

But then, there was a lot about his good friend that he'd never figured out, including how the devil Lark had managed to keep his stuccoed, flat-roofed building, which was protected only by a transparent wall of chain link and cleanly swept asphalt, as the only structure on the block that hadn't been targeted by taggers.

Entering the gate, Roberto wound around the outdoor basketball hoops noting that the area was so conspicuously tidy, one might wonder if the owner hid behind trash bins with a twenty-two, picking off spray painters like a farmer dispensing a flock of nuisance crows.

Of course, Lark was much too civilized for that sort of thing. He'd prefer to assist the young vandals to become emotionally in tune with the subliminal motivation and suppressed hostility that was camouflaged by overt expression in their, ahem, art. In other words, he'd talk them to death.

Roberto heaved open the huge gymnasium door and was greeted by the echo of bouncing basketballs, scuffling sneakers and a cacophony of high-five street slang. Several boys were sinking hoops at the far end of the cavernous arena; some teenaged girls were clustered by the pop machine, eyeing the ball players and giggling; a lively game of billiards was in progress and several arcade-type computer games were also getting a workout. Three adult volunteers were supervising the ruckus.

At the far end of the building, Larkin McKay leaned against the wall outside his office, engaged in solemn discussion with a slouching, baggy-trousered adolescent. When Roberto approached, Larkin gave the teen's shoulder a friendly cuff, exchanged an over-the-head hand slap, presumably the street equivalent of "see you later", and sauntered over, grinning. "Hey, Bobby. Since this isn't your scheduled volunteer night, I assume that you've either been struck by a double dose of civic duty or you've got a warrant for one of my kids."

"Now, you know that I don't pick 'em up, Doc. I just put 'em away."

"A fine line, counselor." As Larkin adjusted his wire-rimmed glasses, his astute gaze swept the room before settling on Roberto. "So, what brings you here on a Wednesday?"

Slipping a hand into his slacks pocket, Roberto rocked back on his heels and tried to act casual. "I thought you might want to grab a burger or something."

The nonchalant performance couldn't fool a man who'd known him for twenty years. "Since you haven't requested the pleasure of my company for dinner since the day you met Erica Franklin, may I assume that there's trouble in paradise?"

Roberto shrugged.

Larkin rubbed his chin, frowning. "How about Chinese?"

"Sounds good. I'll drive. You pay." Roberto spun on his heel, heading for the door.

Larkin fell into step beside him and tossed a chummy arm around his shoulders. "Nice try."

They crossed the asphalt yard to the alley, climbed into Roberto's car and drove a couple of blocks to The China Pearl, which was one of the Brotherhood's favorite meeting spots. The owner greeted them warmly and escorted them to their usual table, an isolated booth situated in the farthest corner of the restaurant.

An hour later, Roberto pushed away the remnants of his Kung Pao Chicken, ordered more wine, then sat back and watched Larkin wield chopsticks like a Beijing native, snatching the few remaining noodles off his own plate before eyeing what was left on Roberto's.

"Help yourself," he mumbled. The offer was unnecessary, since Larkin's chopsticks were already circling the spicy chicken bits left on his companion's plate.

When he'd dispatched the final morsel, Larkin dropped his napkin on the table and smiled. "Thanks, Bobby. Next meal is on me."

"This meal is on you."

"Okay, but since the IRS only allows deductions for patient expenses, I'll have to bill you for my services."

"What services? All you've done is eat everything except the tablecloth."

"Not true, Bobby. Why, all through dinner, you've been telling me how Kenneth Mallory's legal woes have affected your love life. Now, I get big bucks for listening to people's problems so the way I figure it, you'll probably end up owing—" he made a production of studying his watch "—somewhere in the neighborhood of $265.00. On the other hand, if this was just a couple of buddies getting together for a chat..." Larkin grinned as Roberto, muttering to himself, pulled a credit card from his wallet. "So, now that the check is settled, tell me what's really going on between you and Erica."

"Nothing's going on," Roberto said, laying the card at the edge of the table. "That's the problem. Erica and I had an argument last Saturday, then she packed up and left. I haven't spoken to her since."

"Where'd she go?"

"To her folks' house." Roberto didn't bother to describe how crazed he'd been to realize that she was gone, nor did he mention that after having spotted her car in the Mallorys' driveway, he'd blended in with the gaggle of reporters, spending hours parked across the street in the hope of catching a glimpse of her.

He'd finally spotted her as she'd driven through the gates, her windows rolled tight, her lips clamped even tighter. She'd looked exhausted. She'd looked beautiful. Roberto had actually considered ramming her car just to have the opportunity to talk to her.

"Why haven't you called her?" Larkin asked.

Reasonable question. In truth, he had called at least a half-dozen times and had gotten only the answering machine. Since he hadn't figured out what he was going to say in the first place, leaving a message had seemed pointless. So he'd hung up and tried later, each time hoping she'd answer and the sound of her voice would trigger the right words. Each time, he'd gotten the damned machine.

Larkin's fingers snapped in front of his face. "Hello, in there."

"Hmm? Sorry."

Larkin leaned back with a thoughtful expression. "Let's try another question. Who are you most angry with, Erica or her father?"

"That's a stupid question."

"Life's full of stupid questions. The point is, do you have an answer?"

"I have no reason to be angry with Erica."

"She chose her father over you. That might have a tendency to irk some men."

"I don't see it that way." Despite the firm reply, Roberto added, "I'll admit that initially I was a bit baffled by why she insisted on defending him."

"Until you learned about Mallory's financial problems and understood why he'd reacted as he had?"

"Yes. Under the circumstances, I could see why she'd be inclined to make excuses for his behavior."

"But you weren't inclined to make excuses for it, were you?"

The question surprised and annoyed him. "Of course not. What kind of world would it be if people were allowed to rob banks for their mortgage payments? The law has to be respected—it's what separates us from animals."

"Well, now, if you used that argument to plead your case with Erica, I can't understand why she wasn't impressed. I mean, here's the father she adores, who has just put his entire career on the line for her mother, whom she also loves, and you compare the poor guy to an animal. Great stuff, counselor. Pompous, but highly dramatic."

Roberto straightened at the word that Erica, too, had used to describe him. "Do you think I'm pompous?"

"Is the pope Catholic? Anyway, the only opinion that matters here is yours."

Sighing, Roberto raked his hair and propped his elbows on the table. "Oh, hell, Lark. I don't know what I think anymore. All my life, I've followed a specific set of rules. Suddenly, they don't make sense anymore. We've got an alleged criminal for whom I feel nothing but compassion and a district attorney, stoic representative of the people, who doesn't give a fat flying fig about anything but his own re-election. Everything's backward and I can't figure out why."

"What's McMahon's problem?"

"I wish to hell I knew. From what I hear, there was barely enough evidence for indictment. Just the tape and Mallory's bank records, which show several unexplained deposits. Damned suspicious of course, but not enough proof to convict.

"Besides, none of Caricchio's companies have had projects before the planning commission during the months in question, so Mallory hasn't recorded a vote that resulted in Caricchio's financial gain. Of course, there are some big votes coming up, but Mallory could always say he'd planned to abstain. The bottom line is that the commissioner's proven association with Caricchio, although highly improper, hasn't crossed the line into the realm of criminality."

Larkin raised a brow, to which Roberto responded with an empathetic shrug. "I know, but that's the law. All Mallory has to do at this point is detail Caricchio's payments as political contributions on his annual disclosure statement and the D.A.'s criminal case is totally hosed. Of course, so is Mallory's political career. That was history the minute Mallory got caught with his hand in Caricchio's pocket."

"So what's the big problem here? Mallory issues a public apology, steps down from the planning commission and that's that."

"Ordinarily that's exactly what would happen but the D.A. is refusing to negotiate because even if he loses, a splashy trial is worth a jump in poll points."

Larkin refilled his wineglass. "Now you know why I went into psychology. Schizophrenia is more predictable than politics."

After Roberto nodded in glum agreement, they sat there sipping dry Chablis, comfortable with silence. It was like that with friends, Roberto thought. There was no compelling need to sustain irrelevant chatter, no fear of the dreaded conversational void. It had been like that with Erica, too, because they had been more than lovers; they'd been friends. Roberto missed that friendship almost as much as he missed her smile, and the silly way the side of her nose crinkled when she laughed.

And God, how he missed those children. Hell, even Buddy had been moping around, sad-eyed and droopy-tailed. Their lives, his and Buddy's, had returned to the dismally quiet, disturbingly organized, damnably boring existence with which they'd once been satisfied. It wasn't enough anymore, for either of them.

Larkin suddenly spoke. "I was just thinking about that time at the Hall, after Tommy was gone and Dev's dad had finally shown up to bail him out. There was only the two of us left, remember?"

"Yeah, I remember. We were so scared, neither of us could pee unless the other one stood guard."

Smiling, Larkin shook his head. "You were the one who was scared to be alone. I had my own demons. I needed to visit Tommy, and explain that I hadn't meant to abandon him. Do you remember what you did to help me out?"

A familiar knot formed in Roberto's gut. "It was no big deal. Let's talk about something else."

"I'd like to talk about this," he said quietly. "It's important to me."

The knot gave a painful twist. Roberto remembered the night in question as clearly as if it had happened hours earlier instead of years. "Sure, okay." Roberto downed his wine with one swallow, then refilled the glass.

Larkin leaned against the booth's tufted backrest, swirling his wine and staring into space. "We planned everything, from how you'd plump pillows under my blanket in case there was a surprise bed check, to timing out the night sentry's routine. You even got hold of a road map with the route to the cemetery all marked out. By the way, I always wondered where you got that map."

"One of the vice chancellors forgot to lock his car. I borrowed it from the glove box."

"Ah, borrowed," Larkin said, exaggerating the word. "And where did you borrow the thirty-five bucks you stuffed in my pocket for cab fare?"

Roberto took another healthy swallow of Chablis. A pleasant numbness tingled along his lips. It wasn't enough. His chest still throbbed; his belly burned with antediluvian fury that had never really healed. "You had a right to say goodbye to Tommy. I wasn't going to let them take that away from you."

Roberto didn't bother to define the ambiguous "them"; both men understood that he was referring to the administrators of Blackthorn Hall. They'd been the enemy, those murderers of children. They'd destroyed lives, butchered young souls. They'd deserved no respect; Roberto had given none.

Across the table, Larkin was regarding him thoughtfully. After a long moment, he said, "You stole that money, didn't you?"

Roberto dismissed that with a flick of his wrist. "Ogden Marlow was a rich pig. A few lousy bucks didn't mean squat to him and you needed it to get to the cemetery and back before dawn." Setting his glass down, Roberto smiled at the memory of how he'd picked old man Marlow's pocket, slick as a whistle, then returned the wallet before the sadistic jerk discovered the damned thing had been missing. Roberto had been proud of himself that day, prouder than he'd ever been before or since. Because he'd done something worthwhile for a brother.

Still, something had always bothered him about that night, a question he'd been afraid to ask at the time because he'd been afraid Larkin might actually consider staying away. Now Roberto took the opportunity to wonder aloud. "I've got to tell you, man, I never could figure out why in hell you came back. If it had been me, I'd have kept on going."

"I was eleven years old, Bobby. Where was I going to go? Besides, there was no way I'd have left you there alone. You were all I had." Larkin propped his chin in his hands. "Would you really have kept on going?"

Smiling, Roberto shook his head. "No, I couldn't have left you alone, either. Without me doing your homework, you wouldn't have made it past the sixth grade."

The anticipated protest never came. Instead, Larkin just gazed sadly across the table. "You're avoiding the point, Bobby. You stole the money."

Roberto's smile faded. "It was a long time ago."

"So that makes it okay?"

"What the hell do you want me to say?"

"I don't want you to say anything. I want you to think, to remember how it feels to be scared, and willing to do anything, even commit a crime, to protect someone you love."

For a moment, Roberto simply stared across the table. Larkin stared back. Roberto finally broke the visual stalemate, focusing on the wineglass he was twirling between his hands. "You think I've misjudged Mallory?"

Larkin steepled his hands in the imperious manner that had always irked hell out of Roberto. "Do you think you've misjudged him?"

"Don't head-shrink me, Lark. I'm the guy who used to hide your sheets after you wet the bed."

"Hmm." Eyes twinkling, Larkin rubbed his chin in a Freudian manner and peered over the top rims of his glasses. "Does that make you feel threatened, Mr. Arroya? Perhaps we should talk about it—"

Roberto threw a napkin at him with an explicit suggestion of how it might be put it to use. They both laughed. The tension was broken. For the next half hour, relaxing over coffee, they joked, chatted, teased each other with good-natured jibes. When the evening was over, Roberto dropped Larkin back at the youth center and drove himself home.

If he'd bothered to turn on the living room lamp, he might not have noticed the frantic red flash on his answering machine. He pressed the button. The machine whirred softly, then Edith Layton's voice hummed from the speaker. "Sorry to call so late but I just heard something from my contact in the D.A.'s office. This afternoon, in the middle of plea negotiations, Ken Mallory collapsed. Heart attack. He's at County General. I thought you'd want to know." There was a pause of several seconds before she added, "I'm sorry, Rob. It doesn't look like he's going to make it."

Chapter Thirteen

The critical care unit was couched behind glass, like an execution chamber. Beyond the windowed wall were five beds, three occupied, all hooked to electronic monitors by a tangle of conduit and cable. Erica's gaze was riveted on the occupant of bed two. If not for the printed label on the footboard, she'd have never recognized that sunken shell of a man as her father. He looked old, gray. Fragile.

Electrodes were fastened to his chest and his temples. Above him, suspended from a stand-alone rod resembling a hat rack, were two plastic fluid bags, the contents of which trickled into a connecting cannula where the medication mingled, allowing a measured dosage to drip steadily into the patient's veins.

At her husband's bedside, Jacqueline gently held the splinted hand into which the I.V. had been inserted. By leaning forward in the wheelchair, her reach was extended so she could caress his cheek or stroke his mussed hair. She hadn't left his side since they'd arrived, nearly five hours ago.

Occasionally the duty nurse would appear at Kenneth's bed to check the monitors and I.V. equipment, then whisper something to Jacqueline, who would clamp her lips together and firmly shake her head. Presumably the nurse had been reminding Jacqueline that ICU visitation was limited to ten minutes per hour, although the staff was thankfully reluctant to enforce those rules. Erica knew her mother would never leave willingly.

Nor would she.

"Erica."

The sound wafted around her like loving arms. It was Roberto's voice, an illusion crafted by her bereaved mind. Closing her eyes, Erica imagined herself ensconced in his consoling embrace, comforted by a touch so tender the mere memory of it melted her heart. She wished he was here; yet knew that he wasn't, that her imagination was playing a cruel trick.

Then she heard it again, his voice calling her name, closer now, from a point just behind her. And when she took a sharp breath, she inhaled his distinctive scent, that unique blend of musky spice that was his alone. Trembling, she raised her gaze and saw his ghostly reflection in the glass.

For a moment, she forgot to breathe. Her fingertips brushed the image, yet she hesitated to turn around, fearing she'd discover that it was nothing more than a trick of light.

"Erica," he said, his voice thick with emotion. "I'm so sorry."

She whirled around and saw Roberto standing there, his eyes dark with genuine sorrow. A sob escaped from somewhere deep inside her as she stumbled into his open arms. Clinging to him, she buried her face against his chest, absorbing his warmth, his comfort. His love. She felt his cheek resting on her head, his breath lifting the feathery hairs at her temple. For the first time since arriving at the hospital, she allowed herself to cry.

He held her, whispering softly, inaudible words of solace that she felt rather than heard. Healing heat from his fingers massaged her quivering muscles, easing the silent terror, warming her to the bone. As she clung to him, needy and frightened, a delicious sense of peace flowed through her veins, a feeling that despite odds to the contrary, everything would be all right.

Roberto brushed his lips over her hair. "How are you holding up?"

With some effort, Erica forced herself to step back from his strength. But not far. Sniffing, she wiped her wet face, grateful that he was still holding her upright. "I'm okay."

"How's your father?"

She bit her lip, angling a glance at the sterile room beyond the glass wall. "He's . . . very ill. It's my fault."

"What?" He grasped her shoulders. "It's nobody's fault, Erica."

"The symptoms have been there for weeks. Fatigue, pallor . . . sometimes he even seemed to have trouble breathing. I should have known. If only I'd said something, forced him to see a doctor—"

"Now, you know better than that. Your father is stubborn as an old mule. I doubt anyone could force him to do anything. Don't take responsibility for this, honey." He tipped her chin up with his thumb. "Besides, taking blame is Carolyn's job, remember?"

His gentle teasing helped relax her. "Ah, yes, my guilt-ridden little martyr. Fortunately, she hasn't taken the rap for her grampa's illness yet, but neither of the girls know how serious it is, either. All I've told them is that he went to the hospital because he wasn't feeling well." Erica glanced through the glass into the ICU unit, wondering if deliberately misleading the children had been a mistake.

Sensing her concern, Roberto answered the unspoken question. "There's no need to worry them," he told her. "You did the right thing."

She gave him a grateful smile before returning her attention to the ashen figure beyond the window. Roberto followed her gaze. From her position beside the bed, Jacqueline slowly looked around, acknowledged Roberto with a thin nod then refocused on her husband.

"Is he asleep?" Roberto asked.

"Yes." At least, Erica hoped that he was, and took comfort from the monitor screens which continued to produce a series of jagged peaks that to the untrained eye appeared benignly rhythmic. "He wakes up every so often and speaks to Mama, then dozes off again."

"I imagine the rest is good for him."

"Yes," she murmured. "I imagine it is. The doctors say that his condition has stabilized. They've scheduled surgery tomorrow morning."

"What kind of surgery?"

"Another bypass. The one he had five years ago is failing." Erica massaged her eyelids, feeling as if she'd swallowed a brick. "According to the cardiologist, Daddy has known for months that he needed more surgery. He didn't tell us because he didn't want us to worry and because... because..." Her throat clogged up and she shook her head, unable to speak.

Roberto slipped an arm around her shoulders, giving her silent strength. After a moment, he brushed his knuckle across her cheek in a loving caress. "Because of what, Erica?"

She took a shuddering breath, rubbed her upper arms and tested her voice. "Because he doesn't have health insurance. It was canceled after Mama's stroke."

"What? That's not legal, Erica. No insurance company can arbitrarily cancel coverage simply because the policy holder submits a legitimate claim. Or several claims, for that matter.''

''I know, but according to Oscar—he's Daddy's lawyer—the company either lost or deliberately refused to cash a premium check then claimed that the policy had lapsed. He's been trying to get it reinstated, threatening to sue and such, but so far the company hasn't budged. When the hospital found out Daddy wasn't covered, Mama had to sign some kind of lien against the house before they'd even admit him.''

Roberto was silent a moment, staring intently at the weakened man behind glass. ''What insurance company are we talking about?''

Erica told him, adding, ''I'm going to make some phone calls tomorrow, although I don't know what I can do. Oscar and Daddy have already tried everything short of filing a lawsuit, which might be our only recourse at this point.''

''Maybe,'' he mumbled, brushing one finger along his jawline in a gesture Erica recognized as one of distraction.

While Roberto was preoccupied with his thoughts, she was lost in her own. How was it, she pondered silently, that he always knew when she needed him? And was always there? ''Are you by any chance clairvoyant?''

He looked up, startled. ''Of course not. Why?''

''I was just wondering how you knew we were here.''

''A colleague called me. She'd gotten the information from someone in the D.A.'s office.'' He cocked his head, scrutinizing her. ''You look perplexed.''

''I am.'' Erica studied him, searching his eyes for any trace of deceit. More than once over the past few days she'd considered the possibility that Roberto had been in cahoots with the district attorney. He had, after all, provided the information that had initiated her father's catastrophic fall from grace. The fact that he was here now indicated that his inside track to goings-on in the D.A.'s office was more than mere speculation—he'd just admitted as much.

Roberto seemed baffled by the intense scrutiny. "Do I have spinach in my teeth?"

She managed a smile. "No. I was just . . . I don't know." Sighing, she rolled her head and absently massaged her aching neck. She was exhausted, drained clear to the bone. "I'm just tired, I guess. Nothing makes sense anymore."

"What exactly doesn't make sense, Erica?"

"It's silly."

He took her shoulders, turning her to face him. "Anything that bothers you, bothers me. Please, tell me what doesn't make sense."

There seemed no reason not to tell him, except that Erica was so emotionally wrung out that she could barely recognize her own name, let alone articulate an obscure intuition that something simply wasn't right. "I'm just confused about everything. For days, McMahon has been on the five o'clock news conducting trial by press conference. Then Daddy has a heart attack—in McMahon's office, of all places—and from what I've heard, our illustrious D.A. was so upset that he had the paramedics use the back elevator and swore everyone else to secrecy. He even sent one of his drones to the hospital to have admission logs reflect an alias instead of Daddy's name. That's peculiar, don't you think? I mean, why would he suddenly be concerned about our family's privacy?"

"He wouldn't," Roberto said, his eyes dark with anger. "McMahon is protecting himself. Unless he has considerably more evidence than I think he has, there's not a snowball's chance in hell that he can win a conviction on the charges he's planning to file. Since the case won't come to trial until after the election, that doesn't matter to him. What does matter is the political boost he'll get by swaying public opinion, touting himself as a bastion against bureaucratic corruption. The last thing he wants now is a sympathy backlash for your father."

Erica didn't want to believe that anyone, even a narcissist like Calvin McMahon, could be so cold. The problem was that she *did* believe it; what's more, she wasn't even shocked. She was numb. "I can't deal with that now," she murmured. "The only thing that matters is for Daddy to get better."

"I know." When he embraced her again, Erica laid her cheek against his shoulder, surrendering to his tenderness.

As he lovingly stroked her hair, Erica's gaze wandered through the glass wall, into the critical care unit where her mother clung so desperately to the man she'd loved for over thirty years. At first glance, one noticed only a stoic woman at her husband's bedside. A more vigilant look revealed the raw panic in Jacqueline's eyes. She was, Erica realized, alone in her agony, the private hell of watching a part of yourself die and being helpless to save it.

For decades, Jacqueline Mallory had by her own definition been an extension of her husband, completely dependent and happily so. There had never been a deeper love than that shared by Erica's parents; they needed each other so desperately that she feared neither could survive without the other. If love was so wonderful, she wondered, how could it cause so much pain?

Falling in love was so easy. A heart swollen with happiness, a world revolving around that special person without whom life would seem meaningless. Cocooned in loving arms, it was so simple to assume that the glow would never fade. But it would. It had to. Nothing was forever. And when disaster finally struck, through betrayal or loss or rejection, the pain would come. Unbearable pain.

"Erica, what's wrong?"

At the sound of Roberto's voice, she realized that she was stiff as a broomstick. She backed away, unable to identify the source of her sudden trepidation. "I was, ah, just thinking about the surgery." Her cheeks heated at the lie, because that's certainly what she should have been thinking about. "The doctor is optimistic, of course, but any surgery is risky."

"The commissioner is a tough old bird," Roberto said firmly, although his eyes reflected Erica's doubt. "I'm sure he'll come through fine."

She nodded, stepping even farther away so he couldn't melt her shaky resolve with his touch.

A subdued expression conveyed that her withdrawal had been duly noted. Thankfully, he didn't comment on it. "What time is the surgery scheduled?"

"Seven a.m."

"You should try to get some sleep," he said, gesturing toward a nearby waiting room. "I'll wake you in time." When her head snapped up in surprise, he added, "You didn't think I'd let you go through this alone, did you?"

A peculiar panic rippled to her toes. She desperately wanted him there; and that desperation was what terrified her. "It's not necessary for you to stay. Really."

"I want to."

"Please." She turned away, clasping her hands. This was something she had to get through on her own. She couldn't need Roberto, couldn't need anyone, or the inner strength that she'd gained since leaving Carter would evaporate like so much steam. If she allowed herself to love Roberto, she'd become an extension of him, just another frantic woman too weak to face life on her own terms. Eventually she'd become a clone of her mother, who was now facing the loss of a love that had been her reason for living. "I think it would be best if you leave."

The silence was deafening. She could feel his acute gaze on the back of her neck. "All right," he said finally. "If that's what you want."

"It is." Another lie. God, how they rolled off her tongue now.

"Where are the girls?" he asked.

"One of my mother's neighbors is taking care of them."

"What's the address? I'll pick them up."

She spun around. "Why?"

The vehement question startled him. "I thought it would be less stressful for them to be in familiar surroundings and carry on a normal routine. They're comfortable at my place and in the morning, I'll take Cathy to day care and drive Carolyn to school."

"That's too much of an imposition."

"Not at all." His voice softened. "Besides, I've missed them."

"They've missed you, too." Erica closed her eyes, gathered her courage, then looked straight at him. "They care deeply for you, Roberto, and that's the problem. I don't want them to love you."

Erica would rather have taken a bullet than see the pain in his eyes. "Yes," he murmured. "I can see that."

"Please, try to understand—"

He laid a fingertip against her lips, silencing her. "I do understand." He gazed into her eyes, as if wanting to say something more. In the end, he simply lifted her hand, brushed his lips across her palm, then released her quickly, strode down the hallway and was gone.

Erica stood there, her heart as empty as the deserted hall. Rationally, she believed that she'd been right to protect her children from the possibility of yet another rejection, another devastating disappointment.

It never occurred to her that she was also protecting herself.

There was a red moon that night. Bloodred.

Roberto stared into his glass, swirling the whiskey he'd poured an hour earlier and hadn't yet tasted. It had been years since he'd felt such an exquisite sense of loss; perhaps not since the day Tommy had died.

All his life, Roberto had been searching for an elusive shadow that, although indefinable, had always hovered just beyond his reach. With Erica and the girls, he'd finally found what he'd been seeking and had even discovered that it had a name: Love.

That discovery, monumental as it was, had been made too late. Erica would never forgive him for what he'd done to her father. Roberto hadn't really expected she would. After all, forgiveness had never been a part of his life. It was, in his experience, seldom given, rarely received, almost never deserved.

Certainly, he didn't deserve Erica's forgiveness, not after having so blatantly betrayed her trust. Regardless of his reasoning at the time, nothing could change the fact that by turning that tape over to the district attorney, Roberto had set in motion the entire chain of events that might, God forbid, culminate in her father's death.

And for what? Some hypothetical professional ethic that grants no license for circumstance yet allows a man like McMahon free rein to destroy lives?

A secret corner of his mind issued the answer. Anger, not ethic, had compelled him to turn over that tape without offering Mallory an opportunity to explain. Roberto had prejudged Mallory as just another power-mad bureaucrat like Ogden Marlow.

And that was the crux of the matter, he decided. The underlying motivation of his morality, the holy grail of his ruthless standards could be traced back to that one defining event of his life: Tommy Murdock's death.

In retrospect, he realized that trauma had implanted the seed of vengeance but his own secret fury had allowed that seed to germinate and grow. He'd become the Brotherhood's avenger, meting out his own brand of justice like the comic book heroes he'd revered as a child.

But somewhere along the way, he'd become a caricature of that which he held in such high esteem. Because he'd lost sight of his humanity, he hadn't recognized a man willing to give up everything, including his own life, to protect the people he loved most.

Yes, Kenneth Mallory had made a mistake, a big one. Thankfully, timing had prevented that critical lapse in judgment from becoming a criminal offense. Caricchio's project was already scheduled for future action by the planning commission but Mallory hadn't had a chance to cast the favorable vote that would validate what was now only suspicion—that the county's planning commissioner was in cahoots with a known racketeer.

The sofa vibrated as Buddy hopped up and laid his chin on Roberto's thigh. *"Hola, mi amigo,"* he murmured, absently stroking the prickly head.

Buddy returned the greeting with a soft whine. Then his ears perked and he anxiously sniffed his master's hand, which had absorbed Erica's scent earlier in the evening. The dog wagged his shaggy tail and barked.

Roberto set the whiskey glass aside. "No, she won't be back. I blew it big time, Buddy-boy. Erica and the girls are gone for good."

The dog's tail stiffened and dropped to the cushion like a dead snake. He bared his teeth, growling low in his throat.

"I know, I know." Slouching down, Roberto let his head loll against the back cushion and shaded his eyes with his arm. "I should have at least talked to Mallory and found out what was going on before I decided what to do with that damned tape. But I screwed up and now McMahon's on a blood trail. At this very moment, the D.A. and his henchmen are probably huddled over a stack of election polls trying to put their own spin on Mallory's illness before the press gets wind of it."

Seeming disgusted, Buddy circled the sofa and flopped down facing away from his master.

Alerted by the dipping cushion, Roberto peeked out from beneath his raised arm just as Buddy presented his rear. *"Et tu?* I thought dogs were supposed to be loyal, no matter what.''

Without lifting his whiskered chin from the mattress, Buddy grumbled under his breath, then heaved a pained sigh and fell silent.

Roberto had been soundly snubbed.

Not that he blamed the dog. By botching every decision, Roberto had grappled with a bad situation and created one a hell of a lot worse. Even though Mallory had been ill long before his Caricchio connection had hit the proverbial fan, there was no doubt that pressure from the indictment and subsequent feeding frenzy by the media had exacerbated his heart condition.

At this point, Roberto firmly believed that McMahon planned to turn the heat up even higher. Should Mallory survive the surgery, the emotional strain of continued harassment and public humiliation might kill him. Guilty or not, accepting a bribe was not now and never had been a capital offense.

But if McMahon was prepared to issue a death sentence, Roberto wasn't. He picked up the telephone.

Two days later, the *Los Angeles Times* carried Devon Monroe's first installment of a series detailing Kenneth Mallory's tragic quest to save his family. Erica read it at the hospital, as her father recovered from the surgery which, according to doctors, had gone exceedingly well.

The article began with a chronological diary of Mallory's career in public service, which highlighted some of his most remarkable achievements: lobbying for and receiving federal grants to renovate public housing projects; establishing headstart programs in neighborhood schools; his fervent campaign to subsidize community day care for working mothers; and the dozens of fund-raisers he'd spearheaded on behalf of local charities.

After several paragraphs of glowing praise, the column then recounted how a series of misfortunes, each compounding the other, had turned a proud man into a desperate one. Kenneth Mallory's past mistakes were also delineated in unflinching detail; but the groundwork already laid gave the reader a sense of empathy for a man driven to the brink of despair by circumstances beyond his control.

The first time Erica read it, she was too shocked to feel anything at all. The second time, grateful tears seeped into her eyes. By the third reading, she cried openly. After all the bitter accusations and public humiliation her father had endured, Erica was touched to the core by an article that was a candid, yet respectful overview of the facts as this particular journalist saw them.

The author of the piece had obviously done his homework. Those details with which Erica was familiar were precise and factual. Some specifics, such as the mention of her father's investment losses during a stock market crash and how he'd been forced to personally finance defense of a lawsuit filed by disgruntled developers unhappy with zoning laws, were a complete surprise. Erica suspected, however, that those previously obscure facts, if as scrupulously researched as the rest of the article, were probably as accurate.

What affected Erica most deeply, however, was the byline. Devon Monroe was one of Roberto's closest friends. There was little doubt in her mind that the frequently quoted "informed source" was, in fact, Roberto himself.

He must have paid a heavy price for having leaked such information, a price far beyond having put his own career at risk. In the past, he'd segregated society based on his own definition of good and evil; now that invisible line had begun to blur. For the first time since Erica had known him,

perhaps even for the first time in his life, Roberto Arroya
had accepted that the worth of a person isn't wholly defined by one act, but by the aggregate comport of their lives.

It was a profound message; but perhaps one sent too late.

Chapter Fourteen

Erica tapped on the master bedroom door. "Mama, are you ready?"

"Almost, dear," came the cheery reply. "Come in." The wheelchair hummed across the room, stopping in front of a vanity covered by cut crystal atomizers and extravagant imported perfumes. Jacqueline scrutinized her reflection in the antique framed mirror, checking her makeup and patting her perfectly coiffed hair. When her daughter's reflection appeared over her shoulder, she smiled brightly. "Where are the girls?"

"Having breakfast. Can I help you with anything... zippers, jewelry clasps?"

"No, thank you. Everything is under control. I just need a little more lipstick, I think. Your father hates it when I look pale. You know how men are." She gave Erica a conspiratorial grin and proceeded to dig through a cache of gold-toned cylinders until she located a shade that appealed to her.

As Jacqueline carefully applied the lip color, Erica noted that her mother's right hand now exhibited almost as much agility, if not the same strength, as did her left. Her progress over the past couple of weeks had been nothing short of astonishing. "I know I've said this a dozen times before, but I can't help myself. You are absolutely incredible. Sometimes I wonder if there's any limit to your capabilities."

"None whatsoever. Over the years I've learned that as a species, humans are highly adaptable and infinitely clever." Jacqueline returned the lipstick to its place on the vanity. "Oh, by the way, dear, would you please ask the girls to put their breakfast bowls in the dishwasher? The realtor will be showing the house this morning."

Erica's stomach tightened at the reminder that despite a groundswell of public support generated by the *Times* articles, her parents were still being forced to relinquish their home. "Don't you think that opening the house should be put off for a little while. I mean, Daddy's coming home today and seeing strangers traipsing through the hallways might upset him."

Her gaze met her mother's in the mirror. Jacqueline studied her daughter's reflection, then pressed the control button. The chair whirred and swung around. "Sit down, dear. I get crick in my neck looking up all the time."

Recognizing her mother's "we need to talk" expression, Erica dutifully perched on the foot of her parents' bed. "Why do I feel as if I'm about to be lectured?"

Jacqueline chuckled. "Oh, my. I had no idea you considered our lovely mother-daughter chats to be lectures."

Smiling at the memory of the hours she and her mother had spent in this very room contemplating her own adolescent angst, Erica felt herself relaxing. "I guess I had a flashback to my teenaged years when I considered the phrase *good morning* as an unacceptable directive."

"Those were challenging times, weren't they?" Jacqueline heaved a wistful sigh. "I rather miss them."

"You're joking, of course. From the day I reached puberty, I gave you nothing but heartache and worry. Sometimes I wonder how you overcame the temptation to strangle me in my sleep."

"Your father stopped me. He insisted you'd grow out of it. As always, he was right." Her amused twinkle faded. "Heartache and worry are all part of love, Erica. You'll learn that as the girls grow older. They'll give you grief, not because they want to, but because they can't help it. As children, it's their job to grow and explore the world, despite our desire to protect them at every turn. Our children bring fear into our lives, true, but they also bring infinite joy. So you see, Erica, a life without love may be safer, but it's only half a life."

Avoiding her mother's earnest gaze, Erica made a production of smoothing tiny wrinkles from the goose down comforter on which she was sitting. Although Jacqueline had deliberately avoided mentioning Roberto's name, there was little doubt as to the underlying message of her final comment. "I thought I'd made it clear that my love life, or lack thereof, is not up for discussion."

"Why, Erica, you've misunderstood. I was simply reminiscing. As for Mr. Arroya—"

"Mother, please."

Jacqueline held up an imperious hand and continued as if her daughter hadn't just flushed to her scalp. "As for Mr. Arroya, if you wish to ignore a man who quite obviously adores you, that's very much your business. Apparently you enjoy loneliness and are looking forward to spending your life as a sexually deprived, withered old prune."

Covering her eyes, Erica moaned and shook her head. "You amaze me, Mama, you really do. Most parents would be pleased as punch that their children had learned enough from past mistakes not to repeat them."

"Roberto Arroya is a man of honor, as different from Carter Franklin as day is from night."

"Yes, but I'm the same as I've always been. If I wasn't good enough for Carter, who had no standards whatsoever, I can't possibly live up to the expectations of a man with Roberto's implacable ideals." Ignoring her mother's stunned expression, Erica hurried on. "Sooner or later, I'd disappoint him. I couldn't live with that, Mama. It would break my heart."

"Oh, Erica." Biting her lip, Jacqueline reached out and took her daughter's hand. "It requires two people to make a marriage but only one to break it. Carter destroyed your marriage all by himself. He never wanted the responsibility of a family. I doubt he even wanted the responsibility of being an adult. In every way that counted, Carter was a spoiled child when you married him. From what I see, that hasn't changed, although you certainly can't blame yourself for his failings."

"I don't, not really." Frustrated, unable to dislodge the obscure terror dwelling deep inside her, Erica struggled to express what she didn't fully understand. "It's just that I have to consider the children's feelings. They've already been rejected once. Carolyn is especially vulnerable. She's suffered so much already. I can't put either of the girls in a position where that could happen all over again."

Jacqueline studied her daughter's face for a moment. "Don't you really mean that you can't put yourself in that position again? Don't use your children as an excuse for your own lack of courage, Erica. I raised you better than that."

Erica's hand froze against the soft comforter. She looked up, stunned by the accusation.

Her mother's stern expression melted instantly. "That was cruel, I know, and I'm sorry if I've hurt you. Perhaps it's none of my business, but since we've all been under the same roof these past weeks, I haven't been able to help noticing that you and the children are miserable. Every time the girls mention Mr. Arroya, you become instantly morose and change the subject. That's not really fair, you know. Since the children will ultimately be affected by your choices, don't you think they're at least entitled to express their opinions? Quite frankly, dear, I doubt they'd be as frightened of the possibilities as you seem to be.''

Erica just sat there, gaping, as her mother reached out to pat her knee. ''But I digress,'' Jacqueline said, slipping back into a more chipper mood. ''This was supposed to be a conversation about how difficult it is for all of us to let go of a place that holds so many memories. The memories will always live in our hearts, Erica. This house is much too big for your father and me now. It's time for us to move on. Kenneth has accepted that. I hope you will, too.''

Somehow, Erica managed to stammer that she would, then added, ''It was you that Daddy and I were worried about. You've always loved this house.''

With a dreamy smile, Jacqueline gazed wistfully around the elegant master suite. ''Yes, it is beautiful, isn't it? I've loved living here. But the house was never as important to me as the people I shared it with. As long our family was together, I would have been happy in a one-room flat.''

Oddly enough, Erica not only believed that, she understood it completely. No structure, regardless of sentimental or monetary value, was worth even a single lost moment with a loved one. Through the power of modern medicine and the grace of God, her parents had been given the greatest gift of all—more time together. Nothing else mattered. ''I know how much you've missed Daddy. You must be so thrilled now that he's coming home.''

''I can hardly wait.'' She indulged in a girlish giggle before rearranging her features into a subdued, matriarchal countenance perfected by years of parenting. ''Of course, he'll continue to require a great deal of rest and quiet to continue his recovery.''

Erica agreed with a nod.

''Well, then, I hope you'll understand . . .'' Allowing the thought to linger a moment, Jacqueline rubbed her hands together, her brow furrowed in a distracted frown. Finally she sighed and blurted, "I've appreciated all your help, Erica, but it's time for you and the children to get back to your own lives."

With a double take that under other circumstances might have been comical, Erica found herself sputtering. "You want us to leave?"

"If you wouldn't mind."

"I guess not . . . I mean, if you're sure."

"I think it best." Beaming, Jacqueline hit the control and the chair hummed backward. "Then it's settled. You and the girls can gather up your things and be tucked snug as bugs in your own little house by supper time."

"But what about Daddy?" Erica blurted, completely bewildered by the sudden eviction.

Jacqueline paused at the doorway. "What about him?"

"Well, it's going to take time for him to regain his strength. He'll need a lot of care and attention."

"Are you implying that I'm incapable of supplying that?"

"Oh, Mama, of course not. But there's so much work to do—"

"I'll manage," she interrupted with a cheerful grin. "Besides, you've given up quite enough, I think. It's time for you to get back to your own life."

Erica studied her mother's self-satisfied expression and decided that something was definitely amiss. This was a woman who, until five minutes ago, couldn't seem to get enough time with her daughter and grandchildren. She had, in fact, been known to drop sly hints about how wonderful it would be if Erica and the girls would actually move in with them permanently. Of course, the reality of sharing living space with two exuberant youngsters might have put a damper on that enthusiasm . . . but Erica doubted it. If anything, their close proximity appeared to have brought both Jacqueline and Kenneth even more joy.

The unceremonious ouster simply didn't make sense. Unless, of course, Jacqueline had another motive for wanting Erica back in her old neighborhood. Roberto's neighborhood.

"Mama?"

Jacqueline looked up expectantly. "Yes, Erica?"

"You're not trying to push Roberto and I back together again, are you?"

"Me?" She laid a hand against her heart, appearing genuinely shocked. "Why, Erica. However could you think such a thing?" Jacqueline pressed the control and cruised into the hallway with an indignant expression and a crafty gleam in her eye.

That day turned out to be exceptionally busy. After dropping the girls at school and day care respectively, Erica dashed to the shop for a few hours, then headed out to drive her parents home from the hospital.

After Kenneth was comfortably ensconced on a makeshift bed in the family room, Erica dragged upstairs to pack their belongings. Despite the grueling pace, her thoughts frequently wandered back to the morning's conversation with her mother. Jacqueline had accused Erica of cowardice, of using her children as an excuse to avoid the call of her own heart.

At first, Erica had dismissed the charge as ludicrous; later, however, she'd wondered if her mother might have a point. Of course, Erica's concern for her children was genuine; but so was her own fear of suffering another loss, another agonizing rejection. As she mulled that bothersome concept, she considered the possibility, remote as it seemed, that one mistake didn't necessarily preclude the possibility of a second chance. Her mother's doomed first marriage came to mind. What would have happened, Erica wondered, if Mama had been so shattered by failure that she'd turned Daddy away? The thought was frightening.

Eventually Erica accepted the sad fact that breaking off the relationship with Roberto truly had been at least partially motivated on her own deep-seated anxieties. If that was the case, perhaps cowardice had been an apt description after all.

As she continued to contemplate the conversation with her mother, one particularly haunting phrase was most troublesome. *A life without love is only half a life.*

The words became an obsession, a continuous whisper in the back of her mind, teasing her, chiding her, forcing her to examine her own motivation in bitter detail. In the end, that phrase stuck to her heart as she made the decision that would change her life forever.

Surrounded by untidy stacks of legal reference volumes, Roberto hunched over his kitchen table studying a court brief that was dry as a California summer. Once, he'd have immersed himself in legal minutiae, exulting in the complexities of form and substance. At the moment, however, he was unable to focus and quite frankly was bored out of his skull.

Frustrated, he tossed down the red pen and leaned back until the chair balanced on two legs. His eyes burned. Rubbing them, he discovered, made the burning even more intense. He glanced at the sink, wondering if a splash of cold water would help. Before he could make a move, Buddy slammed through the doggy door, yelping frantically, and nearly knocked the chair over.

"What the—" Roberto grabbed the table, righting the chair with a jarring thunk while the hysterical animal circled the table with a sniveling whine that grated his master's already raw nerves. Pushing away from the table, Roberto glared down at the agitated mutt. "What the hell is wrong with you?"

Buddy barked loud enough to roust a corpse before dashing out of the kitchen. Roberto heard the mad scratching of doggy toenails on the front door just as the bell rang. He swore under his breath. The last thing he was in the mood for was a vacuum salesman or anyone else for that matter.

Stomping into the living room, he snapped "Get down" at the pawing dog, who blithely ignored the command and continued a zealous attempt to scratch his way through the wooden door. Thoroughly peeved, Roberto yanked the door open, prepared to send the trespasser packing. Instead he simply stood there, gaping, not sure his mind could believe what his eyes were seeing.

There, flanked by her two beautiful children, was Erica Franklin holding a bow-studded cheese basket and wearing an uncertain smile. "Hi."

It was the last thing she said before Buddy pushed by his master's legs, dived outside and was instantly beset upon by the two screeching girls. In less than a heartbeat, the entire porch erupted into a frenzy of giggles and barks.

Oblivious to the joyous bedlam, Roberto's gaze was locked on Erica's face, the face that had haunted his dreams since the day he'd first laid eyes on it. She moistened her lips, cleared her throat and managed to make herself heard above the din. "Things have gone, well, kind of wrong between us. I was hoping that we might be able to put all that behind us and start over again." She held out the basket, a duplicate of the gift she'd brought on her first visit, and took a shaky breath. "Hello, Mr. Arroya. My name is Erica Franklin. I'm your new neighbor."

Roberto tried twice to reach for the basket before his numbed limbs finally responded and he was able to accept it. "Thank you, Ms....Franklin, was it?"

Her smile was brighter than the setting sun. "Please, call me Erica."

They stood there, gazes locked with smoldering intensity until Carolyn, who'd been hugging Buddy so hard his eyes bulged, suddenly released the gasping animal and threw her arms around Roberto's waist. "Mr. 'Roya, Mr. 'Roya, guess what? We stayed with Gramma for a long time, 'cause my grampa's heart *attacked* him!"

Shifting the basket to one arm, Roberto squatted down to the child's level. "Is your grampa feeling better now?"

Her eyes were huge with excitement. "Uh-huh. He came home today and we made him a really neat bed downstairs so he could watch Gramma cook supper."

"I'm glad to hear that, sweetheart."

"And guess what else?" She sucked an enormous breath, clasped her hands under her chin and quivered with anticipation.

Roberto couldn't stop himself from affectionately stroking her cheek. "There's more?"

The air rushed from her lungs all at once. "We get to sleep in our own beds tonight and Mommy says we get to stay in our own house *forever.*"

"Forever? My, that's a pretty long time."

Cathy toddled through the doorway. "Can I please have a cookie?"

Erica hastened to correct the child's manners. "Cathy, that's impolite."

"But I said 'please.'"

"That doesn't matter," Carolyn added helpfully. "You're not ever s'posed to ask."

"But I want a cookie!"

Carolyn jammed her fists on her hips. "Well, you can't have one."

"Can too."

"Can not."

"Can *too!*"

At Cathy's final screech, Buddy flattened on his belly with his paws crossed over his head. Erica, obviously frazzled, slid Roberto an "excuse me" smile before dispensing an explanation of proper etiquette to the thwarted youngster, who folded her fat arms and stuck out her lip in a pout so adorable that Roberto burst into uncontrollable laughter.

Three pairs of startled eyes—four, if one counted Buddy's—swung in his direction. Roberto just sat back on his haunches, clung to the stupid cheese basket and howled all the harder. He knew that Erica was staring at him as though he'd lost his mind, and maybe he had, but he couldn't help himself. It was the chaos, that delightful pandemonium of arguing kids and a barking dog and a frustrated mother trying to explain the unexplainable to a totally unreceptive child . . . it was simply too wonderful.

Eventually, he was able to wipe his watery eyes and choke out enough words to indicate that the kids could, indeed, help themselves to cookies. Cathy scuttled toward the kitchen without so much as a thank-you-kindly but as Roberto started to stand, Carolyn suddenly latched on to his neck and hugged him tightly enough to cut off his air supply. "I love you," she whispered.

Then she planted a moist kiss on his cheek and scampered after her sister, with Buddy following right on her heels.

The sweet gesture and loving words touched Roberto so deeply that his heart swelled like a balloon and his chest felt so full he could barely breathe. His eyes burned again, this time from a rush of emotional tears that embarrassed the hell out of him.

Ducking his head, he stood, swung around to place the basket on the coffee table and swiped at his moist eyelids before turning to face Erica. "So, your father's home from the hospital?"

Her eyes looked a little red around the edges, too. She issued a nervous cough. "Ah…yes. The doctors say that he's making a remarkable recovery. But you already knew that, didn't you? According to the floor nurses, you've called nearly every day to check on his progress."

"It seemed the least I could do, considering the role I played in putting him there."

Erica reached out as if to stroke his cheek, but pulled back without touching him, then folded her arms. "None of this was your fault, Roberto. You had no choice in what you did. I was wrong to have implied otherwise."

"I had other choices," he whispered, looking away. "Although admittedly, I didn't recognize that at the time. I know it probably doesn't matter now, but I wish I'd done things differently."

"I know you do." A gentle tremor in her voice gave him courage to meet her gaze. There was empathy in her lovely eyes, and something deeper. "I also know that when you realized my father was being unfairly persecuted, you took a tremendous professional risk to even the playing field."

He hesitated, chilled by the implication that she, or anyone else, might actually recognize that he'd leaked the information that had been the basis for Devon's story. "I don't know what you mean."

"Come on, Roberto. Since it was your childhood buddy who wrote those newspaper articles, it hardly takes a rocket scientist to figure out who his 'informed source' was. As a matter of fact, I found the passages portraying the proud grampa teaching his granddaughter to ride her birthday bike particularly enlightening, since you were the only person outside the family to observe that particular ritual." She gave him a wink and a sly grin. "Don't worry. You're secret is certainly safe with me. As for Mr. Monroe, journalistic ethics require him to spend life in prison rather than reveal a source."

"Are you kidding? At the first hint of a contempt charge, Devon would throw his notes at the judge, complete with my name, address and beeper number."

Erica's expression grew serious. "What you did took a lot of courage. I'm grateful to you."

Sighing, he raked his hair. "Don't put me on a pedestal, Erica. I don't deserve it. Believe me, I never intended to subvert the judicial process. I've always believed, and still do, that your father, like everyone else, should answer for his mistakes. The only reason I reacted was because the district attorney was making a mockery of the law to push his own personal agenda." He angled a wary glance and was relieved to see no anger in Erica's eyes.

Instead, she nodded calmly. "I understand that."

"You do?"

"Yes. But that doesn't negate the fact that you were willing to put your own career on the line and risk everything for a cause you believed in." She licked her lips again, and absently plucked a loose thread on the cuff of her emerald print blouse. "Daddy regrets what has happened and is willing to accept full responsibility for what he's done. He's resigned from the planning commission, of course, and has made arrangements to pay back all the money he received from Mr. Caricchio. In return, the district attorney has been kind enough to drop the charges."

Roberto issued a disgusted snort. "McMahon never had enough evidence to win a conviction in the first place. Besides, only when his office was besieged by indignant letters supporting your father did our illustrious D.A. conclude that his political aspirations wouldn't be served by further annoying his constituents. Don't confuse a snake for a fat worm just because it doesn't strike every time it has the chance. It's still a damned snake."

Erica studied him thoughtfully. "So, does that mean Daddy can keep Caricchio's money?"

It took a moment before he recognized the amused gleam in her eyes. "Sure, why not? Where Caricchio's going, he won't have much use for it. At least not for the next fifty-plus years."

Smiling, Erica slipped her hands into her slacks pockets and poked a piece of carpet fuzz with the toe of her shoe. "I don't think that matters to Daddy. All he wants now is to wipe the slate clean and start over."

"Good for him." Taking her cue, Roberto, too, stuffed his hands in his pockets. That way, he wouldn't be tempted to take her in his arms and kiss her senseless. "How about us, Erica? Should we wipe the slate clean and start over?"

Still studying the carpet, she shrugged. "Is that really what you want? To start over, I mean."

"No."

She peeked up, startled, then quickly lowered her gaze. "Oh."

"What I really want is for us to pick up where we left off."

This time, she lifted her head and studied him without flinching. "And where would we go from there?"

"To the next step, I suppose."

"Which is?"

"Well…" He hooked a finger in his collar and tugged his tie loose. "I guess the next step would be for me to, ah, confess that I—" cough "—love you."

He felt, rather than heard, her soft gasp. "Do you? Love me, that is."

"I, ah, think that's what I said."

"I want to hear it again."

Roberto felt his neck heat. "Look, I've never said those words in my life and now you want me to say them twice in one minute?"

"Yes, please."

"All right." Squaring his shoulders, he looked her straight in the eye as the words slid out as if his tongue had been greased. "I love you, Erica, more than I could have ever believed possible. You've changed me, made me a better person, because somehow you've burrowed your way inside and become part of me. I don't know how it happened, but it did and I couldn't change it if I wanted to. I love you with all my heart and I think—I hope—that you feel the same way about me."

He paused, his pulse racing, awaiting her reply. All he received from her was a weak sniffle as matching tear tracks moistened her cheeks. "Hey, feel free to jump in any time here," he said. She dug through her pocket for a tissue. He shifted nervously. "Any time at all, just speak right up. Tell me how you feel."

She dabbed her wet face. "I feel . . . wonderful."

He frowned. "Perhaps I should have been more specific. I was inquiring as to how you felt about me."

"About you?" She tucked the damp tissue back into her pocket. "Well, let's see now, you tend to be a bit uptight on occasion and although most people might be disconcerted by your habit of arguing with a dog, I think it's rather quaint. Besides, human perfection can be rather boring, don't you think? And certainly no one could ever accuse you of being boring . . . or perfect, for that matter.''

"Erica—"

"On the other hand, no one could ever accuse me of those things either, so all things being equal—although things are rarely equal, of course—"

"Erica, please!"

"The only possible conclusion is that I must be in love with you, too."

"For crying out loud, Erica—" Roberto stiffened. "What did you say?"

"That I love you," she whispered, laying a warm palm against his cheek. "And I will love you for the rest of my life."

Seven weeks later, Roberto and Erica were married in a picturesque chapel overlooking the Pacific Ocean. The occasion was captured on film by Devon Monroe, who was assisted in his role as official photographer by his lovely wife, Jessica. Larkin McKay served as best man; Marge, The Sandwich Shoppe's new assistant manager, was matron of honor.

A radiant Jacqueline Mallory descended the aisle on her own two feet, aided only by an usher's arm and a carved teakwood cane. The flower girls performed admirably, despite Carolyn having executed her duties with such enthusiasm that half the guests were showered by fragrant petals and poor Cathy, struck by an unexpected bout of stage fright, ducked her head, clutched the basket like a football and charged down the aisle without so much as a glance at the amused congregation.

Erica was ravishingly beautiful, a vision in white lace and seed pearls, who seemed to float down the aisle on a pillow of air. After giving his daughter away, Kenneth sat beside his wife, grinning with pride.

As Roberto took his bride's hand, murmuring the words that would bind them forever, his soul was at peace. Through Erica's love, his heart had been drained of destructive anger.

For Roberto Arroya, the Blackthorn legacy had ended.

*   *   *   *   *

Watch for THE REFORMER,
the final book in Diana Whitney's
***BLACKTHORN BROTHERHOOD** mini-series,*
coming in 1996, only from
Silhouette Special Edition.

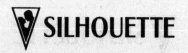

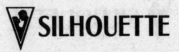

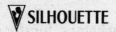

▼ SILHOUETTE

>SPECIAL EDITION<

COMING NEXT MONTH

D IS FOR DANI'S BABY Lisa Jackson

That Special Woman! & Love Letters

She'd been forced to give them up—baby and father. Now Brandon was back and Dani was determined to find her child. Would Brandon forgive her for keeping their baby from him?

MORGAN'S WIFE Lindsay McKenna

Morgan's Mercenaries

Jim Woodward volunteered to save an old flame who'd been abducted, but he didn't plan on taking a partner—certainly not a *woman*! Pepper Sinclair was just going to be a dangerous distraction!

STRONG ARMS OF THE LAW Dallas Schulze

When Kate Sloane agreed to testify as a witness for the state, she had no idea she'd become a voluntary hostage to a sexy stranger who was armed and dangerous…

A MAN AND A MILLION Jackie Merritt

When Theodora Hunter inherited a large fortune, she suddenly became one sought-after lady. One man offered her security but it was the town's bad boy who really had Theo's pulse racing!

THIS CHILD IS MINE Trisha Alexander

She'd grown up poor but now Eve was successful beyond her wildest dreams. Reunited with the man who'd walked out of her life years ago, she couldn't help wondering about the child he never knew he had…

AND FATHER MAKES THREE Laurie Campbell

Sarah Corcoran had enough trouble raising her rebellious nephew. She didn't need Ryan—the man who'd seduced her twin sister years ago—making her job any more difficult. Not even if he was the boy's father!

the exciting new series by
New York Times **bestselling author**

Nora Roberts

The MacKade Brothers—looking for trouble, and always finding it. Now they're on a collision course with love. And it all begins with

**THE RETURN OF RAFE MacKADE
(Silhouette Sensation, March 1996)**

Be on the lookout for the next book in the series, **THE PRIDE OF JARED MacKADE**—**Silhouette Special Edition's 1000th book!** It's an extra-special event not to be missed, coming your way in May 1996.

THE MacKADE BROTHERS—these sexy, trouble-loving men will be heading out to you from Silhouette Sensation and Silhouette Special Edition alternately. Watch out for them!

SILHOUETTE

Desire

COMING NEXT MONTH

WILDCAT Rebecca Brandewyne

Man of the Month

Morgan McCain hadn't wanted a new partner, but he couldn't afford to buy Cat Devlin's shares. So he was going to have to live with her and like it!

A WOLF IN THE DESERT BJ James

Men of the Black Watch

Matthew Winter Sky had rescued Patience O'Hara from a gang of lawless drifters, but he knew she was jeopardizing the success of his mission. What could he do with her now he had her?

THE COWBOY TAKES A LADY Cindy Gerard

When Sara Stewart propositioned him, sexy rancher Tucker Lambert surprised both of them by turning her down. Almost any man would have done, Sara hadn't really wanted *him* and, for the first time, that was important to Tucker.

A WIFE IN TIME Cathie Linz

Spellbound

Somehow Susannah Hall and Kane Wilder had been transported back in time and were posing as man and wife. Susannah had old-fashioned values, while Kane was wrestling with old-fashioned lust...

THE BACHELOR'S BRIDE Audra Adams

Rachel Morgan was having a baby by a wealthy, powerful man—a man she couldn't even *remember*! A man who wanted to be her husband!

THE ROGUE AND THE RICH GIRL
Christine Pacheco

Nicole Jackson hired Ace Lawson to take her where she needed to go, but she hadn't planned on being stuck with him. He might be able to teach her about life, although he knew nothing about true love...

▼ SILHOUETTE
Sensation

COMING NEXT MONTH

THE ONLY WAY OUT Susan Mallery

Andie Cochran had escaped the clutches of her ruthless ex-husband
until he abducted the child she loved more than life itself. Now she had
no one to turn to except another very dangerous man—a man who
awakened passions she'd thought long dead…

But she had no choice; she had to rescue her child.

REGARDING REMY Marilyn Pappano

Southern Knights

Remy Sinclair thought he'd found the perfect potential wife. She was
everything he wanted—apart from the secret he was determined to
uncover. With her brother's life in jeopardy, Susannah had to spy on
Remy. But could she really choose between the lives of her brother and
her lover?

KAT Linda Turner

The Rawlings Family

Lucas Valentine was a hard man, who had learnt never to trust a
woman—and that went double for the headstrong lady rancher who
was his new boss. He was going to keep his distance from her whatever
it took because she had a way of keeping a man lying awake night after
empty night…

THE RETURN OF RAFE MACKADE Nora Roberts

The MacKade Brothers

The town was buzzing over Rafe's return. He was as handsome and
reckless as ever. Would newcomer Regan Bishop be impervious to the
legendary MacKade charm?

Look for the second novel in this wonderful mini-series from
Nora Roberts in Silhouette Special Edition in May. THE PRIDE OF
JARED MACKADE is a very special book, which is fitting as its
the 1,000th Special Edition!

FREE

Return this coupon and we'll send you 4 Silhouette Special Editions and a mystery gift absolutely FREE! We'll even pay the postage and packing for you.

We're making you this offer to introduce you to the benefits of Reader Service: FREE home delivery of brand-new Silhouette romances, at least a month before they are available in the shops, FREE gifts and a monthly Newsletter packed with information.

Accepting these FREE books and gift places you under no obligation to buy, you may cancel at any time, even after receiving just your free shipment. Simply complete the coupon below and send it to:

SILHOUETTE READER SERVICE, FREEPOST, CROYDON, CR9 3WZ.

No stamp needed

Yes, please send me 4 free Silhouette Special Editions and a mystery gift. I understand that unless you hear from me, I will receive 6 superb new titles every month for just £2.20* each postage and packing free. I am under no obligation to purchase any books and I may cancel or suspend my subscription at any time, but the free books and gifts will be mine to keep in any case. (I am over 18 years of age)

1EP6SE

Ms/Mrs/Miss/Mr _____

Address _____

_____

_____ Postcode _____

▼ SILHOUETTE
Intrigue

COMING NEXT MONTH

CRADLE AND ALL Rebecca York

43 Light Street

Abby Franklin's dream of cuddling her new baby turned into a nightmare when little Shannon was kidnapped. But *who* had taken her baby wasn't as critical as *why*. The question was tearing husband Steve Claiborne from Abby. And only Abby could bring her family back together...

LADYKILLER Sheryl Lynn

Dangerous Men

Policewoman Nadine Shell had been seduced by DJ Ben Jackson's voice on the nocturnal airwaves, but was the man of her late-night fantasies the murderer she was seeking? After all, Ben had mysterious connections to a string of suspicious deaths...

MYSTERIOUS VOWS Cassie Miles

Mail-Order Brides

'Maria' had amnesia. She couldn't remember her real name or her background. And she couldn't remember the mysterious, brooding man who claimed she'd agreed to marry him. Would saying 'I do' to Jason Walker be a deadly error?

WHISPERS IN THE DARK Heather McCann

As Shannon Hollister settled into her new home, a murderer lurked in the shadows, impatiently waiting to make her his next victim. Mike Finnegan wanted Shannon too, but all his efforts to lure her elusive heart failed. Until she realised someone wanted her dead and she needed the comfort of his arms...